RIVER JIM

A WORLD CLASS PISCATOR

Gary E. Belschner

Illustrations by Rosemarie Belschner
Cover Design by Jennifer Belschner

CONTENTS

This book is dedicated to the amazing women in my life:
My mother Gloria who is an inspiration to us all,
My two perfect daughters, Rachel Marie and Jennifer Rose
And to the light in my life, my wife Rosemarie.
It's also dedicated to the teller of tall tales everywhere.
Never stop….

AUTHOR'S NOTE

Fishing has been an important part of my life from the beginning. My father, Earl Belschner, was from northern Minnesota and a two-week midsummer vacation at the lake was a staple for our family. Many of the early Jim memories are twisted recollections of my early fishing life. Many characters are based on real folks and for that I ask their forgiveness.

In keeping with excellent fishing stories everywhere there is actually nothing true in this book, with the exception of some of the historical references.

I hacked my way
THROUGH A WALL
of **WALLEYES...**
DRAGGING MY
CANOE
BEHIND ME.
—DEAN CIMMIYOTTI*

*From his best selling book, *Eat Walleyes or Die!*

CHAPTER 1
MY NAME IS JIM AND I'M A FISHERMAN

Now, some folks might think that fishing is my hobby or my passion or my career even and they would be right. But it is also my life. I'm not ashamed of it. It is my belief fishing is one of the most pure and straight paths to enlightenment. It is a vehicle from which we can learn everything this life has to teach. I know lots of folks picture a fisherman with a beer can in his hand, a crushed ball cap and a wasted day loafing to which I reply, "True." Some folks think men fish to get out of painting the house, fixing the fence or mowing the lawn and I say, "True." Oh those things need to get done and in their correct time they do. One of the great things fishing teaches us is that it is not wrong to wait. In fact it is healthy to wait. I believe we train ourselves to feel things are necessary that are not. I'll be happy when the garage is clean, I'll be happy when the car is washed, I'll be happy when the toilets are cleaned … and on and on and on. Patience, people.

Listen to the wind blow, feel the boat rock and sense the gentle tug on the line. Easy now.

I was born a fisherman. My people have been fishermen since time began. I did not ever question what I would do with my life or who I was. I understand that in this I am beyond lucky, I am truly blessed. It's as if I was born high in the Himalayas where the entire purpose of life is to know what life means and to become comfortable with the answer. Unfortunately in the West it seems we have built a culture that strives to be distracted from even the most basic questions. We have created solutions that allow us to be free of our need for understanding the true meanings of life. "Oh, I am a bad person but I am forgiven because someone else did all the work for me. I can keep on being miserable and mistreating everyone as an expression of my misery... but of course I am forgiven even before I do the thoughtless things I intend to do." Those of us who do not use this particular solution can use countless more. We distract ourselves with our careers and even the basics of our lives. We fill our moments with minutia to desperately ignore the fundamental questions that cause the continuous dull aches in our hearts. Oh, don't get me wrong. I'm not sitting on a pedestal sitting above everyone saying I am immune to these things. I am not a perfect fisherman. But I recognize that through fishing I can lift the veil and see something true beyond the fog.

Think of all of the metaphors that use fishing: "Fish or cut bait," "fishing for a compliment," to "bait" someone, a person "trolling" for a date, "plenty of fish in the sea," "hook, line and sinker," he's a "bottom feeder," to "hit a snag." I could go on beyond being fun anymore. It is obvious fishing is deeply woven into the fabric of our lives. Buddha is often pictured with a cane pole. And my own Jesus was the ultimate fisherman. Many of his quotes are wrapped in fishing metaphors, such as "cast your nets upon the water," "I will make you fishers of men." His favorite, Peter, was a fisherman and he went with him on the sea. He calmed the waters, told them to cast their nets on the other side of the boat and they filled their nets, he fed the masses with the fishes and loaves, he walked on the water.

Now I don't know about religion. You might get some hint from what I wrote above I don't put much faith in what I perceive as the manipulation of one thing into something else. I love Jesus. I can't find one thing in what he did to argue with. If you think about it that is quite amazing. He preached love and understanding. He showed mercy and said, "He who has sinned the least, cast the first stone." He forgave the harlot and simply asked her to "sin no more." The only violence I recall him exhibiting was when he threw the money changers out of the temple. Money seems to be the great monster that perverts so many things. When I look at organized religion today the greed and excess make my blood boil more than anything else . . . except for perhaps politics. The way supposedly religious people use religion to support their personal bias is truly pathetic. Jesus said, "Render to Caesar what is Caesar's." Judas tried to make him fight a war to throw Rome out of Jerusalem. Jesus would have none of it. He was dramatic in the example he set of keeping politics and religion separate. He was spot on. It is interesting to me that in the parable of the Good Samaritan Jesus used a Samaritan. They were the lower class of his time and looked down on by Jews, but he had Jews walk by the man in trouble and only the lowly Samaritan helped him. It was not a knock on the Jews themselves as Jesus was obviously proud to be a Jew. It was a message regarding the lowly to show us we are all the same. He changed the water into wine. They called him and his friends "wine bibbers," but I think he recognized it is important to relax and have some fun. Yeah, I love Jesus. He was right on. I'm not sure the folks that wrote stuff beyond the Gospels really got what he was trying to say. Of course time and translations and the pressure of politics and the influence of kings has affected the story, but I cling to what Jesus did and leave it to the next life to fill in the rest. For all of you folks that believe every word please don't be offended. I could be wrong but I am betting, even if I am, the Jesus I know will forgive me.

The very act of fishing is a metaphor for what we need to do in life. To be successful we need to use the right bait. The same goes for business, love, sports and on and on. To be a successful fisherman you need to understand your prey and their habits. You need to understand their environment, the lake you are fishing, depth, bottom and clarity. This is just like business, love, sports and on and on again. We can reflect on our lives in ways that perfectly mesh with fishing. We need to know ourselves. We need to be patient and quiet. We need to be focused and notice the small things. We need to learn to enjoy fishing even when they don't bite. What a beautiful world we live in and what better way to watch it?

The mystical ties to fishing might not be something you have thought about. What you are about to read is the story of my travels on and off the river, as a young boy and as a man. I think you will see what I'm talking about when you hear what I've been through. So it is true, fishing is the foundation on which I build my life. I have no choice. I might have been anything in this world we find ourselves in but I am River Jim and I am a fisherman.

~ CHAPTER 2 ~
THE FAMILY BORDELL

I was born James Buchanan Bordell on May 1, 1940. My parents didn't really feel any kin to our fifteenth president but they liked the way the name rolled off their tongues (so I'm told). My father, being a moderately rabid fisherman, had taken my mother bass fishing. It seems in those days a person could fish the spawning seasons with the state's blessing and my father was taking full advantage by loading up on largemouth. They were hitting everything from crawlers to crank bait so naturally when my mother, fat as a tick and a month overdue, began complaining of pain, my father was not perhaps paying her the attention due. The way Dad told it, he had just hooked the catch of the day when her water broke. "That bass was all of nine pounds and a jumpin' fool," he confessed. "The fish was breakin' water and your mom was breakin' water! She was yellin', 'He's coming, Pa! He's comin'!' and I was yellin' 'I got 'em, Ma! Get the net! GET THE NET!'" Well, somehow they landed both me and the bass. They wrapped me in fish paper in a cleaning shack.

(Pop insisted on cleaning his catch before they went to the hospital. He used to say the trick to tasty fish was a prompt trip to the fish shack and a quick introduction to ice.) But all's well that ends well and I guess it couldn't have been any different anyhow.

My father, as you might have already figured, was a man with tastes much like my own. He loved the wilderness and would rather fish than breathe. He emigrated to this country from a German seaport called Wilhelmshaven in 1935. The town was used as a major port in World War I and as such was the target of a lot of U.S. and British hardware. What with another ruckus seeming to be on the way, my daddy figured it was time to find calmer waters. His family had been fishing people in the North Sea and, more specifically, in a bay called Jade Busen since the beginning of time. However, the planting of 70,000 mines off the German coast by the Allies toward the end of the war made fishing a totally different experience. Dad said it was kind of like "the lady or the tiger." When they got a good pull on the net they didn't know if they should jump for joy or jump for cover. Also, he claimed that all the German submarine traffic so shook up the fish that they too headed for new horizons. He used to say that even the good Lord would have had trouble filling a net in those days in those waters. So an eighteen-year-old Wilhelm Bordellschmonham hopped a freighter for New York City and the Promised Land.

The trip over was largely uneventful and the freighter was soon sliding peacefully into New York Harbor. Now Daddy was not what you would call a first-class passenger. He had bribed the first mate of the ship with a golden family heirloom to get on and so was deposited on the docks with the same lack of ceremony. Now you might think it would be hard for a German immigrant to make his way in the then-largest city in the world, but it was not as difficult as it might seem. My father had a reasonably good formal education and could even speak English fairly well so he soon found his way to Bedloe's Island (now Liberty Island), and an immigration station. In those days it was common for people like my father to just walk in and wish to immigrate. In fact, they were welcome. That he could speak English made it even easier. The helpful folks at the station, however, did not like the length of his name (they had to write it fifty times on forms), so they christened him William Bordell and left it at that.

The fishing industry in New York was not the same as in the old country so for many reasons my father decided to observe for a while. He got himself a job selling instead of catching fish. It wasn't the most glamorous job but it allowed him to get to know this modern-day Rome and to get a feel for what it would take to survive in the land of opportunity. It was while delivering a fresh cod to a fancy delicatessen that Dad met the woman who was to be my mom. The way he tells it, when she first laid eyes on him she "commenced to moan and groan, her eyes rolled back in her head and she fainted dead away." While I expect that may be a bit of an exaggeration, I guess she did see something she liked because they took up to courting soon after they met. Now this was about the most unlikely couple you could imagine. My mother's maiden name was Van Stitt and her family was one of the most influential families in New England. In fact, my mom was voted the "most desirable" by a New York publication called *The Blue Bloods' Bible*. Well, you might say that her folks were a mite disappointed in their daughter's choice of a man and they set out to end this distasteful union. Now in those times, as in these times, money was power and the Van Stitts had a lion's share of both. You can imagine the odds against a poor German immigrant even lasting a round in this battle. They began their siege by trying to buy off my dad. When that had no effect they moved to have him deported. It was touch-and-go but while they were trying to have him sent packing in New York, Daddy was quietly gaining his citizenship in New Jersey. The next move was to see to it that he could find no markets for his fish. They did this most effectively. There was not a restaurant or market that would let him in the door. But Dad lived on Flatbush Avenue and when the folks in the area became aware of what was happening all he had to do was walk up Flatbush and down Fulton and he could sell all the fish he could handle. Next, they cut off his supply. Well, that caused a real problem. Being a master fisherman, he was able to survive by fishing off the docks and selling his catch. But his dreams of wealth and independence were rapidly fading.

Now you might well wonder what my mother was up to during all this time. She was an intelligent and fiercely independent woman and very much in love with my father. Every lash laid upon his back made her wince, but even love made in heaven must bend under the weight of such abuse. My father was a proud man and not one to consider a bride's finances for his personal gain; however, he was most aware of her change in position should they continue their relationship. As his dreams of security were fading, his plans for his sweetheart were fading as well. He loved her too much to marry her into poverty.

This was where my mother sprang into action. Seeing her

true love drifting away, she, like a cornered animal, became instant motion. First, she legally changed her name to Bordell, then she formally disowned her parents. Next, she moved into a hall closet in Dad's tenement apartment house and began rummaging through trashcans for bits of food to eat. This, of course, was more than Dad could stand. He also now saw that her money meant much less to her than he did, so they were married immediately. They had a big wedding in the streets of Brooklyn with singing and dancing and lots of folks throwing up on their shoes. A grand time was had by all.

My mom's folks never did get over the "social wall," and the last thing they ever said about the affair was in the pages of the *New York Times*. My grandfather was quoted as remarking, "Someone as fishy as a fish vendor married to someone as rich as my daughter could only beget a politician, to our family's eternal disgrace. So from hence forward we have no daughter." They did not, however, loosen the binds on my father's trade, so after a few less than rewarding months, my parents packed up and moved west. They wanted to be as far away from the New York society perspective as possible. Also Dad was tired of the big water but not of fishing. So they headed for an area with some of the greatest inland fishing in the world, west-central Wisconsin.

Now they didn't start out with a pocket full of cash, so the trip took a bit longer than they had hoped. In fact, it took most of a year. But they were young and in love, so hardships were adventures and setbacks were diversions. Mom and Dad were never afraid of hard work, so they were never hungry but there were a few nights spent out in the boondocks with nothing over their heads but a blanket of sky. I think the experience of going through cities and then through the countryside left them both with the feeling that their future lay in a rural area. So that fit in nicely with their plans to discover Wisconsin. Since they were fairly open about where exactly they would put down their roots, they decided to cross the state and settle around the lake or river in which they caught the biggest fish. That may sound a little crazy to you all, and I'm not sure they would have stayed in a place they didn't like but, like I said, they were young and it was more of a whimsical notion to put their fate in the hands of God.

They came south of Lake Michigan through the Chicago area so the sight of peaceful farms of southern Wisconsin truly looked to them like the Promised Land. I believe they might have had some idea where they were headed for the simple reason that Dad never considered a spot until he hit the central part of Wisconsin at Oshkosh and Lake Winnebago. Up until the time of their departure from New York neither of them had done any freshwater fishing at all. So the trip was also a learning process along with everything else. By the time they reached Lake Winnebago they had become fairly adept at the game and were already showing signs of above-average luck. They hit the lake at the southwest corner and decided to camp there. By this time they had purchased a tent and camping gear so they snuggled into the countryside in peaceful harmony. It was now in the late spring of the year so the weather was warm and the land was rich with the promise of life reborn. It was on this night, my mother says with conviction, that I was conceived. They were camped on the part of the lake where the Fox River enters so they fished within that area. Their luck, as usual, was very good and in a short time they had landed enough for a grand breakfast and had released a couple of limits of largemouth, several wall-eye and three very nice northern.

They had discovered walleye when they fished Lake Erie, near Detroit, and after that they always made an effort to fish lakes that offered them a chance at a walleye meal. Like me, they considered them the biggest challenge to catch and one of the tastiest treats around. Now I won't say they'd turn their noses up at any game fish, 'cause fish are like women, each is beautiful in her own way, but the ones that are hardest to catch seem to taste the sweetest. That may sound funny coming from me, a backwoods bachelor, but I've loved before (another story), and I love 'em all, in my way. Someday I still hope to share my cabin (do I pine?).

Back to Winnebago. Even though they did very well, the biggest catch was a nine-pound northern, which they released. I believe they already were thinking farther west so they didn't spent any more time on that fine lake but packed up and were on the road by noon.

I haven't mentioned their mode of transportation. They rode train to start out. They would work at odd jobs until they had enough money for another short-hop train ride and a little extra savings besides. Well, at that time there were lots of jobs for hard workers so they began to get some ahead. That tiny bankroll turned into a sturdy, used Model A Ford pickup. My father was raised working on marine engines so he kept that little buggy running like a deer. From the shores of Winnebago they purred west to the future and more fishing.

It became apparent as they wheeled across the state that it

would take two or three lifetimes to fish every body of water they were passing. So they checked their Esso map and decided beforehand the stops they would make. Their next landing spot was at Lake DuBay at Mosinee. The Wisconsin River enters the lake there and my father, having fished river deltas in the ocean, believed you would find constant fish activity if you worked in that area. I believe that at certain times of the year this is true, but by no means is this a year-round phenomenon. At any rate, that's where they camped and that's where they fished. Their luck held out and they caught a fine mess of pan fish. My mother still talks about the way those fish tasted. I don't know if they were starving or what, but she claims they were the sweetest meat fish she had ever introduced to her mouth.

You might well wonder how my mother was taking all this poverty and sleeping on the ground. The plain truth was, she loved it. I believe that even before she met my father she was tired of the life she was living. Back then people weren't as free as they are today. It would have been impossible for her to even wear a pair of jeans, and for her to think of talking to some segments of the population was unthinkable. She was forced to talk a certain way and walk a certain way. However, even at a young age she found it impossible to take that whole thing seriously. At the age of ten she was a master at popping her knuckles, belching, and placing her cupped hand underneath her armpit, pumping her arm, and thus creating the most obscene of all human sounds. Only the hired help derived any pleasure from her efforts. Perhaps if she had had a little more direction (her folks were always off on holiday), she might have been molded into a more satisfactory model of her line. As it was, by the time the adults realized the extent of her abnormality, it was too late. I think her departure was actually a relief, not only to her confused parents, but to the whole New York social scene. But most of all it was a relief to her.

Back at Mosinee, the Bordells were packing the truck. Even though the fish were the sweetest, the agreement was for the largest. So they fired up their everyman car and headed into the country, feeling as much happiness and freedom as their hearts could hold. Their next destination was Chequamegon Waters Flowage near Perkinstown. Of course, everyone knows where Perkinstown is, but for those who don't, it's a hundred or so miles northwest of center. I'm told that it was the name that attracted our blissful travelers, and the area didn't disappointment them. The day was perfect (they were on a roll!), with blue skies and fluffy white clouds softly, slowly heading somewhere. The wind was warm and just strong enough to fluff their hair. They found a secluded spot to park the truck and set up camp then decided that before even fishing they would discover the water, and perhaps take a dip.

As the story goes, the shoreline was so beautiful, the day so ideal and the couple so in love, they strayed quite a ways. Soon the remote area and the bliss overcame them and they (for what I can figure from the blushes and giggles of my folks) went skinny-dipping. Afterwards, with the gentle, warm coaxing of the woods, they fell into peaceful sleep. This is where the imps of the forest took over, leading a small patrol of Boy Scouts to the exact spot where the couple slept. My mother woke up to the faces of two giggling twelve-year-olds and three leering thirteen-year-olds. She screamed and grabbed my father's pants.

He jumped up before he could fully grasp the situation and ran in three tight circles searching for his trousers. In the meantime the scouts had figured it was time to head for the hills so went crashing through the woods. My mother now had grasped the situation and began laughing hysterically, choking out the words, "We're bare! We're bare!" My father, on the other hand, was half asleep and totally confused. All he could understand from my mom was, "bare," and hearing the crashing, having never seen the Scouts, thought she meant a completely different sort of bear. So, he heroically picked up my mother and jumped in the lake. Fortunately it wasn't very deep and before he could run through the water to the dangerous depths my mother had contained herself enough to choke out some words to halt his stampede. As you can imagine, they had such a fine laugh that they came as close as two adults could to drowning in three feet of water.

When they were sure the Scouts had scurried, they put on their civilization skins and made their way back to the truck. There they had severe hangover giggles and decided that to live in this area might prove embarrassing. So they avoided fishing (what if they caught the biggest fish there?), repacked the truck and headed back down the pike.

There is nothing like the road. You know it has never disappointed me. It has scared me and it's made me want to be home, but it's never ceased to surprise me. Now, I'm not talking about the super freeways we have today. They're nothing but caponized concrete. It's hard to image myself in such a hurry that I would subject myself to such a journey. I know a lot of people like driving on those things, and I really do understand, but to me it's kind of like watching a test pattern on the TV. But the road, now that's a different story! The next time you're not in a hurry to get somewhere, just aim in the direction that you want to be, and go. A great little gizmo for your vehicle is an auto compass. That, together with your adventuresome spirit, will show you the country as it really is . . . living art!

My folks, at this time of their lives were definitely woven deeply into that rich tapestry. They had escaped Chequamegon and were heading toward the intersection of the Chippewa and Flambeau Rivers. They had been fishing all lakes and decided to try their hands at a river. They couldn't have made a better choice in rivers because those two rivers, I believe, hold some of the largest game fish in the state. They found an abandoned homestead a mile or two south of the intersection on the east side and made their camp. By this time night was moving in on them and the skies had finally decided to water the land so the young couple huddled together in the small canvas tent and fell asleep to the sounds of gently falling rain.

Well, while those two are sleeping I think I'll take a moment to talk fishing. I haven't gone into much detail about the techniques my folks were using. I can tell you it was a far cry from the methods we use today. For one thing there were very few mass-produced lures. If you were creative enough to imagine what a fish would like, you had to make it yourself. There were a few plugs on the market and spoons were around by then, but it was nothing like it is today. Then there were the rods. Most of them were wood (hickory, greenwood, palm, etc.), or bamboo with the newest rage, a heart of steel. Organized fishing had always, up to this time, considered trout to be the civilized quarry and most store-bought equipment targeted this market. But that was in the process of changing. The reels of that time were either fly reels or what they called casting reels. To cast with one of the latter, however, took years of practice. My folks had converted saltwater gear that Dad used in New York. It consisted of heavily varnished bamboo poles, light for saltwater but quite a bit heavy for freshwater use, Penn casting reels that were much superior to the new light duty freshwater reels they were selling at the time, and line that was 40- or 50-pound test made of a combination cotton and silk. It was crude by today's standards but quite capable, in the right hands, of catching fish. They had not invested in a boat, as of yet, so all their efforts were made from shore. A lot of folks put a lot of importance on boats for fishing but I can tell you some of the most serious and successful fisher people that I know never leave the shore. Next time you pull up to a lake, walk on over to the old lady with the floppy hat fishing from a beach chair. Check out the old dude with his rod propped up in a forked stick, or the kids who rode their bikes down for a day of fishing. I think you will be surprised what you find. You might also be surprised to know that most of them are trolling from shore.

That's right, trolling! You see somewhere in history that word got confused and found itself in the wrong part of our vocabulary. It really means using a bait that is alive that attracts fish through its own natural motion. The proper word for dragging a lure behind a boat is trailing, and I don't care what Webster's says. To be fair, I guess there are two ways to look at language. One is to look at the true meanings, the other is to define by usage. I favor the former. Think of what would happen to the English language if they rewrote it to the way I throw words around! No, it's better to have a sturdy backbone that stays the same. Then let folks create and abuse the rules for their comfort and amusement. All that stuff is like the fat hanging on the bones (do I wander?). Time to wake up my folks.

By the time the young couple crawled out of their cave the sun was rising into a cloudless sky. The grass was still wet and the trees dripped sprays of diamonds with each puff of the wind. The air smelled and felt as clean as the first morning and for all the world my folks could have been Adam and Eve. They just stood around drinking it all in. I'm sure that all of you have experienced moments that are like a glimpse of heaven; this was such a time.

They may have just sprouted wings and flown right into the fire but for a granddaddy musky that chose that moment to reach the length of his body out of the river and snatch a tasty fly. Now to some folks that would have just been a part of a perfect picture. To my dad it was ample reason to put off paradise a while and run for his rod. Within moments he was dropping a handmade plug the length of your forearm about twenty feet upstream from the musky's launch site. He walked down the river, slowly following the gentle current and all the time twitching his rod tip to make the plug quiver like a boat-struck perch. He saw the "V" in the water, planted his feet and waited for the strike but it didn't come. The fish had gone deep and under the lure. My father reeled in quickly to prepare for another throw but before he could get it to the shore the monster came straight out of the water with his homemade in his mouth. I'm not sure who was the most surprised but both had very definite ideas as to what was going to happen next!

The fish peeled off line and headed for Eau Claire. My father's thumb was on the spool of the reel trying to slow down the loss of line. By the time he turned the fish he had run out all but a few yards of his line. Now he ran down the shore line, as best he could considering the brush and tangle, trying to recover some of the lost ground. In the meantime my mother had grabbed the net and was following close behind. First my dad gained a few yards then the fish stole them back. All the while they moved farther downstream. The fish had the advantage of the current and was using it for all it was worth. They rounded a bend and came upon a river fisherman's worst fear, a log jam, and the big pike was heading right for it. My father was forced to make his move before the fish was completely spent, but he had no options. He once again planted his feet, squeezed his thumb on the reel and hung on. Slowly the noise of the string hissing off of the reel quieted. The rod bent almost in two and for several moments all you could hear was the soft moan of the river while everyone held their breath waiting to see what would hold and what would not. First a foot, then a yard, the big fish slowly began to come around. At first Dad would gain a couple of yards then the fish would jerk back out half. But soon its strength sapped and the exhausted fish was captured by my mother in a net which was about half as deep as the fish was long. All three of them lay on the bank, too spent to move.

The fish was the first to recover and begin slopping around on shore. My father next weighed the fish with his trusty pocket scale and found it to be a hefty thirty-eight pounds. This was not a record but was the largest freshwater fish they had ever seen. They had no use for that much fish so they gently removed the hooks and laid him right back in the water. My mother had to hold him right side up for several minutes before he had the strength to motor off under his own power. The two of them sat on the banks of the river grinning like a couple of kids. My father looked like he had been beaten with a whip. His arms, legs and face were full of scratches from his dash through the shoreline brush, and his thumb looked more like hamburger than the digit that sets us apart from the apes, but all in all you would have been hard put to find a happier, more satisfied man. They both were fairly sure they had found a home. But they still had a large part of the state left to cross, so in keeping with their plans they loaded up the truck and once again headed west.

They stopped at several small lakes and rivers during the next couple of days but nothing of any size was netted and nothing real interesting happened. The night of the second day away from the Chippewa/Flambeau they found themselves camping at another small lake that someone along the way said was worth the stop. This lake, however, happened to be one of the finest fishing lakes I've dropped line in. It not only supports some of the finest musky fishing I've seen but also delivers walleyes in the twelve-to-fourteen pound class with regularity. Now, I'm not going to name this lake 'cause I fish it quite a bit, and I'd rather not have it covered by fancy, high-seated power boaters bombarding the bottom with waves of every description and filling the lake with secret sauces of all flavors guaranteed to make any and all fish lose their natural caution and attack with abandon the latest and certainly most scientifically tested lure on the market. Did I say that? Well, anyway, let's just say it's kind of a big, round lake in Polk County, Wisconsin, and there they sat.

They had been having a fine time, and really had caught a lot of fish, but they couldn't in all truth imagine a larger fish than their thirty-eight pounder. Course they didn't really know where they were (I could've told 'em!). You probably figure I'm leading up to a big fish story and I'm not going to disappoint you. They were about to tie into a fish so large that a lot of the folks in the area quit swimming in that lake after they saw it. Women fainted and kids had nightmares. Grown men grew pale at the sight of it. Most folks say it was a musky but some swear it was more alligator gar like they grow in the Mississippi. I guess it's just hard to imagine a musky in the nine-foot range. But I've seen fish in that lake, fish that don't get caught. Every once in a while they just kind of rise out of the deep water for a look. Then they settle down deep again to rest and grow. I don't fish 'em myself. I love catching the big ones, as you know, but this is different. There's something holy about those fish, something bigger than the truths we live with. They don't seem to show themselves to too many people so I take it as a sort of trust and I leave them alone. But believe me when I tell you, they're there and the lake is special.

The sun was just beginning to rest on the horizon, looking more like a flaming tomato than a slightly yellow, medium-sized dwarf star, and the sticky hot summer air made the whole world feel kind of like an All Star Wrestler's armpit. It was an evening that made survival close to impossible without the assistance of a cool water swim. Fortunately, they were in God's country and the solution to their dilemma existed a mere thirty feet from their tent flaps. So they crossed that span and surrendered to the lake. They had just about brought their body temperature back to normal when my dad noticed what looked to be a big log floating about fifty or sixty feet from them out in deep water. Now that would be nothing to be concerned with; however, they were in a lake and everyone knows that logs don't swim, so considering all the facts and considering that this particular log was moving along at a fairly good clip, they became concerned.

At first they thought it to be an animal of some kind. Then they saw a very distinct, very large, dorsal fin and immediately left the water. By this time my folks had been fishing freshwater long enough to know that with the exception of a sturgeon (my father was familiar with sturgeon from the old country and knew this was not one), there were no fish in the area as large as the one they were watching. They were looking at a fish that was about the size of a canoe. Most people would think of going for help. My father went for his rod. My mother went for the net. They stood on the shore searching for some sign of the creature they had both, thank goodness for their sanity, seen. It was only moments but it must've seemed like an eternity before my mother saw the ripple. She pointed out in the lake . . . THERE! My father dropped his now-tested foot-long homemade plug ten feet past the water motion. It hit the face of the lake with a slap and lay perfectly still.

The whole lake became perfectly still, and the couple stood looking out over the sunset drenched water, listening to their heartbeats. After the longest thirty seconds in history, my father gave the tip of his rod an almost unnoticeable flip. The motion ran down the line the forty feet or so to the big plug. It twitched. Small rings ran out from the lure and grew like tension. The lake, once again, grew perfectly still. The couple stood frozen as if captured on a tourism postcard offered to passersby at some roadside attraction. My father was about to repeat the procedure when the wooden decoy simply sank into the lake. The two stood gazing in amazement at the spot where it had been. Then very slowly and steadily the rod began to bend. My father let the tip go down, then jerked it back with every muscle he could command. The next thing he knew he was yanked off his feet, skipping along the surface of the lake like a flat rock, clinging to the rod with grim determination. Fortunately, the lake was only thirty or forty feet deep at the most and Dad had lots of line so the big fish couldn't pull straight down. But pull he did and my father went along for the ride. My mother, in the meantime, made a dash for the nearest cabin and help. The folks in the cabin were Fred and Sandy Hanson up from Chicago for the summer. Fred was quite a fisherman himself and had caught lots of big game fish. But he was not prepared for the fantasy he was about to step into. My mother was screaming something about a monster and all he could see in the lake was a large wake (Dad), plowing across the surface. He ran back into the cabin and returned with his rifle, figuring to shoot first and identify later whatever it was that was causing the ruckus. Mom stopped him before he could fire a shot and explained the totally unbelievable situation. He, of course, didn't believe a word but since he really couldn't identify what was churning up the lake and he could hear what sounded like semi-human screams coming from the direction of the foam, he held his fire.

By this time folks all around that part of the lake were beginning to gather on the shoreline, craning their necks to see what had cracked their peaceful egg and splashed them onto a skillet of chaos. When they figured out that whatever it was it involved a man in some kind of trouble, several of them got into their boats and motored out to assist. My father, fearing they would cut his line, managed to wave them off, and they took up positions just far enough away to jump in if need be.

Time and Dad dragged on. The sun set while the minutes became hours. The great fish swam on with little loss of power. My father hung on with the same strength of resolve. The sky was just beginning to show hints of pink in the east when conditions changed. The fish suddenly turned 180° and swam with a sudden fury at my now exhausted father. If it had decided to attack its tormentor or if it had just randomly turned the 180 we'll never know because by the time it had covered a hundred yards of line at unbridled full speed it was too spent to go any further. So my father and the fish bobbed quietly, belly up, in the middle of the lake.

My father's world came back into focus about an hour later in Fred and Sandy's rented cabin. The good folks of the area had plucked him and the fish from the water, placing Dad on a feather bed and the fish on a charcoal bed. The thirty or so local folks had voted to keep the fish a secret because of the effect it would have on the lake. No one wanted the attention or the people it would bring so they got rid of the evidence in the best way they could think of—they ate it and buried the bones. The folks never measured or weighed the fish, so Dad never knew the exact size, but he used to say it really didn't matter because no one would believe it anyway. Now I'll leave it up to you to believe 'cause my dad never lied to me in his life and this is just the way he told it to me. Just look at some of the treasure in your heart that you know to be true. Imagine some scientist taking it out, laying it on a sterile table and cutting it apart with a knife. It would take someone with the same treasure to recognize that all those little pieces are jewels. Next time you're fishing, look down into the deep water and believe. One of those monsters may just show himself to you. Be that as it may, the result of all this is that from that day forward, my folks were residents of Polk County, Wisconsin. To them, it was home.

CHAPTER 3
YOUNG JIM

It wasn't too long after the folks put down roots that I came along. They say it was obvious from the start that I had a special rapport with the fish community. I wasn't a month old when they decided to pack a lunch and hit the river for a little fishing. From what Dad says, they were catching small rock bass and minnows with tiny flies. He said they were more into the picnic than fishing on this particular day but wanted little Jimmy to catch his first fish. So they tied a very small dry fly to a string and tied it to my big toe and set it in the river.

Like I said before, this part of the river was known to hold small rock bass, minnows, and once in a while a small blue gill or sunny. The water both up and downstream became very shallow so the only inhabitants got there in high waters of spring and my folks were comfortable leaving me to tackle these finned monsters by myself. Of course they were only a few feet away, and even at the deepest part of this pool the water was only three to four feet deep. Now, how that northern pike got into the pool,

I do not know. People liked to picnic in this spot so you would think that someone would have seen a seventeen-pound pike in a pool no larger than a Buick. But, the odds were never much of an obstacle when it came to my fishing. I'm told that one minute I was giggling with a tiny minnow wiggling my toe, the next I was being dragged into the pool. The pike, upon feeling the drag of my weight, panicked and ran downstream into the shallow water. This was fortunate for me because it was only inches deep and slimy with moss, so all I was getting out of it was a rather quick ride. My mom and dad sprang into action, chasing their pike-drawn papoose down the creek. The fish now looked like a salmon swimming in inch-deep water, fighting the odds for some primary purpose. Had the water deepened I would have been in trouble, but it was miles to the lake and much too far for this pike to snake. So within a hundred yards or so my parents caught up with me, screaming like a banshee. All I got out of the trip was a sore toe, a few minor bumps and a seventeen pound pike. My daddy mounted this fish and it hangs in my cabin to this day. It wasn't the biggest fish I ever caught but, by golly, it wasn't a bad first.

It became obvious in other ways that fish were attracted to me. My mother used to take me swimming, holding me in her arms while I giggled and splashed. It wouldn't be five minutes and there would be so many fish in the area that the water would boil around us from all the activity. My mom said it was plain unnerving, so after a while she would only take me swimming in the bathtub. Even now I can't stay very long in water with fish. There get to be so many hanging around that I get scratched to pieces on their fins. My dad put me to good use right from the start. When I was just a baby he rigged up an inner tube that I could safely dangle in and dragged it behind the boat to "chum." I guess he caught some beautiful fish that way but he stopped doing it 'cause he said there was no sport in it and besides the neighbors were going to have him arrested for what they figured was cruelty to a child. I can tell you though my daddy was never cruel to me and in that tube I was as safe as I was in my mother's arms. But Dad was a really good fisherman in his own right, so he didn't need my help anyway.

The first clear recollections I have of this world are wonderful things. My folks were kind and loved me. I remember their warmth. I remember the sound of the river. From the first and to the last that is the sound that most makes my heart sing. It makes me feel secure, a part of all life. I believe that in the sound of the river you can hear all the sounds that ever were. If you listen you can hear pyramids, the elephants of Hannibal, the songs of David and the Ten Commandments. It's all there. Just like the blood in a person, it's the life-blood of creation. I believe you could take a citified scientist and sit him by the river for a day and make him listen. Let him start out with a scientific purpose or something. I tell you, by the end of the day he'll have a faraway look. You think it's not so? I'd bet my favorite fishing hat on it.

Another one of my earliest recollections is the cry of the loon flying over our cabin. You people that have heard that know what I mean. If there are folks out there that have not, please, for your own sake, this very summer head up to lake country in Wisconsin or Minnesota, rent a cabin or just camp out by one of the thousands of marvelous lakes. Not only will you find great fishing but in the evening or early morning you will be treated to a song that will thrill your soul. That sound has such love and joy and sadness in it that it's like a description in a few seconds of what life itself is about. It's like an audio kiss from the lips of God. Take my advice, you won't be sorry.

Some other childhood things I remember are my early toys (my favorite was a hookless plug my daddy carved) and the fine smells of my momma's cooking. You know all that talk about loons headed my memory to a story about them when I was a kid. I believe you might like to read stories rather than history, and I know I can show you what it was like better through a story, so why don't I give up this play-by-play broadcast and stick to some color. I think you'll find it relaxing. Throw a log on the fire, put out the dog and listen to this one. If it had a name I guess it would have to be the dance of the loons, and you know it's all true.

~ CHAPTER 4 ~
DANCE OF THE LOONS

I was awake, fed, dressed and waitin' on the porch of my folks' cabin when Scoot stepped into the light. I always pride myself in the ability of knowin' when someone's comin', especially through the woods, but Scoot was different. He was the only person I've ever known who could sneak up on me. I mean, he would just appear. I must say at times it would annoy me. I'd be sitting, like this morning, listening to the woods and the soft purr of the river, feeling one with it all, knowing that anything not part of it would be so apparent that I would sense it for a mile (that's truly the way it is), then I'd open my eyes and there he'd be, grinnin' like a black jack-o-lantern.

Yeah, Scoot was different. I guess I could never sense him because he was part of the woods himself. But at nine I was too young to figure that out so I would just get a mite ruffled.

"Where you been?" I said on this one occasion. "I been waitin' half a lifetime, and early mornin' bass wait for no man. Let's get a move on."

"Now, calm yourself, Jim," he laughed. "You know I'm ten minutes early. What's the matter?"

He already knew, so I wasn't going to give him the satisfaction of sniveling about it again.

"Not a thing on God's green earth," says I. "Let's roll."

Off we hiked through the woods, heading for our favorite bass lake. The lake was about a mile through the center of a deep woods, and being four o'clock in the morning those woods were as dark as the pupils of a madman, but we knew them like a mother knows her baby and had no need of lights or fear. We padded silently through, the only sound being the tinkle of lures in our little tin boxes.

Scoot was quite a kid alright. He was easily the best educated, best mannered, richest kid in the county. He was, like I said, black, and my best friend. His father was the inventor of pizza pie. Now I know that most folks think that pizza came from Italy and it's true that they did have similar pies, but from all I can gather there was nothing truly like our modern day pizzas. How the Italians got the full credit you will see. Scoot's dad invented the pie in the Deep South in the early 1930s. He made it for all the folks in the area and they all said go North and make your fortune. They got together a modest investment group and sent him to New York. His name, by the way, was Emanuel Miller (Scoot's is Mildred, so you can see why we called him Scoot!).

Emanuel figured if he really wanted to make it big he would have to appeal to all the races. In the thirties that was not even an option for a black man. So he hired an Italian tap dancer to front his pizza palace. The man's name was Antonio Pizzaterio. At first the food was called spicy tomato pie. With the growing popularity of a new type of serve-yourself dining, the restaurant became the Pizzateria, serving the now famous "pizza pie." Antonio had been down on his luck (the fall of vaudeville hit him hard) so he was happy in his new role. He was also an honest man and tried to give Emanuel credit for the pizza, but Emanuel would have none of that. He was satisfied to just sit back and become fabulously wealthy. He was also very aware of the responsibilities of success and helped the poor of New York in many behind-the-scene ways.

Emanuel educated himself in schools all over the world, and by the time he was married and had his firstborn son he was the perfect picture of success. But he missed the country and in the mid-forties he moved to Wisconsin. You might think he'd have rather moved back to the South but his home had changed a lot and not all for the better. He had made all his investors rich by most standards and money had affected them all differently. The games some of them played with the new bought toys in their heads were not fun and not something Emanuel thought he could go home to. I'm not sure what brings people to a spot on this earth but conditions all align and there you are. You know what I mean? At any rate, he still had a huge respect for education and had private tutors for Scoot his whole life.

It's odd to me that some people think blacks are less than whites in some way. Emanuel being the way he was, and Scoot using all those big words and all, I thought for most of my young life that the Negro was the natural aristocrat of this world. When people were mean to Scoot when we were young he handled it so well and he came out looking so good that I could never understand what they were getting at. Nigger, if you don't know of all the poison in it, doesn't sound any different than any other name. And the people that would go out of their way to bother him were usually so physically or mentally grotesque it is easy to see why I felt that this tall, good looking and intelligent black kid was so great. Besides, I loved him like a brother.

As we made our way up to the lake we could see, even in the dark, that it was covered with a dense fog. The cool summer nights hit the warm lakes and make an instant vapor. Usually the chilly air blows in from one direction making it seem as if God is pouring a thick fog sauce out over the water. But, to two hardcore bass fishermen, the conditions were perfect. Scoot and me were the proud owners of the tippiest tin boat ever made. It was an eight-foot job that, when we climbed in, left about six inches above the waterline. It was so bad that he and I were the only ones who could fish from it. We had tried to share it with other friends only to have to retrieve it off the bottom. We had traded two days of our lives for it, chopping and hauling wood to raise the money to buy it, and were as happy with it as two kids could be. Even though Scoot's dad was rich, he never spoiled his son with toys. He was smart enough to let him earn things so that when he looked at the things he had worked so hard for he could see the worth in them. It worked well 'cause in that boat we could see solid gold! With the amount of fishing we did, we got so we could handle it like it was a luxury liner. We pushed off from shore without a noise and were instantly swallowed by the fog.

"Hoo-whee, Scoot," I whispered as the craft seemed suspended in another dimension, "this fog is as thick as buttermilk."

"Yes," he replied, analyzing the situation, "it's a bit like joining Jonah in the belly of the whale. I'm not so sure that I can tell which way we're going, can you?"

"I'll tell you what," I giggled, "I'm glad this lake ain't no ocean 'cause I was lost after the first ten feet! It don't matter much, though, we'll just row till we hit some ground and then fish the shallows."

And row we did for what seemed like an hour.

"Great balls of napo-gel, Scoot, either we're traveling in circles or this lake is bigger than I thought."

"Yes, it would seem we've slipped into a cosmic crease. I know that between the two of us we can keep to a straight line, and I seem to have this persistent feeling we are approaching somewhere that we don't belong."

"I hear you talkin', Bucko," I croaked. "Every hair on my head is standin' straight as a cane pole. And I keep thinkin' that I'm hearin' something. . . There, did you hear that?"

The boat glided noiselessly across the lake and silence surrounded us like a noose. Then just ahead there came a very soft flutter and the sound of lightly splashing water. We remained as quiet as a thought and stared with eyes as big as saucepans into the mist. Gradually the noises increased in volume and variety. The splashing became clucks and the clucks became chortles with a gentle whoop thrown in for good measure. In the middle of it all came the distinct sound of soft, feminine laughter. As the sounds grew the fog thinned and soon we found ourselves on the edge of a ring of mist, staring at an unbelievable scene. The ring was about one hundred feet across with a small island in the center. On the island were sitting, naked to the world, five young women, as beautiful as paradise with long black hair salted with white spots. They laughed and splashed their feet in the water. They combed each other's hair and sang a soft song. They seemed not to notice us and I believe we could not have moved if we'd wanted to, so we watched with rapture-filled amazement.

They sang, "To loo, to loo, to loose your love, hisssad, hisssad, hisssad is my heart. Woo woo me, woo woo me, woo woo me, my dear, your touch is the moon of the night."

Their song was at the same time joy and sorrow and they seemed to live it as they sang, once radiating pure love and joy, then emanating a loss that made us cry unashamed. Through it all ran a very strong thread of desire that made us aware of our developing manhood. They held each other and caressed each other with a passion that was for one moment the tenderness of a mother, the next the warmth of a lover.

We were so transfixed by the scene that we didn't notice at first that the island was being encircled by five very large male loons. The big birds swam round and round to the rhythm of the song, adding at the perfect times their own soulful cries. At first the women sang only to each other, but gradually their attention shifted to the beautiful male birds. The loons stopped their circling and began to move in and out, to and from the island in rhythm, each opposite a beautiful maid. The whole of eternity was, for the moment, a throbbing pulse of music and moans as the tempo increased and the longing became a frenzy. The giant males beat the water into foam with their powerful wings, first attacking the shore, then escaping away to spring once again to the land. The women's song became a wail as they crawled to the water on their bellies, squirming in the warm sand with pounding, gyrating motion. They reached out to their partners, pleading as the attack and retreat continued. Slowly, the song changed again from words to high-pitched cries more loon than human.

Then, very slowly, a physical change began to take place. The women turned over and arched their backs, shoving their breasts and bellies to the sky, their chests heaving with each breath still in rhythm to the music of the males, and the hair on their bodies began to grow and change into feathers that were growing black and long all over their naked flesh. They moaned and stroked themselves as if the purely sexual nature of the transformation would drive them mad. Within moments the women were gone and in their place were five large and beautiful female loons. They each joined their mates and ran across the water, jumping into the air, winging higher and higher out of the fog into the first pink light of dawn. The sound of their cries, "Loolooloolooo, loolooloolooo," burst with an unconfined joy that shook us from head to toe, then faded, leaving us once again adrift in the mist.

We sat in the gently rocking boat for several minutes staring off in the direction of the fleeing birds. Our eyes met each other. "I never said this before, Scoot, but watchin' that was even more excitin' than fishin'."

"I'm just glad we haven't reached full puberty," he replied, "I think it would've been more than we could handle."

As we sat, afloat, pondering our altered reality, the mist began to lift. It escaped up a small valley that bordered the lake, sucked like dust into a vacuum, leaving the lake smooth and shiny like a no-wax kitchen floor. We found, to our amazement, that we were a mere fifty feet from the very spot we had slid off the shore. We decided that we had had enough action for the morning and headed home. As we walked back to the cabin we were as quiet as a lamp but our thought lights were glowing bright.

Just a short ways from my home I turned to Scoot and said, "Scoot, I was thinkin' there have been few times fishin' that were as excitin' as that. You remember that big bass I coaxed off the bottom when nothing in the world was bitin'? That was something! And how about that time me and you hit that wild pack of walleye in rain so thick we couldn't see the ends of our poles? Or what about the time . . ."

I rambled on, watching Scoot out of the corner of my eye. He never said nuthin', just grinned, but that was Scoot, he grinned a lot.

~ CHAPTER 5 ~
WHISKERS

I guess I've kind of made it sound like every time I put my line in water I catch a monster fish. I must admit right here that that's just not so. I've spent many an hour sittin' on the shore watchin' a bobber do nothing but bob. To be honest, if I did always catch fish, I doubt if I'd do my fishing at all. The challenge every time I pick up my pole is what sets my blood boiling. The settin' and thinkin' part of fishing is a part of the sport that I love too.

The good Lord did it right when he made the hot part of August unproductive. You can catch enough fish to keep it hopeful but most of the time is spent sleeping in some shade with your rod restin' between your toes. And it's never too hard to talk yourself into a cool skinny-dip in the river. Yeah, I'd say it's the perfect sport. All that talk of summer reminds me of another tale in my youth, if you don't mind. It sort of centers around a grubby old dude that used to live around these parts and a day in the hottest part of summer we spent with him. I don't know anyone who knew his real name, he was just known locally as Whiskers.

I'd say I was about ten at the time. I was old enough to have a pretty free run of my world but still too young for many serious responsibilities. I'd have to say that ten is a fine age to be. Scoot and me and a kid by the name of Billy Wax spent most of that summer exploring the wonders of the Wisconsin backwoods. The year was 1950 so there were no electronic diversions to gobble up a kid's mind and time. We had to suffer with a life that had for its chief source of entertainment lakes, rivers, and a never-ending forest and of course the incredible creatures, both human and other, that resided within.

One such individual was Whiskers. He was, without a doubt, the most unkempt human I have ever known. He was about five feet nine inches with oily grey-black hair. I think the hair itself had black in it, but knowing Whiskers it could have been all grey—or all black for that matter. He sported the nastiest, scruffy beard God ever gave a man, hence the name. I knew him for many years, and there were bits of food in that beard that I knew for just as long (getting the picture?). He wore a pair of long johns all year round (same pair) and you couldn't tell where the long johns ended and old Whiskers started. He lived in a one-room cabin by the river with his live-in zoo. The numbers varied with who was in heat or what season it was but there were always ten or twelve dogs in there, several cats and wild critters by the score. Like I said, they lived in the cabin. They ate, slept, and exercised all their body functions in the cabin. I honestly believe that Whiskers never, not once, cleaned it out. I never went in the place and I never approached it from the downwind side. But, even with all of his quirks, he was always worth the visit.

Rumor had it that he had been a lawyer in a big city firm but got disgusted with the payoffs and paybacks and general corruption within the system so he chucked it all for a life of grime. I believe that that is true because, even though he rarely talked B.C. (before crud) he was one of the most intelligent persons I have ever known.

One story he did tell was about a meeting he had with the heads of a large company who were interested in milking more production from an already overtaxed assembly line. He watched for days the superhuman efforts of the men to keep up to the demands of the foreman. Everyone seemed to be giving all he had. This was in the early thirties, and with the depression these jobs literally meant the difference between eating or not eating to the families of the workers. So they put up with the semi-criminal conditions. But this made it tough for Whiskers (no one knows his B.C. name). He was about to give up when he had a brainstorm. He took out his pocket watch and timed every employee when they went to the outhouse. It took an average two minutes per man. Then he instructed the company to cut square holes for seats and timed them again. Sure enough he had trimmed an average fifteen seconds per visit from the downtime! Considering that there were fifty men in the plant making an average 1.3 trips to the outhouse per day, that meant he added 16 minutes, 55 seconds per day or 1 hour, 37 minutes, 30 seconds per six-day week or 84 hours, 19 minutes, and 36 seconds per year, roughly, to the productive hours. The management was elated. He was recognized in the business community as an "up and comer" and invited into the inner circle of the local Republican Party. He proudly claimed to be the cause of some of the early problems in labor and had a particular satisfaction with the tension he caused their movement. He was secretly pro-labor, so was proud that he had helped "get them off their rear-ends" in their struggle. He would say it was time for them to "crap or get off the pot," it went on and on . . . Whiskers had lots of salty stories so you can see the attraction for us country boys.

The early part of the morning was already exposing itself, hot, when I joined Scoot and Billy Wax at Problem Rock. They were both sitting on top of the giant stone, chins on their knees, brows furrowed, gazing into the void as if straining so hard for a solution to some riddle that they were in danger of rupturing their resolution finders. Problem Rock was a huge bolder dedicated to the problems of the local youths. On it were chiseled thirty years of love and lost love. The rock was not only for affairs of the heart, however. Anyone with any type of problem could, as legend would have it, sit on top like a tiny bird on a huge egg and hatch out a solution to whatever was weighing them down. So sat my two buddies.

"Hey Scoot, Billy Wax. Boy if you don't look the part of the worried birds! If you work that rock any harder I believe you may crack it for sure." My grin didn't put a dent in the atmosphere. "OK, boys, let old Jim in on it. I can't stand the sight of you workin' on all that worry by yourselves."

Well, it seems that Billy's folks were having money problems and were considering heading for the city and the promise of more work. They owned the small general store in the area and even though the local economy was pretty good the store's rural location kept it from any of the real prosperity. Moving to the city was, to the kids in our area, a nightmare we didn't even talk about. We were only sixty miles or so by road from St. Paul, so we had all been in the city at least a couple of times. The trips were adventures and were worth some brag but the thought of staying there was like the idea of living in a cartoon to us. A fun place to look at but no place to live! So I climbed up to the top of the rock and there we sat, like three befuddled fleas on a bald man's head, staring into the void in hopes of spotting an elusive hair.

Finally, when I thought the sun would boil my brains I said, "Boys, it just ain't no use, I'm smart enough to know what I don't know and business is high up on my list. I think we ought to put this in the hands of someone who knows the rules of this game. It will be an unpleasant trip in some ways but I see no other way. We need to sit at the feet of a business Buddha and around here that can be only one person."

They both looked at me and nodded. Scoot whispered the name that filled all of our minds, "Whiskers!"

I haven't said much about Billy Wax yet so while we're startin' off towards Whiskers I'll fill you in a bit so you can get a sharper focus of him in your mind's eye. He was a year younger than Scoot and me and small for his age so he kind of looked like a tagalong brother to the casual observer. But once a person met his eyes they could easily see that this kid was a stranger to fear or hesitation. His mind had the same edge with a flair for the sarcastic. The combination of these qualities placed him in the center of many a tussle. (I should say "placed us," 'cause Scoot and me had to, more times than not, come to his rescue. Many times his mind was ready more than his body was able!) He was also, in most folks' opinion, "cute" and the subject of many a young lady's attention. Billy Wax was also an avid fisherman, not nearly as lucky as Scoot and me, but a fisherman nonetheless, which was the glue that bound us together. He definitely gave our early lives a color that otherwise would have been missing.

Whiskers' shack was about five miles downriver from my folks' cabin, but only three from Problem Rock. The only access was by a well-worn path or by canoe. Since we had no canoe, we chose the path.

"I hope this geezer is as sharp as you guys say," puffed Billy as we reached the highest hill on the river. He had never met the old man, so he knew him only from Scoot and me.

"Oh, I don't think you'll be disappointed," replied Scoot.

"Naw, I suspect you two will take to each other like trout to dry flies," I laughed. "I'm just waiting to see who will eat who!"

"It will be interesting to say the least," came back Scoot. "I would say Billy Wax may be out of his weight class."

"I don't care about all that," said the kid. "If the old toad can help my folks, I'll clean up his shack so it looks like a palace. I'll even give him such a fine shave his face'll look as pretty as a baby's behind!"

"Oh Billy Wax," I shook my head, "you know not of what you speak. I think I'd save my promises till I met the man. And I truly believe if he can't come up with something, there's nothing can be done."

We were pondering that thought when we hiked out of the woods into the field in which the shack sat. As if a switch was turned on the whole world exploded into howling, barking and whining, mixed generously with the most colorful cussing you could imagine. The animals were not mean, thankfully, and they parted like the Red Sea as we approached the hovel. Even from the upwind side as we came near, our eyes began to water.

Whiskers remained in the hut until we stopped, then his head popped up in an open window. His hair was matted and pointing west, his beard was full to the brim with decomposing food bits generously mixed with slobber, pointing east. He stared at us with wild bloodshot eyes.

Then the dogs were silent and the only thing we could hear was the sound of the river. I suddenly wondered if it knew what a blight was on its shore. The bubble was broken when Whiskers cleared his throat and spat what came up, aimed outside the window at Billy's feet. Billy stared at the quivering blob, then at Whiskers, then at the blob, then barfed up breakfast all over the side of Whiskers' shack.

Whiskers came running out of the shanty like a man possessed. "My house!" he screeched. "My home, you've defiled my temple!" We all just stood there watching him rave. "You've got no respect!" he cried. "What did I ever do to deserve this? What would your mother say if she knew you acted this way?" He looked pleadingly at Billy Wax. "Why don't you just hit me? Come on, you little piss-ant, hit me!"

He held out his chin to Billy. Scoot caught Billy's arm just as he was about to deliver the blow. This gave Whiskers the fuel he needed to commence to bellow anew.

"Violence!" he screamed. "I knew it, a man's not safe even in the bosom of his own home. Take cover! Take cover!" He ran around in circles then dove screaming through the open window back inside his shack.

The silence folded around us like a hen's protective wing. There was no sound from the hut. Time passed and even I was beginning to think that maybe coming was a mistake when Whiskers' head popped up in the window again.

"Hey Scoot, hey Jim, who's your friend?"

"His name is Billy Wax, Whiskers, and he's in the need of some of your brain power," I replied.

He looked Billy up and down and said, "Eat fish," then disappeared from the window again.

If Scoot and I didn't know better, I suppose we would've left then and there but we recognized genius and stood in the hum of the river's sound again. After a few more minutes he popped up again.

"Howdy Jim, Scoot, Billy. Something I can do for ya?"

I explained the reason for our visit. While I was talking the old man would moan and cry and bang his head on the window frame to show how upset he was at Billy's predicament. When I had told the whole tale, he came out of the shack with his head down and his hands clasped behind his back. He paced back and forth like a caged tiger. Finally he paced to the river's edge and dropped to the ground with a thud. There he sat staring into the foaming motion. He sat and sat, long into the heat of the day. We were glad to be away from the major stink of the cabin but soon were broiling under the midday sun. Whiskers never moved. He wore his long johns and on the bottom he had on a pair of patched and re-torn wool pants. The only motion on him was the sweat dripping down the exposed flesh, vanishing into the half-soaked wool.

After what seemed like a lifetime trying to be quiet, giving whatever support we could to a thinking man, we succumbed to the pull of the river. We swam quietly at first but soon lost all restraint and were splashing and laughing like two ten-year-olds and a nine. The sun was beginning to drop in the sky when we climbed out and put our clothes back on. We sat upwind from Whiskers, who by this time looked like a soggy statue. Finally he raised his head and looked at us.

"You know that water will rob you of your protective oils, don't you? Leave you naked before disease. It's a little known fact these days. Hundreds of years ago they knew. I never let anything get between my oils and me." I thought that was pretty obvious.

"But, Whiskers," Billy said, "what about my folks, the store and all?"

"Well, Waxy," said the old man, "I've given that some thought."

Billy cringed at the play on his name. Had it been at any other time with any other person, he would have been at their throat. But even if Whiskers wasn't helping him, he would have thought long and hard before grabbing hold of that soaking wet, slimy old man.

"What your folks need is a hook, something to pull in the crowds. Used to be the woodstove would get folks to come and spin yarns but nowadays folks are too tense for that. Then there was the Motorola but everybody has one now. You need something with zip, something that reaches out and grabs 'em. Know what I mean? There's only one thing could save that store. You need a telly-vision. That's right, a television!" says he. "One of the niftiest little gizmos I ever came across. When I was back East it was just startin' to come into vogue. The idea for it is pretty old by today's mechanical marvel standards. It was in the early 1870s, if I recall right, that a guy by the name of May found that the electrical resistance of selenium was greatly reduced under illumination. They call this photoconductive action. Now the river tells me that just this year they've developed a thing called a "vidicon" that is gonna . . . Well, I'm ahead of myself. Basically a cathode ray uses electron beams to reconstitute the image at the receiver because the basic principle of transmission. Boys . . . boys . . ."

The only one who was at all in contact with what Whiskers was rambling on about was Scoot, and even he was lookin' a mite cross-eyed. Like I said before, we had all been in the city and so we knew what he was talking about. The picture machine was the rage and half the downtown storefronts sported one. But we were forty miles from the city (as the picture flew), and I couldn't imagine that we could see a moving picture all that distance.

"Mud puddles," said Whiskers. "Sure you can get it. Just put your receiver antenna high up on the store. You're on a high part of the county there, and I'll bet there ain't a single higher hill from you to St. Paul!" He commenced to laughing and jumping around and singing, "I did it again, I did it again, old Whiskers ain't lost it! That store will be the center spot of the county; wait and see, boys."

We all began to see the logic and joined him with whoops and hollerin'. After we exhausted ourselves we all lay panting in the later afternoon heat.

"Well, I expect you boys will be stayin' for dinner," voiced the old man. "I've got some fine bullhead been sittin' for about three days and in this heat that ought could spreadum on bread like jelly. I think there's even some bread around here somewhere, if the dang animals didn't root it out. I wonder if I could market bullhead jelly. You know if I didn't have so darn much money from B.C. I might just be persuaded to leave my little paradise here and make another fortune. I believe I just might do it! Yes sir, bullhead jelly . . . couldn't fail."

We made our apologies and before he could protest made an escape to the safety of the woods. As we got out of the range of his voice he was digging through the mounds of trash to find just the right jar to stuff that rotten fish in.

Well, the Polk store on E survived thanks to Whiskers and to Mr. Wax, who saw the wisdom of the scheme. It showed courage for him to risk the money for the new machine, but with the antenna high on the roof he was able to get a reasonable picture so folks from all around were introduced to Howdy Doody, the Honeymooners, Jack Parr and the rest of the magical world of television. It would be years before any number of them would be able to afford their own sets and by that time the store would be a habit for many miles around and on a firm financial footing. Billy's dad gave all the credit to the old man and for years carried jars of a slimy, pinkish yellow goo called Whiskers' Bullhead Butter. The jars would disappear and Whiskers would replace them every month raving about how, if he didn't have so much money from B.C., he would go out and make another fortune. But between you and me, there was a spot behind the store that was the brightest color green, and it never faded until the old man died and the store ran out of that magical blend.

❧ CHAPTER 6 ❧
DREAM

I have a recurring dream. Doesn't seem I have it as much now that I'm older but it used to come around quite a bit. It seems like something very basic in my life. I still have it once in a while. It still leaves me in a sweat. For some reason it feels like it rings true.

I'm walking in the woods that I love. It must be the middle of summer because everything looks in full flower but nothing has that over-used look of late August. The day is warm and bright with a steady breeze. I think when I first started having the dream I probably felt very fine indeed. Even now, at the beginning, before I start to remember, I enjoy the perfection of the day. But soon I have a feeling that I've been there before (well, I have . . . many times), and that something is not as it should be. I can foretell something that makes me very uncomfortable but I can never quite remember, can't quite visualize what it is.

Now, I know this woods in all directions as far as a man can walk in two days. It's my home. But I haven't walked a mile from the center of my world when I come to a path. I don't know this path but deep down in my soul I know it very well indeed. It's an ancient, well-trod trail, wide for this woods and covered with serpent-like roots, thick and powerful. I somehow stop and stare up its mouth while my heart begins to pound like a base drum. I don't stop to decide whether or not to use the trail. That decision seems as if it was made the day I was born. But I fight and it's like trying to fight the wind. The farther down the path I go the stronger the feelings become. I would like to run and hide but something pulls me on, like the moth to the flame.

I notice at first one, then several animals. They peer at me from behind trees and brush. The deeper into the forest I go the more bold they become. They only stare at me. They make no move to run. They only stare. Their eyes have a questioning look. As the dream drags on it becomes a pleading look. I just stare straight ahead at the clear blue sky between the trees that line the path, but I know the eyes of the animals as if I were looking into each. And I know the question deep in my soul, but in my dream I only know that I know it, not the words themselves. They become as a sea that parts as if I were Moses, but no. He was a great king, leading a great people to their promised land. I lead no one nowhere. I am very much alone. Except for the creatures that seem to look to me to stop whatever madness is taking place. I want to tell them I don't know how. I want to show them it's not my doing, not my choice but I have no voice and I have no words if I could speak, only feelings, old and powerful. They begin to whine and moan in a universal language. Some nip at my feet as if to bring me to reason.

Now the track becomes steeper and the animals cease their

protestations. They climb behind with heads down also apparently driven by what must be. My heart has become a physical discomfort. It beats within me with a violence that threatens to burst the cavity in which it lies. My breath comes hard and deep and not from the climb. After what seems like an eternity, I see up above me the path widens and spills out onto a cliff. The last few steps are the hardest. The beating has become very slow but so strong I can feel the blood being pushed through my veins. If I could I would throw my heart up and spit it out and be done with it. My air comes in huge gasps, and the wind has begun to blow. I make the last few feet and fall to my knees, able only to stare at the ground.

Slowly I find the strength to raise my head. Below me is a deep canyon and through it runs my beloved river. I believe that somewhere on my river is such a place or, I should say, was such a place. I feel very much out of time. I see the forest that surrounds the river and feel a great love in me that I know I have but seldom take the time to feel. As I raise my head a little more I see on the horizon to the west the great city, reaching tall into the rippling heat waves in the sky. The wind blows hot into my face and my eyes begin to water. My vision becomes blurred for an instant and I have a feeling that I know something is happening but I can't see clearly.

There is a sudden flash in the west. I wipe the tears from my eyes with my sleeve and strain to take another look. Above the city grows the heart of my nightmare. A huge mushroom cloud. I am incapable of motion and stare in helpless disbelief. Slowly the giant cloud spreads out, covering everything in its path. As it nears everything becomes very clear and I can see perfectly for miles. I watch as the animals are swallowed by radiation. The meat is dissolved off of their bones before their running bodies can hit the ground. The winds of destruction blow in all directions. I watch as the land and its inhabitants are erased from the face of the earth. The winds blow up the river valley. The water dissolves in an instant. The fish are frying as they hit the river bed and dissolve immediately. It winds up the valley to the cliff upon which I kneel. It's so sad. I know that I'm weeping and I know it has always been so. I am struck by the flesh-eating gale and become exposed and alone. Where the animals are I don't know. I only know I am alone in the cloud, on my knees. The wind is deafening and I bow before its ferocity.

Then I hear, softly at first then becoming louder, the sound of a hand-cranked organ's song: "La la la tink a tink a tink; la la la tink a tink a tink a tink; lo lo lo tink a tink a tink a tink; lo lo lo tink, a tink a tink."

Now I see, lowering itself down from within the cloud, a wooden vessel. It sort of looks like an old telephone booth but only much larger with lights all around it top and bottom. Its lights blink on and off making a circle and creating a kind of carnival atmosphere. It lowers slowly, very slowly, to the rhythm of the organ's tune. Everything is in slow motion and I stare up at the approaching trolley. I know it's coming for me . . . like it always has . . . like it always must be. As it sets next to me, the operator, a kind of distorted yet smiling Meher Baba holds out his hand to me. Still full of fear yet knowing what is must be, I take his hand and step into the craft. He nods at me with eyes that have always known me and we begin to rise.

I watch with regret for all the things that I did, that I never did, that I would never have a chance to do or undo as the land that I love disappears below to the sound of a hurdy-gurdy tune: "La la la tink a tink a tink . . . la la la tink a tink a tink . . . lo lo lo tink a tink a tink . . . lo lo lo tink a tink a tink . . ."

IF CIGARS HAD *been invented in* **WISCONSIN,** **MEN IN POOL HALLS** ALL OVER THE **COUNTRY** *would be smoking*

—FRED HANSON

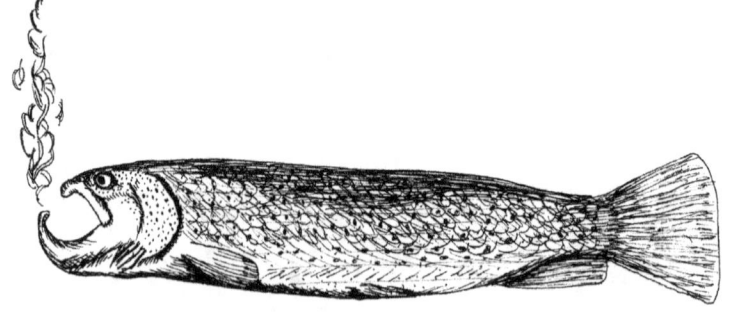

CHAPTER 7
OLYMPICS FIRST ROUND

As I reached my manhood my world began to change. I guess this is the natural progression of things but it was something that I was finding hard to accept. High school only lasted four years. If I could have I would have stopped time and stayed indefinitely in that fun-saturated time. Yep, we had more than our share. And adventures—I could fill three books with stuff we did that's hard for me to believe really happened. I guess it's all part of the magic of growing up.

But time drags on and takes all of us with it. Scoot left me for medical school and became one of the world's greatest brain surgeons. I'm not at all surprised, as smart as he was. He also had a gift with a fillet knife that was not to be believed. Billy Wax became a soldier, for which he was also suited, and then he was lost in the Vietnam War. Even though it hurt awful badly it didn't really surprise me either. God forgot to give that boy his fair share of fear. Story is, he saved a whole mess of folks in his dying moments and, around here, we're mighty proud of him. I went off to college myself and became a liberal artist. That's someone who can dabble in lots of things but none of them seriously. I came home with the feeling that, now that I was educated, I had a responsibility to go out in the world and make a fortune.

So off I went to Minneapolis to make a life. I tried every kind of job you can imagine. I started out at one of the giant twin city– based companies, Honeywell. I spent all of three weeks there. I am the most undisciplined individual you can imagine and I have a couple problems that make me a fairly undesirable large company prospect. I'm not a joiner. I can't gather with large groups. Everyone has a scam that they want you to agree with and most folks just seem to be able to nod and pretend to be interested. In that, I'm afraid, I fail. I have tried but my face refuses to go along. It seems I offended a few folks. I also find very few things to take really seriously. I know when work has to be done it has to be done correctly, and that I would do. But to truly believe it is somehow significant was beyond my capabilities. We were involved in high-tech research so were also involved in products that had military applications. Being involved in all that also hurt me deep inside. I tried as best I could, but I'm afraid it wasn't very good. So we parted ways, a no-fault accident.

I tried several other things, from real estate to insurance but felt kind of like a small fry in a school of musky. Finally, I started driving cab at night, while I looked during the day for something more suitable. I found that I didn't mind hackin'. The people of the night are an interesting lot and I gathered quite a few interesting stories. That's kind of what it's about, isn't it? I mean, when it's all over you want your life to read well, don't you? Anyway, I found that during the daylight hours I was doing more fishing and sleeping, in that order, than job seeking. I found a small lake right in the middle of town that held some fine bass and pike and lots of pan fish.

I was doing this routine for about a month or so when I started noticing a man in a suit watching me. He came every day for what I assumed was his lunch hour. He never said anything and I was getting to the point where I was going to ask him to come on over if he wanted to watch, when he came up to me. Turns out he worked for a company that made fishing lures. He was much impressed by my skills and wanted me to go to work for the company and help design and test equipment. So after finding out that he was on the level and the company was interested in me I signed on that very day. I've been on the payroll of Arboblaster ever since. They're a fine company and have treated me very well.

I worked in their inner city plant for almost a year, where we designed some of the modern day standards. But at the end of the year I was pale and sickly. I guess I'm a delicate fish and being in the murky city water was taking its toll. I went to the head of the company and told him my story. He could tell by looking at me that one way or another he was going to lose an employee. He was a good man, and a very capable fisherman, so we began to research the options. I was the best fisherman in the company with a natural instinct for what fish wanted. They didn't want to lose me.

Finally, they came up with my present status. I design and test lures right out of my own cabin, which they built for me next to the site of my folks' old cabin on the river I love. Talk about blessed! You know how Jesus was fond of fisherman? Well

I believe he still has a soft spot in his heart for them. I know I've been looked after. Well, I worked that way for a couple of more years without too many stories. It was a peaceful time and I guess I was about as happy as a single man can be, doing exactly what I pleased.

Then came 1963 and a president looking for someone to represent the U.S. in an unofficial event in the 1964 Olympics. John F. Kennedy was looking for a few good fishermen! I was approached by our Wisconsin representative, Lucky Dave Lackloman. He had heard of me while on the campaign trail and wanted me to compete in a statewide competition. If I won at state I would go on to a national fish-off. Well, I wasn't so sure this was a good idea, or legal by Olympic standards. I worked in the fishing industry and was, by definition, a professional. They assured me that I was eligible for the position because this would not be a sanctioned event. In fact, it was more along the lines of a personal bet between Kennedy and Khrushchev. It seems that Khrushchev was going on about the superiority of Soviet everything when he started on about fishing. Well, not many folks know it but Jack Kennedy was a fair fisherman himself, and by the time his Russian counterpart had come around to that sport he was tired of the pompous leader's raving. So he bet, as the story came to me, that U.S. fishermen were not only superior to Soviet fishermen but the finest in the world. So the ground rules were laid and it was decided that it would be an unofficial event in the '64 Olympics. Now that he had put his country and ego on the line, JFK began to search his Camelot for a lure-throwing Lancelot.

It was in the spring of 1963 that I was approached to compete in the all Wisconsin fish-off. At first I said I could not. I felt that I owed Arboblaster and would never quit my job. I knew a good thing when I saw it and for me this job was the best. So the folks in charge of rounding up worthy contestants went straight to our company's headquarters in Minneapolis and talked to our top management. They explained the benefits of having a contestant in the field and pointed out the obvious advantages should I win. Well, I guess those old boys didn't need a whole lot of convincing because they drove down to the cabin that very day. They told me I was the best there was and that, if I would wear an Arboblaster cap and T-shirt, and if any lures I used would become part of the Arboblaster line, and if I would do extensive advertising for them if I won, then I had their blessing. I guess I'm kind of like an old dog, if you once throw me a bone and scratch my ears I'll follow you anywhere. So I didn't even need to sign their new contract 'cause I would have done all of those things for them anyway. I liked what they were doing for fishing (they were instrumental in early repopulation efforts in heavily used fishing areas and were always concerned with environmental issues, even before it was popular), and I liked what they had done for me. So I was an Arboblaster man all the way! I love my peace and quiet and if I could have seen what notoriety I was going to get I might have run and hid. But I also love a challenge and said yes. Besides, I was beginning to think that maybe, just maybe, I was the best there ever was.

The contest was organized in a flash. Within a month of the original wager fishermen all over the world were deeply involved in local competitions. Because not all states had salt water access it was decided that it would be an all-freshwater event. That suited me just fine because, although I believed I could fish the "big water," I had never tried.

They divided Wisconsin into four sections for the preliminaries. The northwest section was section four, with our first head-to-head commencing in a town called Luck. I found out later that a local politician had a cabin on the lake and pulled a few strings to get that location. I guess he figured the publicity would increase his property value and also his nephew was in the competition, so he hoped to give him an advantage. The stench of politics is everywhere! I myself had never fished the lake but knew it to hold a fair population of bass, northern and walleye with the normal abundance of pan fish. The rules were really well thought out. The idea was not to choose the luckiest fisherman but to choose the best. So it was decided that points would be awarded for several categories: largest fish of each species, most fish, most varied species and finally presentation or style. I was as excited as a kid.

The contest started at five a.m. on the first day of May in 1963. The weather was gray with a fine mist turning any and all dry to instant wet. The competition was at this stage open so the banks were literally lined with hopefuls as the clocks headed down the homestretch for five. I was in a twelve-foot Alumacraft boat with a three-horse Johnson motor. For a small lake this was a standard and I would say a large percentage of my competition were outfitted the same. The lake is a fairly small one being less than 400 acres and only twenty-feet deep at the most. It's not the most imaginative lake they could have chosen either. It is almost round with very little structure. There are a few small rivers, really just trickles, going in and out, but besides that no bays or arms of land, no middle lake sandbars or other obvious "hot spots." But there was, by reputation, a good quantity of fish in the lake so I waited excitedly for the starting gun. When the bang finally came everyone jumped into their boats with enough noise to scare even the most brassy fish back into hibernation. People had not started to carpet the bottom of their boats yet, so hard shoes on bare metal do bangs make. I, at that time, always wore a pair of corduroy slippers I had purchased for just that reason. But with all the surrounding racket it didn't really matter that my boat slid silently out into the newly violated pool.

I had intended to fish bass to begin with, casting surface lures from about thirty feet offshore toward the land, but it was an obvious strategy and it turned out every other man had the same idea. Before I could even begin, a giant ring of fishermen were encircling the lake. I motored out to the center and watched as the boats began to circle. I felt like I was in the center of a giant carnival ride as the boats motored round and round. I don't believe any self-respecting bass would succumb to such a barrage so I began to set up for an alternative attack. There were three or four other boats out of the daisy chain and I made a mental note of who might be my real competition. It was still early in the season so I figured I might pick up a few walleyes at the river locations. This was one of my Dad's favorite tactics so I borrowed one from him and camped at the southwest end of the lake where Butternut creek heads for the ocean. I rigged up one of my walleye specials and dropped her in the pond. This "special" was a small hook with a very small bobber about two feet up the line. I put a medium sized sinker another foot up and a fine fat leech for the call. The sinker sits on the bottom with the bobber holding the bait up and in view. The two feet of line allows the leech (or minnow or worm) to perform in a natural manner making an effective troll (remember trolling?). Also walleye are light hitters so they can drag that sinker a ways before they pull directly on my pole and feel real resistance. It's a method I still use and find to be, under the right conditions, very effective. It proved out again this time because within a very few minutes I was boating my first fish of the day. It was a four pounder and considering the fact that I had heard this lake held only smaller fish, I happily put it on the stringer. I tried to be as sly as I could in hiding my success but by the time I was boating the final fish in my limit I could have walked to shore over the fishermen who crowded around me. The largest walleye I caught was an eight pounder, the smallest was the first four pounder and I was satisfied that it would take some doing to beat my stringer so far.

Since I had filled out on what I consider to be the most frustrating of game fish in the first hour of the game I decided to spend the next hour exploring. This was before the days of depth finders so we had to use other methods to figure out the bottom. I had a pyramid shaped piece of lead made that I would drag over the bottom of a lake to get an idea of its structure. I would run the motor very slowly with heavy weight tied to my pole. When the water became even a little shallower it was obvious and large rocks and submerged trees and such stood out like perch in a pickerel pen. It was slow by today's standards but still quite effective. So I spent the next two hours circling the lake, making notes on anything worthwhile. The bottom dropped right off to ten feet then tapered down to around fifteen feet, flattened out, and then dropped gradually to a final twenty feet, which held true for almost the whole center of the lake. I found one variation, a sandbar that was ten feet surrounded by twenty feet. It was not a large bar, only thirty feet or so long and six or seven feet wide, but I felt at some time of the day it might produce a northern or two. We would see.

The lake had succumbed to total confusion. Most of the bass fishermen had quit circling and were trying their hand at other, hopefully more productive, tactics. During the explorations I had picked out my most serious competitors. From what I could see I believed there were only two. There was an old lady in a floppy hat fishing out of an old wooden scow. Her husband, I assume, was rowing the boat. She was as big a woman as I've seen on water and he was as skinny as a rail. She was fishing with primitive equipment, a cane pole, but was doing very well. Her stringer was already causing a wake behind the slowly moving craft. My other competition I knew very well. He was mentioned earlier in a tale about my folks, and was, probably the best natural fisherman in the area. Many folks would talk about who was better, him or me, and several had come just to watch what they figured would be a two-man duel. It was Fred Hanson, the man who'd witnessed my father's fish surfing.

Fred was a Chicago man who spent every summer on Bone Lake, which is fairly close to my cabin. He and his wife, Sandy, had been coming to the area since the beginning of time and were good friends with my folks. Fred was what you would now-adays call a party animal. He loved the pretty ladies and he loved his pint. He could tell a joke or hear a joke and end up laughing until he cried. Sandy was the only way she could be and still maintain her sanity. She was quiet and tolerant. My folks were conservative, by comparison, and would party rarely. Usually, it was Fred who would really shake them loose and my dad and he spent several nights on their knees behind the cabin "baying at the moon." My dad and mom were devoted to each other and could never understand Fred's casual attitude with the ladies. Sandy was a very special lady, which made the situation harder to figure. I just think Fred was part goat and figured it was his personal obligation to see to it that everyone had a good time, including the ladies. But if anyone had problems, Fred was the first one there. He would give of himself until you would think it would turn inside out, and everyone who really got to know him loved him. He was the original "lovable rogue." One of his other talents was the ability to catch lots of fish and that's the one that concerned me now.

When I took my spin around the lake I not only checked out the bottom but I checked out my competition. I could tell Fred was doing very well indeed. He had the exact same rig as mine, a twelve-foot Alumacraft with a three-horse Johnson motor. He had something I didn't have, however, a driver. His grandson, Rick, was at the rear, expertly guiding the boat at Fred's direction. Rick was a ten-year-old Chicago boy who loved the woods and his grandfather. The two of them became a well-oiled fishing machine. I could see I had to get down to business.

By the time I was ready to wet a line the sun was beginning to hint at the kind of heat it was going to kick out of the day. I decided I would troll (trail?) the north shore of the lake and try to shake loose a northern or two. The reason I chose this area was because there were weeds right at shore that came down to about the fifteen-foot mark. I believe in dragging a plug right off this kind of weed line for pike production. It was tough going to begin with. My first pass I harvested several weeds and a slimy little bullhead. I hate those fish and for some reason consider it my obligation to clear the lakes of them, so I threw the little booger in the bottom of the boat. My concentration was definitely off. This was my first real competition fishing and my insides were tangled in knots. When the fish don't want to bite I do this thing where I mentally demand them to surrender to me. I know it sounds like I've popped my cork, but it has rarely failed. After a few minutes of this kind of telepathic calling I feel a change come over me and I feel as if I'm in direct contact. That's when, like a long distance runner, I begin to pull away. That's what happened this day. I began to catch fish every time I dropped my line in the water. At first people crowded around, thinking I was in a hot spot, but soon they quit even fishing. They just began to watch. The only drawback to my style of fishing is that fish of all kinds respond. For every fish I wanted to put on the stringer there were ten or twenty I threw back.

By noon it was obvious that the field was narrowing down. Fred and Rick were fishing the relative shallows in the northeast corner of the lake and they too had begun to draw a crowd. I couldn't see the Ma and Pa Kettle team but there was a crowd in the southwest corner of the lake where Butternut Creek lives, and if I didn't miss my guess that's where they were working. I wasn't too sure what the judges were looking for in relation to style but since I was really in high speed I knew I could catch fish on anything and I began to show off. I had several rods with me so I began to use every technique I knew. I used everything from spinning gear to a cane pole. I stood up in the boat with my fly fishing gear and filled out on bass from five to eight pounds. Catching an eight-pound bass on a fly rod is as exciting as it comes and the crowd went wild. I even caught a twenty-pound northern on a drop-line, much to my finger's dismay! Then my success coupled with the appreciation of the crowd began to get to me. I had pretty much filled my limits on everything with fish that I felt were good enough to win so I really started to strut. I stood on the seat of the boat and told the onlookers I could catch fish on anything. I asked them to throw me anything and I would catch a fish on it. I put hooks on everything from key rings to sunglasses and caught fish on everything. One sweet young thing even donated her brassiere, to the howling delight of the crowd. I tied a red and white daredevil to one end and promptly landed a six-pound pike with it. You should have heard those folks scream every time that pike jumped and those double "Ds" came flying out of the water. By the time we had motored in to the scales I didn't think even Fred had a chance to match the day I'd had.

The "odd couple" were the first ones that could compete to the scales. They had filled their limit and had the largest blue gill I had ever seen. They would easily win largest in that category. When they laid out my catch I controlled the lead in all other areas. My top fish were a thirty-two-pound northern, an eight-pound walleye, an eight-pound bass and a two-pound crappie. The rest of my limits were equally impressive. By the time Fred and Rick motored in I was feeling pretty cocky. My security was short-lived, however, as I watched them unload their boat. Fred was obviously confident and also obviously feeling no pain. He shuffled a little soft shoe and sang a dirty little ditty as Rick hauled out his catch. I could tell at a glance, he had a larger bass and a larger walleye. When the weighing was done, we were dead even in points. Then it came to style. I was again sure that I would walk away with that one. But Fred was no slouch when it came to playing the crowds. I guess he had come prepared, starting out singing quietly and sipping his pint while Rick whistled along. He brought a large board along, which he laid on two seats and at the finale was dancing atop the board, singing at the top of his voice with Rick banging a drumbeat on the side of the boat and singing in perfect harmony. All the while Fred was hauling in the fish as fast as he could reel. I just wished I could have been there. So anyway we were judged a dead even. No one could have imagined a tie and the rules had nothing to say about one. We all stood in dead silence as the judges scratched their collective heads.

Then out of the silence came a very gentle "thump." Everyone turned to the row of boats on the shore to see where it came from. It was soon followed by another "thump . . . thump . . . thump." It was definitely coming from the bottom of my boat. One of the on-lookers nearby peered over the side and slowly reached down into the craft. With a disgusted look he lifted out by the tail one ugly, nasty, slimy little bullhead. It was the only one of its kind caught all day so, with that single fish, I use the term loosely, I captured another largest of breed, another most of breed and best of all, the contest itself! Fred was great about it and toasted me countless times. The last thing he said before his mind surrendered to the void was "Jim, remember, you can pick your friends and you can pick your nose, but you cannot pick your friend's nose! He looked at me as if to apologize and added, "Jimmy, it just can't be done." With those words of wisdom, he passed out cold.

CHAPTER 8
INTERSTELLAR CAMPING

I guess it was about 1955, midsummer in our part of the country, and the time of life that just begs for a campout. It didn't take too much to get my friends out for a night on the river, in fact we had a semi-permanent campsite that we had cleared and used on average one night a week. The gang at this stage of my life was Billy Wax, Scoot, Michelle (Mike), a kid named Andover Scrubb and me.

Now I'm sure that most of you out there are aghast at the thought of four fifteen-year-old boys and one fifteen-year-old girl on a campout, but you didn't know this group. We had grown up together and would fight to the death for each other. I'm not saying she wasn't worth looking at, not at all. She was slim and strong with raven black hair and eyes blue as deep water. She still acted pretty much like the rest of us but her pretty, soft features and liquid motion when she moved, together with a body that was quickly becoming more Michelle than Mike, was beginning to set us apart. But she had always been a tomboy so we refused to think of her as anything but one of us. She was very grown up in some ways and was private in her sexuality. We hadn't skinny-dipped as a group since we were nine or ten. While we swam she always disappeared and vice-versa. There was a lot of love and respect there and at fifteen the mindless rut was still weak and confusing. She had her own tent and equipment but we put all of our heads toward the fire so we could talk together through the night.

This was the last year this was possible though. Mike's folks called me over to their house at the end of the summer and had me sit down. They explained that Michelle was getting to the age where she was turning into a woman and to avoid any problems that would hurt us all they would not let her camp with us after that summer. I felt terrible and so did she, but we both knew they were right. We were starting to feel those rumblings. I can honestly say after that summer every time the gang went camping I felt someone was missing. It was never quite the same. But that came later, now we were just rolling out the tents and all the heads were facing the fire.

I suppose I should tell you about Andover Scrubb. He was a real case. The kid was a bit off from the rest of the crew. He was no good at fishing and as out of place as a well-worn Barcalounger in the woods. You might wonder why he was with us. Well, there were two main reasons: one, we had all been together since we could walk and two, he had a great sense of humor. No matter what kind of mess he got into he always supplied the comic relief to make getting him out of it worthwhile. He was a short kid, at least half a head shorter than me and at fifteen I was no giant. He was covered from head to toe with a generous layer of baby fat that was milk white and clammy to the touch. Shaking his hand was like grabbing a pike. It left you looking for a towel.

Although he was very smart, he wasn't particularly brilliant in school. He had an obsession with being a World War One Stuka pilot so spent much of his class time planning "Stuka raids" on unsuspecting female victims. This involved pretty harmless "fly-bys" involving a run up with flapping arms extended spraying vocal Stuka bullets at the generally grossed-out female victim. He tried to be careful in his chosen targets so as not to attack and destroy any well-defended areas (boyfriends, etc.). Every once in a while his attacks would get so frenzied his Stuka bullets would spray unintended targets and Andover would find himself the target of some football player's wrath. But upon being attacked he could instantly cover himself with sweat, transforming from Stuka pilot to Clam Man. When he was grabbed his attacker's hands would immediately be covered with slime or "clam sauce." This sauce was so nasty as to easily repel the most ferocious attacker. Together with Scrubb's moaning and whining and pleading he was so disgusting even the most aggressive champion would be turned aside. After he was left alone with us he would get up off the floor, look around to make sure the coast was clear, then proceed to strut around like some cross between a bantam rooster and slug chanting, "I am the man! The MAN I AM! The unbeatable MAN OF CLAMS!" He was a national treasure. We just called him Clam Man.

Now, to get back to the fire. I hope you don't think I'm babbling on too much but you can't appreciate some of the things that went on if I don't paint a reasonable picture in your mind's eye of some of these people. I remember them so clearly it's like

I could turn around and there would be the Clam Man, grinnin'; Mike, strong and unafraid; Billy Wax, as defiant as an unbroken colt; and of course Scoot, with eyes that looked deep into your head and willingly shared the good and the bad he found there. Yeah, they were the best, and we were done setting up the tents and just rolling out the sleeping bags. Mike, like I said before, had her own tent, me and Scoot shared a pup tent, and Clam Man slept with Billy. Fortunately they had a three-man tent, so Billy set up a "no man's land" in between them. If Clam Man should roll over in his sleep he was awakened to the sound of Billy threatening to take his trespassing parts off. Of course, Billy would never touch him. Even he was no match for the "Man of Clams."

The sun was just beginning to give up for the day so we gathered wood and struck our match for the night. We prided ourselves in our woodsmanship and were so confident in our abilities that we always brought only one match. We figured if we couldn't raise a fire with one match we deserved to do our campin' in the dark. This would also mean no trout, which was one of the highlights of the night, so we were ceremoniously respectful of that match. We always left the strikin' to Scoot and the trout catchin' to me. Mike would fry the fish (there was already that much woman in her) and Clam Man and Billy would do the general chores like gathering water and wood. We moved around like a well-oiled machine. No chore was given to anyone, we just all knew what we could do best and happily did it. Within minutes there was a fine fire crackling, Mike was buttering the pans and I was hiking up from the river with the five fine rainbows we would consume that night. By the time the trout were done Scoot and I had helped the other guys set up a camp to be proud of.

Those trout were the stuff that legends were made of. I mean to say they were as good as any I have in my life tasted and brother I've tasted them all, from Fish Corners to France. There were none finer. By the time we had savored our meal, cleaned up and crawled into our canvas survival skins the night was in full control and the stars were visible even over the warm flow of our fire.

We lay in silence for a while, just soaking in the beauty of the midsummer night. The river sang its gentle song and the breeze blew softly through the pines and birch that formed a canopy over our campsite.

"Did any of you people hear the news on the radio before coming out this evening?" asked Billy Wax, a look of concern on his brow.

"Not I," I said.

"Not me," said Mike.

"My dad's radio is busted in the truck," said Clam Man. "All it gets is the engine sound goin' through the gears. Powerful stuff, ya know? I don't know how my dad can listen to it." He shook his head.

"I have a feeling I may be sorry for asking, Billy," began Scoot, "but why do you ask?"

"Well, my friend," he grew larger with self-importance, "I haven't mentioned it before but I almost didn't come tonight."

"Come on, Billy," whined Clam, "you ain't gonna start that stuff again are you?"

"I know I've told a tall tale or two before," admitted Billy, "but this one's for real." He looked sincere. "As real as that shadow over there . . . sayyyyy, did that move or am I reactin' to the moon or something?"

We all looked in the direction that he pointed and sure enough there was a shadow that, if you really hadn't thought about it, could have been a tad unnerving but none of us could see it move. Clam made a gagging sound somewhere in his throat.

"Clam, if you wet this tent I'll rip your face off!" yelled Billy. "I don't know why I always gotta sleep with you anyway. Why can't I come over and bunk with you, Mike? I'll be good."

"You never been good for nothin' before, Billy. Why should I think just 'cause you say it you'd be good for something now?"

"Aw, you just couldn't keep your hands off of me, that's all you're afraid of," came back Billy.

Mike winked at me and Scoot and grinned. "I expect you're right, Billy Wax, best leave well enough alone. No sense in playin' with fire."

"You wouldn't really leave me, would you, Billy?" Now it was Clam Man's turn. "I mean it's always been you and me. I mean what about all of those sweet things you said after everyone was asleep last week. You said if I let you, you would be my friend forever."

"You sick swine," was all that Billy mumbled as he put his head down on the pillow. "I just wondered if you all heard what I had heard, that's all."

"You're gonna tell us anyway," I said in a resigned tone. "Let's hear the bad news."

"Well," began Billy, now firmly in the driver's seat, "the fact is, the radio said there was a UFO landing over near Milltown last night, probably Martians. Story said it scared one farmer so bad it turned his hair white as a January rabbit. Went from coal black to snow white . . . OVERNIGHT! Now this is one tale I don't have to make up, no sir, this is the straight poop!"

What with Buck Rogers on TV, UFOs were quickly becoming a national pastime. That summer the TV seemed to realize the commercial potential in reporting all the sightings. Seems like all the nuts were being shook out of the tree at once. One guy even claimed a spaceman bred his wife and that his son was a new super-breed. He was busily trying to collect money to start his new "Universal Seed Church." There are a lot of strange fish swimming up this stream, ya know?

Scoot was the first to react to Billy. "You don't mean to tell us that the fearless Billy Wax almost gave up his night on the river because of a few puny Martians, do you?"

"And leave you to fend for yourselves? Not likely. But I believe in those things . . . I just got a feelin'. . . and I'm not so sure I'm gonna enjoy meetin' one of them. I mean, what if they're all horrible . . . what if they're all . . ." Billy paused, groping for the right word.

"Like Clam Man?" Mike finished off the sentence.

Clam Man jumped out of his sleeping bag, exposing to the world his ultra baggy boxer shorts with puppies on them (I don't know where he found boxers like them in 1955). He was naked on top and his thick layer of baby fat seemed to follow the rest of him around but never catch up. His belly hung over the elastic of his shorts, hiding from view at least a litter of puppies.

"I AM THE MAN," he began. "I was sent to this world by my leader . . . the wise and wonderful KING CLAM himself!" He danced and waved his arms like a drunken sumo wrestler. "You puny earthlings will bow to me and later serve my king!"

"Clam, get back in here before you get all sweaty and commence to stinkin'," pleaded Billy.

Clam stopped his jumping around and looked very serious. "I will do as you say earthman. My time has not yet come. I could, with a wave of my hand, turn you all into vanilla and chocolate pudding." He looked at Scoot. "But for now, I wait." He threw back his head and laughed like a madman showing lines of gumbo in the folds of his neck that probably had never seen the light before and probably dated back to infancy. I casually wondered at all the other hiding places he had as he climbed back into his bag.

"Well, I just thought you guys would be interested, that's all." Billy tossed a small piece of wood into the fire and remained silent.

The rest of us surrendered to the draw of the flames and stared intently at their flickering motion. The tents were far enough away to be safe from sparks and general overheating but close enough so we could feel the power of the flames on our faces. The river took up the conversation, starting up its story of time beyond as if it had only paused to catch its breath. The frogs and crickets urged the water on and a high flying loon cried his cry making the moment golden and permanent. Time seemed to stop as we were devoured by our individual mental ramblings. One by one our heads set to rest on our pillows. Just as I was drifting off I heard Mike say, "Thank you, God, you done it good." Scoot mumbled his agreement, "Amen!" Then we all dropped off to sleep.

I'm not sure if it was the light, the noise or the motion that woke me up but it took me a while to come all the way around to consciousness. I think I must have been dreaming of bright lights and noise and vibration because there is no real memory of, you know, Bam! I'm awake. It's more like, am I still dreaming? Then no, this is no dream, but I'm already on my feet. I looked around and we were all on our feet in various stages of panic. Mike was screaming at the top of her lungs, but the noise from the lights was so loud you could just see her mouth open and her head shaking. Scoot was trying to maintain his composure. He was trying to run through all the options of what our visitor could be vocally but at the same time he was running back and forth waving his hands like a Southern Baptist surrendering to the Spirit. Billy Wax was busy yelling threats and throwing sticks and rocks at the light. I was watching it all but I honestly can't say what my body was doing. The incredible Clam Man was standing in the center of us all, as if made of stone. Suddenly all at once the lights dimmed, the vibration stopped and the noise ceased except for a continuous "woosh . . . woosh . . . woosh . . ." as a giant disk hovered a mere fifty feet from us. We all stopped our raving and stood transfixed.

I would say that there are few experiences in my life that compare to that moment. I mean, your mind is in deep woods mode, you are far from the maddening crowd, all the little molecules in your body are moving so slow and easy that you are probably not even aging. Then someone throws a switch and you are flying through the air in a total state of panic. I'm talking chaos. Now it's quiet except for the steady "woosh . . . woosh . . . woosh . . ." and you're staring at a spinning saucer that had to cover forty acres. It's enough to fry your mind!

Gagglestisstphissssssss . . . . ! Along the side of the ship lines appeared then widened to expose a door with a now lowering ramp. We all regained a touch of commonsense and scrambled to hide behind trees and tents and peek. All of us, that is, except for Clam Man. He stood like a statue and stared at the ramp.

"Clam, get your butt over here," Billy whispered. "This ain't no time to try out bravery." But if you looked close you could see that Clam was shakin'. He was shaking so fast that if you didn't look close you couldn't tell he was shakin' at all.

Then it appeared in the door. It was about the height of a normal human with longer legs and arms and less body. It had a large round head that had a liquid motion to it. What I'm trying to say is that it had features but they seemed to be changing.

The thing lifted a long arm and pointed a bony finger at Clam. "HOWWWW WOOULD YOOOOU . . ." At this point there appeared on the front of Clam's boxers a small spot. It quickly became larger and larger. He showed the creature the backs of his eyeballs and then, with a back as straight as an ironing board, he fell to the ground into the security of another state of consciousness. This obviously confused our visitor. He continued with less confidence, ". . . like to be Queen for a Day?" He looked around then back at the Clam. "Awww, Kingfish," he said. "What is I gonna do?"

It was about this time I noticed that when he said that his face changed to look exactly like the TV character Amos Jones from *Amos and Andy*. Then he must have noticed us peeking out of our hiding places. He visibly brightened and shouted, "Hey, kids . . . what time is it?" with a face that used to belong to Buffalo Bob. "It's Howdy Doody time!" Then he stopped, as if waiting for a response. "Let's hear it from the peanut gallery!" Next his face was wooden looking with red hair and large freckles. "Who's your pal, kids? Howdy's your pal!"

It was beginning to be obvious that this creature was trying with all he had to communicate with us. We slowly stepped out into the clearing. "That's it, that's it, kids. Don't worry, Mr. Bluster isn't around." His face began to change. "Less me see, less me see," he said, looking over at Mike. "What's we got here. If it ain't as fine a specimen of feminine pulchritude as I ever see'd, or my name ain't Algonquin J. Calhoun." He held his head up when he said the name and shook his bony finger at the sky. This guy had obviously seen too much TV. I stepped forward.

"Can . . . you . . . understand . . . me?" I tried to talk like a person would to a Martian.

The thing's face kind of hovered in a nondescript mode. "Yes," was all it said.

"Can you speak without changing?"

"Yes," was again its reply.

"What do you want?" I asked.

We watched as his face changed a few times then landed in a serious, business-like face. "And now," he said, "the news. It began long ago, in a town, not much like this, with people, not like these, for reasons no one can know." He paused for impact. "Can anyone really know?" I caught his searching eyes. "But wherever you go . . . there you are so here we are. Are we there?"

I could empathize with him at that point. "Why have you come?" I asked.

"The cosmic cry," he said, as if that should clear everything up.

"What is the cosmic cry?" The question had to be asked.

Now his face was wavering again. It settled in on Alice and

The Honeymooners. "Don't you know, Ralph," he (she) said, almost in tears, "don't you really know?" I shook my head. "It's when you hurt in here, Ralph, you know, in here." She put her hand on her heart. "I'm not just talking about us . . . about here . . . I'm talking about the whole lousy world, Ralph. When it gets big enough, it cries, like people, Ralph. But it's the whole world. And we hear it. It's the cry, Ralph . . . the cosmic cry."

We stood staring at this powerful being.

"What can we do?" This time it was Scoot asking.

His face turned into the sincere Amos. "Well, brother," he began, "what can we do, well we can do . . . all we can."

"That's it?" questioned Scoot.

"That, my man," the creature held Scoot's eyes, "is everything!"

He walked back up the ramp and turned as he reached the ship. His face slowly changed again, this time taking on the familiar round shape of a smiling Jackie Gleason. His bulldog eyes were filled with pools of liquid love.

He was nodding his pudgy face. "I love ya, Norton," he said. "Trixie, I love ya! But Alice . . . ah, Alice. Baby, you're the GREATEST!"

He turned and was swallowed up by the great craft. The lights became bright and the engines screamed. The ground shook and in the wink of an eye, the saucer was gone.

I would guess our visitors communication skills were honed on a reception of a TV frequency. They must have figured that was our reality. It worked OK, I guess. Anyway, we sure got the message! Clam woke up a few minutes after the creature left and claimed he was zapped by a paralyzing ray gun that also made him lose his water. Luckily he had a change of clothes. By this time the eastern sky was showing the first signs of pink. We all crawled back into our bags to finish out the night. I'm sure not a one of us did any sleepin' though. I think we all felt like cradling the world in our arms, you know, like a baby. Tellin' it things aren't that bad, not really. Please don't cry.

But we were just kids with hardly any idea of what pain and suffering were about. In our part of the world we were blessed beyond measure. In other parts of the world there was starvation and war. We were in a mighty cold war with communists and trying to adjust to the idea of possible world destruction. Just this new nuclear reality was, I'm sure, enough to make the strongest of worlds weep. We all shuffled around for a few days in a kind of shock, each of us trying to deal with our altered reality. I guess we finally found some comfort in the fact that there were some other folks out there who cared. I guess we won't know until that big crisis happens, the one we can't back out of, just how much our friends can help, but from the impression we got I think there might be an unexpected ace in the hole.

CHAPTER 9
ALL-STATE

Well we were off and running in the not-official international fishing Olympics. After the battle royal we'd had in the regional competition I figured the next stage for the Wisconsin State champion could only be a letdown. I guess, in some ways, I was right. The competition with Rick and Fred in the same heat was not to be equaled until I hit the international level. But I did run into some great fishing!

The lakes they chose for the next leg of the tournament were the two lakes, Lost Land Lake and Teal Lake, located in the northern part of the state about twenty miles west of Hayward, Wisconsin. We were allowed to fish both because they are connected by shallow but navigable water. I had not fished the lakes but had heard that there was a very fine musky population along with every other local species. I have fished there many times since the '63 season and now stay at the very nice Teal Lake Lodge where I enjoy the company of its owner (an excellent fisherman and guide), Tim Ross. But back then I was on my own in another strange neighborhood.

The morning of the tourney exposed a clear day that promised to be a scorcher. Now there were only four of us, so the craziness of the last round would not be repeated. Basically, this day was devoted to just toe-to-toe fishing. I began with a surface lure that I had made that was a lot like the modern "jointed jitterbug." It was a hinged plug with a metal "plow" on its nose. It was made out of balsa wood so it floated very high in the water. When retrieved it shook its head, causing bubbles and pops and a wake as wide as a motorboat. Now, it's hard to imagine what animal in nature this thing imitates but I can tell you for sure it drives bass wild!

The mist was still lightly rising from the surface of the lake when we pushed off from shore. You can sometimes tell from the shore what the bottom of a lake is like. The ground gently sloped up away from the water, and I assumed that the bottom probably had a gradual grade out to the more significant depths. There were many trees down, attesting to a healthy beaver population. I chose an older log, half sunk, half floating, to try out this new day. The log was just about perpendicular to the shore so I positioned my boat as if it were pointing at me, about thirty feet out. I dropped my lure three feet from land next to the bobbing remains of the tree and waited.

I like to imagine a scene in nature whenever I fish. What would a fish think about a presentation? How could I convince him that everything was as it should be, and this bobbing chunk of wood and metal was a tasty treat sent free of charge from the fish gods, just for him? When using a surface lure I imagine that anything in nature that small, that would hit the water with that kind of force, would be stunned, and I try to make the plug act accordingly. First I let it lie for a full minute at least. This allows the fish to first swim away from the splash, then to slowly swim back to take a closer look at what made the ruckus. All fish are curious and I guarantee they will, with very few exceptions, come back for a look. It's up to the fisherman to convince them that the lure is alive and a worthy meal. After my minute, I give my rod tip an almost imperceptible bump. This causes the lure to twitch like it was just beginning to come around. Then I let it sit again. Now a hungry bass will often strike at this point. If they are heavily fished or not too hungry they will retreat and you must wait again. I will only wait perhaps half a minute this time (remember, we're trying to act like a living thing regaining consciousness), then shake it a little harder. If our fish hasn't hit by this time I believe the longer we sit the less our chances that he will, so now our bait becomes a creature that suddenly realizes he is in danger but is disoriented. We pull him in a foot or so, then stop, then pull another couple feet, then stop, acting as if it doesn't quite know what to do. Then reel him straight to you. A good lure has a designed motion for a direct retrieve so now it's up to that motion to tempt your fish. Try to make him look natural all the way to the boat because a fish may follow it a long way before returning to shore. If you maintain a natural look when he sees the lure again he may be convinced it's alive and hit. One thing to keep in mind is that no two things in nature are exactly the same, so when you present your lure, use variations of your main theme. Above all, use your imagination!

My mixture of practiced expertise and God-given luck held out once again and before I could stop for coffee I had my limit of largemouth. They were really beautiful. I can't say enough about these two lakes. Not only is the fishing excellent, but the area is also very nice indeed.

My next objective was my old friend, the walleye. I didn't know this lake, as I've said, so I decided to trail some bait and take a tour at the same time. My choice was a very popular bait at the time, a Prescott spinner with a minnow. That is a rather large hook (by today's standards) with a silver spinner about two inches up a steel leader. I attached a medium sized shiner and used a medium to small sized sinker, depending on depth, about two feet up from the whole unit. One of the nice things about the Prescott is that you are just as apt to hook a northern or musky as a walleye. Since I was after them all I began to drag this universal "get."

Usually you can target either a walleye or northern or musky by the speed at which you motor. The slower speeds are for walleye and the faster for the more aggressive pike. We had put in at the northernmost corner of Lost Land Lake so up to this point I had been fishing there. By the time I hit the connecting water between the lakes in the southeast corner I had boated three musky, one sixteen pounder, one twelve pounder and about a three pounder that I released. Even though I was trailing slowly, I couldn't buy a walleye. The water was fairly shallow and had its share of weeds so I decided to check out Teal Lake. The waterway was through a large swamp and had to be all of a mile long. I didn't fish at all through it but saw lots of tempting V's from fish scooting away. I thought that I was going to get stuck in the shallows a couple of times as the whole passage is at most five feet deep, and at the least I dragged bottom. But somehow I managed to squeeze through.

I had just entered Teal Lake and was in about ten feet of water when I was scared so badly I thought I was gonna have a heart attack right on the spot. I was lookin' straight ahead into the calm waters of the lake when just off the right side of the boat a fish jumped. Now that wouldn't have been so frightening except the fish was, without a doubt, near the two-hundred-pound mark. That would have been unnerving enough but the dang thing jumped clear out of the water and landed so close to me I got a bath from the splash. It was a landlocked sturgeon. Now, I'd seen sturgeon before but not that big and I'd never had one try to jump in my lap! I'm just glad I still had several hours of fishing in the hot sun 'cause lake water wasn't the only thing soaking my shorts!

As I reread this part of my story I see it moves with all the excitement of a cookbook. I'm sorry for that but this leg of the contest wasn't all that lively. I never really knew my competition and the only times I really crossed their paths was at the start and at weigh-in. I caught some fine fish but none in the size range or with a style worthy of my lengthy verbosity. It was just "bread and butter" fishing, and I loved it! Needless to say, I won at the scales, losing only in one category. One of the contestants had hooked into a forty-three pound musky. The fisherman's name was Andrew Tillotson from the southwestern part of the state, and from what I gather it was a great battle. But it was his only major fish of the day, and it is definitely his story so I'll leave the tellin' of it to him.

CHAPTER 10
MISSISSIPPI CAT

I am Jim and the river is the river and the womb of all that is, was and is left to be. She is the mighty giver and relentless taker with a consciousness and purpose she shares with no one. She is always coming, always going and always there. She speaks of peoples past, of prehistoric glory and defeat, of the passing of civilizations that could never die but fall before time like dried leaves in the wind, spiraling down and down to meet the ground and finally to become the ground, then the tree, then the leaf green and the mighty civilization anew that can never die . . . the river.

She allowed gentle Indian women to pound their clothes on stones at her banks. She listened as they sang songs filled with the life of other creatures of the land, the bravery of the eagle, the swiftness of the deer, the power of the great bear. The river, a part of, yet always apart from. Set only on her own path, the carrier of the blood of life, relentless. She watched the big change, the coming of the masses. She saw, in a short span, the gentle squaw and the brave warrior become first the defender of the land, then in a time so short even the river must have been amazed, they became the hollow eyes and skin-covered bones of the alcohol-soaked living dead. The pounding hoofs of the buffalo were silenced and became the screech and belch of the train and automobile.

And the river herself was changed from the bringer of life to the taker of garbage. If she minded I cannot say, if she cried I do not know, but as she has done for forgotten years past she did as she was asked and her waters ran with the poisons and she stank. But the white cancer that ate at the land was not mindless and not entirely without control. It felt the loss and recognized the danger if the river were gone. It struggled to survive and in doing so began to respect the river, not like a brave respected the chief, or like a holy man respects God, but like a cook respects his fry pan because of the use he can get out of it. For whatever reason the river would continue, as it had through other challenges and other mindless civilizations, as it had since God first wound the clock of time and sent it spinning into the void, and as it would until the clock returns to his mighty hand and he breathes "enough," and time will be still and life will be, once again, beyond knowledge.

Be that as it may, I am Jim and the river here is clean, and on that day the sky was warm and blue and it is for me to fish. I slid my canoe from the shore to the river and surrendered to her flow. For fish are my quarry and to fish she will lead me. She does not fail.

My canoe slides without sound through the swirls and dips on the river's mighty back. Soon it will moan in delight at the part it was created to play, forever floating back and forth in an endless game of tag with the waves. But it moans so softly it is drowned beneath the river's constant tale like a moan meant only for the ear of a lover. All the while passing the shore, the land, that must stay behind.

The land listens, too, to the tales of long ago and far away that the waters bring. It must listen and dream. That is why the land nearest to the shore is so unstable, like a drifter. When the stories become too much for the land to bear it leaves the shore, diving into the river to find adventure of its own. Only man's concrete and stone can stop it, and only for a time because even concrete and stone will one day fall to the lure of the river's song. And a man that lives by the river is without defense. He is pulled to her time and again, to share the adventures, to become a living image within her dream. I am such a man. Adventure is my goal. The kind of adventure that comes when a man and the river become one and transcend the sum of their parts. When they are poured into one another and become something new altogether. And what they have become can never be known until they are no longer this new creature but their separate parts once again and can look back and reflect.

I was pulled down river swiftly and I steered the craft with the practice that allows one to be free from effort, free to feel life and to dream. The river was void of human sign and I was the mighty Indian hunter. I did not hunt the great bear or elusive deer. I hunt the fish. My weapons are not the stout spear or sacred bow. They are the rod and reel, but I am the hunter nonetheless. My eyes stare around each bend to find my quarry. I must leave the area in which I am familiar because it has to be that way. I felt it in my soul and I did not question. I began to paddle, with the full strength of my mighty arms. I pulled at the river, throwing my canoe downstream. The trees flew past but I did not notice for my chin was tucked into my chest and I bent to the task of great speed. Time flew past like the shore, and when I raised my sweat-soaked brow I realized I had been traveling most of the day. I knew I would spend that night in the woods, far from my cabin. The pine needles would be my bed and the stars my blanket. This was fine to me. It fit my mood. The river was much wider here. The only thing familiar to me was the everlasting song of the river. The shore I had never seen. There was still no sign of man and for that I was grateful. I remained a great chief. I baited my hook and lowered it over the side. The river was so wide that the waters moved very slowly. I put on a weight because the depths were dark and great.

Then I waited. I heard the wind through the trees and felt it slowly dry my skin and I waited. It is a joy to do so. It is as much a part of fishing as any other, and all true fishermen love it with as much respect. So I wait. I think of how my great God blesses me. How much he allows me so much of the things I love. What a truly great God he is and I feel his presence everywhere. As I sat the river moved me slowly, farther from my world. I knew it had a reason and I surrendered to its will. As my mind wandered through the countless possibilities of what was to come, it became tangled in one fantasy after another. I began to drift not only in my canoe but in my mind.

But wait! What's this? Could it be a knock at my fish door? Yes, it was! My heart jumped like the lover who, thinking himself abandoned lies forlorn upon the motel bed but who jumps for joy at the soft "tap, tap, tap" upon the seedy hollow exterior love-nest door. I sat upright, my muscles tense, my fingertips sensitive to the significant pull upon the line. I felt my rod slowly but firmly . . . bend. Again I waited. The rod loosened up. Then again the steady pull. This time I did not wait. I pulled back the rod with a sharp and sudden jerk. It was as if whatever was on the other end did not even notice. The rod remained the same. I began to reel. There was no regaining my line. Now I was sure that I had hooked a large log rolling downstream with the current. Surely a fish would make some movement of life. I prepared to cut my line to begin again when I suddenly realized I was traveling downstream faster than the river's flow. Not much, but definitely faster. I had found my adventure. I had hooked something and if it was a fish, it was a mighty fish. Lord, it was a mighty fish!

It was later than I had thought, and before I knew it the sun was sending its last farewell rays over the horizon. The creature (I thought of it as such because I could not imagine a fish with such power), swam on. It did not slow down or speed up. It just continued, as if heeding the demands of some primal calling. As if my attempts at capture were something so insignificant they were unworthy of notice. And the sky turned black. There was no moon. There were no stars. I could only see shadows. It was as if I had crossed over to a reality in which all the world was a negative of a photograph.

As the night moved on the weather took a turn for the worse. The wind began to blow and the river, now more like a long, narrow lake, began to chop like the sea. Yet the creature dragged on. My hands began to cramp and my arms felt like lead weights. Rain broke from the sky like the emptying of an enormous bucket. I was soaked in an instant. The wind drove the rain like needles, pelting my skin. The waves tossed the small craft like a tiny piece of driftwood. I was forced to tie my line to the front of the canoe as I held on for dear life. Yet the creature pulled on. The lightning began soon after the rain and I was out on water in a full blown Midwest thunderstorm. Not a good place to be. But my only options were to ride out the storm or cut loose the line. That I would never do, so I hung on. I never saw the twister. I guess that's a blessing. But I heard it. I heard it from a long way off, it sounded like a roaring train running out of the stations of hell. I knew what it was at once. I don't know if I cried. I was too wet to tell, but I thought I was going to die. I could see pieces of the earth flying through the air and I began to feel sand and grit pelting my face. I lay down in the bottom of my boat, gripping the little mariner's cross I wear around my neck, and I prayed. The last thing I remember it seemed as if the canoe was spinning but it might have just been in my mind because right then, in a probable defense of my sanity, I blacked out.

I think the thing that first brought me out of my deep sleep was the heat. Or maybe it was the water lapping at my face. In any case, when I opened my eyes all I could see was too bright to recognize. Slowly they adjusted and I realized I was lying in the bottom of the canoe with my face resting in what was left of the storm. It must have been well into the day because the sun was high in the sky and very hot. When I peered over the side I realized two things at once. I was in the middle of a huge lake that was thickly populated by humans, and I was still in tow by whatever it was that was below the surface. The river was, at this point, a lake, and was dotted with crafts of all descriptions. The only kind of craft I could not see was anything as small as mine.

All I could think was that I wanted to first capture my prey, then as quickly as possible get back up river to the sanctity of my own world. It was a true miracle that my line had held. It was a heavy line, about thirty-pound test, but I could not believe it passed the test it was given the night before. Normally I use a much lighter line but I believe it was my role as a mighty hunter the day before that led me to use my "big game" equipment. As I look back it might have been kinder to all concerned if I had had the lighter stuff on. Then it would have broken and perhaps saved my quarry from what was to come. But it didn't happen that way so I was left to the task of capturing whatever it was that had me in tow.

I had tied the string to the front of the canoe without cutting it so it was a simple task to untie and resume control with my rod. I had made up my mind that I was either going to turn the fish (what else could it be?) or break the line trying. I did not fancy the idea of an unplanned trip to the Gulf of Mexico. I pulled the canoe ahead and recaptured the line necessary to put the canoe over the fish, then I lifted with all my strength. Much to my amazement the fish began to rise. Slowly at first, then more rapidly, I began to regain the line. I pumped the rod up then wound in line as I let the tip down. Again and again I cranked and pulled, all the while searching the depths for what was below.

All at once it seemed like the whole bottom was rising. I pumped and pulled until I could finally make out the outline of a great fish, a great catfish. I had heard tales of these bottom fish reaching sizes where divers are afraid to swim in the same areas with them, but until now I thought them to be exaggerations. With one sweep of its great tail the fish dove out of sight and at the same time almost dragged my small craft down with him. I struggled to release line and still remain taut enough to stop his escape. Again he slowed and finally turned and I dragged him to the surface. He dove again and this time when I dragged him up he remained. Slowly he rolled over, exposing his white underbelly. I had never seen anything like him. My canoe was a fourteen-footer and he was longer by a giant tail. I sat staring at him, myself in utter exhaustion. I made up my mind that I would make for the nearest shore. There was no way that I could paddle this giant creature home. The shore, however, was also a long way away. It was a dark line on the horizon. I tied the rope that I use to tie up to shore to his giant snout and attached the other end to the rear of the canoe. Then I put paddle to water and began the arduous task of dragging a beast this size with a fourteen-foot vessel. The sun was blazing hot and the going would be laborious and slow. I just thanked God that the fish could float.

I had not paddled far when the heat of the day coupled with the warm midsummer water brought out the creatures that all fishermen hate and fear the most. My flesh crawled as I heard the first insistent buzzing, first only one, then a couple, then countless numbers all at a slightly different pitch, all gradually becoming louder and I knew they would soon be upon me. As I looked up toward the shore I could see them. They were still just specks but were all gathering. Now it was as I had feared, they were coming my way. I could hear as they came closer that it was probably the worst of their kind. Some breeds are not too harmful to fishermen but from the ever-growing volume of noise and from the way they had packed up I had very little doubt that these were some of the worst, the inconsiderate water skiers. And there was nowhere to hide.

The only thing I could do was to tuck my chin into my chest and continue paddling. I would just pretend that I didn't feel any fear (if they sense fear they will tear you up!), and I will even wave if they come too close. Wave and smile like we are old friends and surely they wouldn't bother an old friend, would they? I paddled in my canoe feeling like a minnow in the middle of a school of large pike, just acting nonchalant. "Hey brother pike, what's happenin'? You betcha. I'm cool, bro. You sure are lookin' marvelous! Nice teeth, yessir, whew!"

The first boat came screaming by, missing me by thirty or forty feet. Two pretty young girls in bikinis waved and smiled, showing long and insidious incisors, as my canoe was lifted a good four feet off the surface of the water by the swell and dumped like so much dead meat back to lake level. The bobbing that followed was at least as bad as the original dumping. I felt my face turn green and if my stomach hadn't been empty I would have emptied it. The next boat came even closer to the delight of its occupants. I held on with all my strength. There was little hope of paddling so I merely hung on.

The next attack was to the rear of the canoe. I can't say whether they could see the big fish floating just below the surface but the boat jumped right out of the water when he hit it about dead center, throwing chunks of flesh a full twenty feet in the air as its prop plowed through the soft underbelly of the cat. I can't be sure if they realized exactly what had happened, but I'm sure that they thought it was great. The female passengers squealed with delight like hogs when their putrid slop is dumped suddenly in front of their pig-eyed, pushed-in snouts.

Each boat felt it necessary to top the attack of the last craft. First the boats hacked chunks from my fish, then the skiers jumped it, carving bloody lines through the meat. The cat twirled as it was hit each time so it was equally chewed all over. I screamed, "No! No! Not my fish! You swine!" I stood up in the canoe with my paddle in hand, swinging like a Louisville slugger. This only excited them more as their attacks became even more frenzied. As I stood there feeling like Davy Crocket at the Alamo, swinging my unloaded Betsy at the attacking horde, an inventive team jumped the fish with their boat and had the skier swim around my canoe attempting to separate my legs from the rest of me. I saw it coming and jumped into the watery foam. My little craft was flipped five feet in the air and would have flown farther if it hadn't been anchored by what was left of my fish. This must have satisfied whatever need it was that drove these young people to madness because after a couple more half-hearted jumps over the bloody pulp tied behind my water-filled canoe, they buzzed off in search of other prey. I hung onto the side of my little boat while the buzzing became softer and softer until all I could hear was the sound of the natural waves lapping up against the remains of my adventure.

It took a while for me to regain my composure. When my heart had slowed down to the point where I could feel safe from explosion, I climbed into my water-filled canoe. I used my paddles to splash out what I could (this is a time tested method of un-swamping a canoe), then used my shirt to mop up the rest.

Then I sat staring forward, afraid to look back at the largest fresh-water fish I had ever heard of. Slowly I turned. The sight that met my eyes was enough to make a grown man cry. All that was left of my prize was the head, from the bulging eyes to the end of his snout. His mouth was gaping as if in a laugh that said, "I got you after all, you took my life, but I stole your glory." The mouth was a full four feet across and I could clearly visualize long legs and a skimpy bikini sliding down that chute. I was sick to my stomach and threw up most of nothing over the side.

I took the knife off of my belt and cut the rope that held what was left of my giant cat. I apologized to him as he sank back to where he had come from. He had lost most of his glory; he was a worthy creature of wonder. I can't say he minded though 'cause as he sank his jaws flapped open and shut and I swear it looked as if he were laughing.

CHAPTER 11
CLAMS

"Come on, Clams . . . jump, you slimy coward!" Billy screamed at the young, quivering, tub of a nine-year-old who stood perched like a soft and flabby Humpty Dumpty on the edge of a twenty-foot ledge overlooking the St. Croix River. "Come on, you porker! Jump or move out of the way!"

"Give a man some room," Clams argued back. "I'm checking the wind velocity, the river currents. These things take time!"

"Time? Time? I'm growing old giving you time and you are SOOOO . . . Clammy! Look at you. You haven't even hit the water and you are dripping wet." It was true. The little fat boy was covered with the sweat that gained him his nickname, "the Man of Clams."

"It is necessary for me to cover myself for a slick entry into the waters below," came back the Clam Man. It was becoming obvious to all that he was no closer to jumping than he had been when he first approached the ledge a full ten minutes before.

A much more sympathetic Scoot stepped in. "Well Clams,

why don't you back off a while? That way you can observe our trajectories and thus prepare yourself for the most efficient entry possible."

"Good thinking, Scoot, my friend." Clams was evidently relieved as he carefully backed away from the ledge. "It never pays to rush these things!"

"Baloney," came back Billy. "You'll never jump, you cowardly slug. You haven't ever jumped and I'm betting you never will! You're pink and pathetic!" The fiery Bill was reaching new heights of cruelty. It was true. Clams was clammy, pink and pathetic, but he was also one of the guys. Billy never knew fear, that anyone could tell, and he had no sympathy for the timid Clams.

"Back off, Billy Wax," fought back the pink one. "I'll slime you head to toe if you don't shut up!" Sliming was when Clams rubbed any or all of his sweaty body on some poor soul.

But Billy was beyond the game and only screamed, "You make me want to puke!" as he dived without looking over the cliff.

Clams puffed up and said something to the rest of the boys but it was obvious that Billy had bruised the normally resilient fat boy. He positioned himself off to one side and watched the rest of the gang take their turns flying off the cliffs to the water below. Billy had pierced Clam's armor. As different as they were, these two boys were also best friends. He should have expected rough treatment from Billy who was hot-headed and not one to hold anything back, but Clams saw the truth in what Wax had said. Fact was, he was scared. It's a hard feeling to live with, especially for a nine-year-old boy in front of his friends.

The day moved on from swimming to other kid stuff but the normally vocal, always humorous Clams was pretty quiet. Later, he slipped away by himself and wandered down the forest trails straight back to the river. Clams just stood by the edge talking to himself.

"You are pathetic," he berated himself. "Billy's right." He stood still for a large slice of time while the warm, soft breeze and the steady moan of the river tugged at his attention. Clams knew he could swim. All the guys could swim almost before they could eat without dribbling. He also knew that if he did jump, he would do so without appreciable injury.

"So what," Clams yelled out, "I am what I am and proud of it!" He stood at the edge of the cliff with his eyes wide and wild and his chest heaving with heavy breathing. "So what if I'm no Billy Wax. So what if I'm not that brave. I am what I am. I don't have to jump. I am the Man of Clams!" His face was soaking wet but not from his normal "clam sauce." Clams, was crying. "I don't mind being different," he explained to the river. "I don't mind being fat. I have good parents, good friends and more fun than I have a right to. It's not bad at all. But damn! I hate being afraid." Clams was sobbing now. "It's one thing to weasel out of a fight when you know you can't win," he continued, but I KNOW this cliff won't hurt me. I know I can do this."

He stood again for a long time. Several times he nearly went over but he stopped himself. Finally, he backed away.

"I don't have to," he moaned, "I don't have to. I'm the Clam Man. No one expects me to be brave. I don't have to."

He backed away from the edge with his shoulders sagging and his spirit crushed. Gently sobbing, he turned from the cliff that had humiliated him so completely and disappeared down the trail.

The wind whispered without words and the river murmured without opinion. The inhale and exhale of life continued on the ledge by the river.

Then a crashing in the woods could be heard coming from the trail. Suddenly the Clam Man burst from the woods running for all he was worth. His belly was bouncing like a Disney hippo and there was fire flaming in his eyes. He face was covered with a grim smile and the world was silent except for the slap of the fat boy's feet as he ran. He hit the rock on the edge of the cliff without breaking stride and launched his improbable flying machine far out into the air. He hung for a year or two in midair then screamed, "I AM THE MAN!" and plummeted into the river below. He hit the water with a perfect one-point belly flop, swam to the shore, then somehow lifted his entire belly onto his chest and like a short, pink, Johnny Weissmuller swaggered into the jungle, the echo of his belly flop and the echo of the deed itself still bouncing up and down the river.

CHAPTER 12
THE NATIONALS

Some of you may be wondering what is happening with my folks while all this is going on, so I'll bring you up to date. As I said before, my cabin now sits next to where our family cabin used to sit. My folks left the place in the mid-sixties and built a new home on the part of the property that borders the road. They were tired of the long walk back to the river. My pa said that when they got older all that rowdy stuff, like runnin' around in the nude and makin' love in the bushes, slowed down enough so they could move back near to civilization and not get arrested.

That didn't turn out to be quite true, they were picked up once when I had to get them from the sheriff's house. Seems Dad was chasing Mom down the road in the middle of the night, both of them "buck naked." There was snow on the ground and they were fresh out of their sauna. The sheriff felt they were a little too far from their place for their own good and for the public image. He knew Mom and Dad didn't want to go to the station, so he brought them to his house. Then he made me come and get them and chewed me out for their shameful behavior. They were in their sixties then and he couldn't quite believe their lack of good taste. He said to me, "And they're not even drunk! They could at LEAST be drunk!"

I was mad as a wet hen driving home with my wayward folks wrapped in the law's blankets. When we got to their house my pa looked at me sheepishly and said with his cutest little smile, "I said we'd slow down, son, I didn't say we'd stop." My mom let out with a little giggle and before long we were all laughing and I thought I was going to bust a gut. I made Dad promise the next time he ran Mom he would herd her into the woods and protect the neighbor's sensibilities.

They would have loved to stay on the river but it was too far for them to walk every day and there were too many low spots between the road and the cabin, which flooded with the high water, so a private road in was not cost effective. They are really proud of me (their only offspring), and came to watch me fish a lot, but they love each other first and foremost and since I left the nest they concentrate primarily on each other. I am close enough so we spend enough time together to satisfy us all. They are in all kinds of church and community groups and always manage to pump life into anything they are involved in. But it is their commitment to each other to maintaining a minimum level of craziness that sets them apart and holds up their quality of life and will, I'm sure, until the day they die.

Back at Nationals, I'm just a fledgling fresh out of the nest and my folks are still planted firmly of the river. I did a little fast talking and got Arboblaster to pay their way out to the national phase of the competition. I got my folks to go by telling my dad I needed him to motor for me. He was a sucker for anyone or anything in need. So when we lifted off the ground from the Minneapolis-St. Paul airport they were on a plane for the first time and sat gripping the arms of the chairs like two kittens on their first car ride. Destination, Georgia and the nationals.

It didn't take them long to relax though. In the short two hours in the air they had gotten to know five couples well enough to promise to write (no doubt my mother would), they got the whole cabin singing hootenanny songs, and then both disappeared into one lavatory to become one of the original couples in the "mile high club" while the passengers belted out, "This Land Is My Land" with harmonies. It's hard for the life of the party to do anything without being noticed, so when they came out trying to look like nothing more than a prolonged trip to the Biff had transpired, the people (who really knew nothing of what had happened but were glad to see them back), gave them a rowdy round of applause. My mother figured they knew everything, blushed like a schoolgirl and hustled, giggling, to her seat, while Dad, confused only for a second, gave them the old "thumbs up" and strutted to his place to a second round of cheers.

While he had their attention Pa just had to drag me into the fray by telling all the folks how I was the greatest living fisherman and was going to be JFK and America's single bait-wielding weapon against Khrushchev and the commies. I tried to stammer that I had not won that honor yet but there was no breaking through the spell my folks had woven them into. They all pumped my hand as we left the plane and wished me luck. My practiced defense in dealing with my folks was to step back a bit from reality and view them as an ongoing show. I surrendered to my appointed role, hugging strangers, giving out autographs and finally making a little speech, letting them know that with God, JFK and them, the American people, on my side there wasn't a commie alive that would be able to sit in the same boat with me. Well, after all, I am my parent's son.

The plane landed in Columbus on the Alabama-Georgia border. This was a fairly large, modern city by 1963 standards, and I'm glad to say we didn't stay long. One of the things I remember the most was the way black people were treated. I'm not going to rant about the injustice—we all have some idea about what the Deep South was like back then. There have been many improvements since, and there is no point in thrashing about in memories that, I'm sure, are best forgotten. Also, I believe that the way northerners treated blacks, at least in the cities, was just as bad and nothing to be proud of. In the South it was just more obvious. It was a sub-nation under siege. The Negro was an angry race and was saying to the world, Brother . . . enough! It would be impossible to relate my tale without some of the prejudice showing up so I hope you remember the year and are not offended.

1963, I remember it well. Vietnam was quickly becoming an evening news fixture replacing the still tense Cuban crisis. The price of a first class letter went to five cents. The national deficit of 10 billion was the largest in history. The Congo was beginning to boil, Khrushchev warned that any invasion of Cuba by the U.S. in the future would be followed by a Soviet nuclear attack. McNamara warned the U.S. would not tolerate any Soviet intervention in any anti-Castro revolt. In a civil rights message,

Kennedy emphasized ending curtailment of Negro voting rights. Albany, Georgia revoked its segregation ordinances. Karl Rovaag was declared Governor of Minnesota in a disputed election in which he won by ninety-one votes. The U.S. agreed to lend Brazil $398 million to combat inflation, confident it would correct the problem. Police dogs were used against Negro demonstrators in Greenwood, Mississippi. The nuclear submarine *Thresher* was lost in the Atlantic with 129 men aboard. Martin Luther King, Jr. was arrested in Birmingham. Seventy thousand people protested to "ban the bomb" in London. Paul Horning and Alex Karris were suspended from pro football for betting on NFL games. William Moore, a white integrationist, was shot to death in Alabama. Sir Winston Churchill announced he was retiring. Telstar II was launched. Sonny Liston knocked out Floyd Patterson to retain his boxing title. President and Mrs. Kennedy lost a baby son, Patrick Bouvier. The Bank of Canada increased its lending rate to 4 percent. "Tie Me Kangaroo Down Sport" was on the radio along with a flood of protest songs including "Blowing in the Wind." Kurt Vonnegut published *Cat's Cradle*. *Tom Jones*, *The Longest Day*, *The Great Escape* and *The Birds* were a few of the movies currently playing. L. Gordon Cooper in the spacecraft *Faith 7* made twenty-two orbits in space and the national segment of the nonofficial Olympic fishing trials was held at Harding Lake on the Georgia-Alabama border in the second week of August.

Let me tell you the second week in August is no time to be in Georgia. At least for a northern boy. It was so hot I felt as if my brains would boil. The locals dressed mostly in white and had their little paper fans that seemed to keep them in good spirits.

They did all the normal things to keep their lives moving but seemed to do them in slow motion. There were very few air conditioners at that time, so their only defense was to take her easy.

When we got off the plane it was like landing in another world. There were two of everything. Restaurants, Negro restaurants, drinking fountains, Negro drinking fountains, lavatories, Negro lavatories, the list goes on and on. You can't imagine all the things they had two of. I made it a point to use Negro everything as did my mom and dad. We sure got under a lot of white skin but being under the protection of a National competition we could do pretty much as we pleased. You might remember a thing on the news when my mom polished a black guy's shoes in the airport but aside from that they really tried to ignore us. "If you love those darkies so much, why don't y'all bring them back to Wisconsin with y'all?" We heard that a lot. There was beginning to be a little national press following the competition so the local powers made every effort to show how happy all the blacks and whites were in an effort to maintain a crumbling status quo. We didn't boycott or do some other things we might have, but we did take a jab or two when we could. And in '63 things were changing very quickly so we felt no need to further muddy the water.

It's funny but I figured that some of the "good ol' boy" fishermen from the south would be mad at us for our obvious pro-black stand, but it was the competitor from Iowa who seemed to be the most annoyed. In fact, for some reason, he hated blacks . . . and us! We really didn't make a big issue of our opinions (after Mom's little stunt), but it was such a hot issue at that time and place the press turned us into some kind of champion of black rights. I personally would rather fish. I'm not a fighter. My folks, on the other hand . . . oh, well. The guys from the South surprised us and were real nice. Some of them tried to explain the South's predicament, but most of them said we were entitled to our opinions and that, in the South, we were free to express them. This toad from Iowa was another story. His name was Horace Placker. I'll never forget. I think he felt that everyone down there hated blacks so he had a license to show off his racial hatred. I would guess that in Iowa he was stifled by those good people's Christian morals. For whatever reason, he set out from the start to hinder me in any way he could to keep me from winning. But he was in for a few surprises.

The contest was to be held on a lake that was divided by the Georgia–Alabama border. It's called Harding Lake and is a flowage on the Chattahoochee River. Man, I love names like that, you know? I mean it just makes my mind picture white plantations, hanging moss, and folks in white suits, straw hats and cane poles. Someday I promise I'm going to put in my canoe and spend a whole summer floating down the Mississippi. If enough of you read this book to show you are at all interested in old Jim's goings on, I promise to write about that trip. There's a whole lot of Huck Finn in my bones. I'll just bet it's the same with you!

Yeah, that is some beautiful country. A lot of poverty, though. Talking to some of the black folk along the way, they don't have possession one. Except a straw hat, cane pole, and if they're lucky, a shack somewhere. There were a lot of poor whites too, but as a whole, the blacks seemed to be all rich with poverty. I guess that has changed a lot. The population has shifted to warmer weather and has brought a lot of jobs with it. But back then that country was covered with poor. As we drove to the lake, every river we passed was lined with black people fishin' for their supper. Many restaurants sported large signs declaring, "We got gizzards!" My dad wanted to stop at one of those but I was sure it would lead to a whole stand-up routine, so I made our driver press on. We spotted a motel near the lake that had "Welcome, Fishermen," on the marquis and pulled into the parking lot.

It seems that the shores of Harding Lake are dotted with these small motels, so instead of housing all of us in one large hotel it was decided that we would be spread out to give the whole area a taste of our business. I thought it was a fine idea because it also gave us a better taste of the area. It was just about suppertime as we unloaded the car and wandered over to the motel café.

"Lawd Almighty, boys, its looks to me like hungry fishermen, yessir! Hungry as a squallin' babe, I'll betcha. Y'all come on in now. Kick that lazy good for nothin' dog out of the way now. G'wan Beau boy, get your wrinkly butt out of the way! I declare that ol' hound could sleep through a tor-in-ado. Fact is, they say his great long-ago granddaddy slept through the entire Civil War and knowin' that one likes I do, I don't doubt it a bit, no sir! Step around him, step around him, that's it. We'd all get old waitin' for that one to move. I jes' sweep him once a day so he don't get too dusty. You don't mind him? That's nice, you're fine folks, I can tell.

"Well, come on now, you're probably weak with hunger. Rest yourself, that's it right here by the window. You lucky today, all right. You dun fell right into the lap of one of the South's finest kitchens. Now, what's it gonna be? Course we got gizzards—everybody's got gizzards. But you want somethin' gonna turn your belly into a pleasure machine, let me whip you up some of my giblet stew. Let me explain. Why I jes' chops up them gizzards and hearts so you can't even recognize them, then I drops 'em in a pot o' bubblin' water an' cook 'em till they're tender. For the las' few minutes I add some goodies from the garden—carrots, celery, poke-sally, onions, peppers, 'bout anything green I see. After I like the smell I drains off that sweet juice an' I adds to the juice a touch of butter and a handful of flour and a handsome taste of the finest dry white wine I ever seed for cookin'. Then I dump in my secrets to bring out exactly what I'm tryin' to say. I lets 'em cook, oh so slow, till the time is right an' I pours it all over the top of my homemade biscuits. Lawd, Lawd, if that ain't heaven it's shore close 'nuf to see it!

"But that ain't all, no sir! When you the best you gots to go that extra mile. With every plate o' stew you gets a half dozen of the finest cockscombs this green earth can grow. I skins 'em myself and stuffs 'em with the most delightful chicken farce your lips ever knowed, then roll 'em in a fry mix and fries 'em as brown as one of my babies' backsides, though Lawd knows they ain't babies no more, no sir.

Fact is, I got two in college and one out there on the road somewhere. Says he's tryin' to make a better world and I know it's true but I worry so. I pray to the Lord to watch him and touch his heart so he ain't so angry. I guess I know how he feels but I jes' want him safe. Oh, this is your boy? Well, I could see that straight out. Well, then you know how a mother worries. He ain't done much with hisself so far but protest, he don't even like me workin' here. Coloreds can't eat here. Seems funny I can cook it but coloreds can't eat it. But, my boy, I mean he ain't like the other two, so smart and smooth, but somehow I feels it in my heart that he's the best of 'em. Oh, I love the others, too, but there's something about that one. Lawd, I hope you watch that boy. How I ramble on! You folks sure are nice to listen so good to a foolish old woman. Now what's it gonna be? Can I do the town for ya? Good, good, good, you made the right choice. Sit back and brace yourself for the taste treat of the century!

Now what you think? Was that grand, or what? I knowed you'd like it. The way you slicked up your plates tells me the whole tale. You know I been sittin' back there watchin' you folks eat and it jes' come to mind that you are the folks that the TV showed at the airport this afternoon. You is the lady that shined that ol' man's shoes. When I seed that I laughed so hard my stockin's rolled clear down to my ankles all by themselves. I won't accept a dime for that meal. No, I won't hear of it. You jes' get on out of here now and don't forget me at breakfast. I'll feed ya at three a.m. so y'all can get a good spot for your boat early. Yep, my stockin's rolled down all by themselves. I'll bet my baby boy was laughin' somewhere hisself. I know'd he would have liked that. Lawd, please watch over that boy. Out of the way, Beau, out of the way! Lawd, that dog is lazy." The moon was full in the cloudless southern sky. The wind softly fluffed our hair as the café screen door slapped shut leaving us in what seemed like a very beautiful Georgia evening.

The organizers had arranged for our lodgings in advance, so we picked up our keys and brought what gear we needed for the night into the motel. The rooms were exactly like one million other small roadside motel rooms across the country. There was a large double bed (nowadays it would vibrate) with a couch next to it. There was a small coffee machine with enough complimentary coffee for one cup and a drinking glass wrapped in paper. The bathroom held a tub and toilet with a strip of paper across the seat to show it had not been violated since its last cleaning. We even had a fine black and white TV in the room. Everything was used but very clean and we were as excited as kids at a campout.

It was about nine o'clock, and the folks decided to hit the sack and watch the tube. I was too excited about what tomorrow would bring to sleep and was more interested in what was happening on the street than what was on the tube, so I decided to take a walk.

First off, I left the motel lights and walked down to the shores of Harding Lake. I stood in awe of its size. It was much too wide to see across and even in the light evening breeze there were rolling waves. That was the first time I had any doubts about my ability to win. I had always caught fish . . . always. I had never fished water like this, though. I had fished in Lake Superior but always in a small area for fish I knew how to catch. This lake held some of the species that I knew but also had some that I did not. And it was so big. I was the king at home but here I felt like a little boy. I remember closing my eyes and saying, "Lord, I guess I'm gonna need your help in this one. I ain't the best of your servants but I think 'cause of how good you treat me you must like me pretty well anyway. I know you showed your disciples where to throw their nets, and if you got the time, Lord, maybe you could show me a spot or two. I know I ain't Peter, Lord, but I know I'd be obliged. Amen."

The slight wind was blowing off the lake, and it felt cool and fresh. The only lights near enough to the motel to see were on an old gas station across the street. I could see folks milling around and decided to mosey on over.

There were two old black men and an equally aged white man there sitting at the pop machine that looked as if they were as much a part of the station as the mortar and stone. They sat looking at the ground at their feet as if they were considering the weight of the world and didn't move an eyelash when I walked up. I stood quietly searching their feet for some obvious center of their attention. I really had nothing on my mind and was in no rush so I stood still, fusing with their collective trance.

After a few minutes one of the black ancients softly said, "Yep." After another span of years passed the other black man agreed, "Yep." More years crept by and the old white gentleman added his opinion, "Yep." As time passed I began to understand. The truths and revelations swam before me like a school of walleye. I added the sum of my newfound truths with conviction: "Yep!"

Three antique faces turned my way. They looked at me with questioning expressions that clearly told me my opinion was absurd. "Something we can do for you, young fella?"

I shook off the thick layer of foolishness that had settled all over me and replied that I was looking for nothing in particular. I explained that I was in the big fishing contest the following day and could not sleep.

It seems they could relate to that because they instantly accepted me into their world. They found an old car seat for me to drop into then commenced with introductions.

"This here gentleman right up against the pop machine is

Clever Tellman," began the the old white ancient. He pointed to Clever who was still looking at his feet but raised his hand for me to take and shake. "Clever here is ninety-three and one of the finest gentleman to sit between a pair of shoes." His handshake was strong and steady. He looked up without raising his head, caught my eyes and nodded, then he returned his attention to the ground and its invisible mandala.

"And over here is Mr. Bowlegs Jackson Brown. Now he's ninety-eight but I don't figure he looks a day over ninety-seven." He chuckled at his obviously well-worn joke.

"Proud to meet you, son," began the man. "You forget that "mister" stuff and call me Bowlegs like everyone else does!" He showed me his gums in a grin that had probably forgotten what a tooth was and shook my hand strong and long.

Bowlegs continued, "This white buck over here is the Colonel and at eighty-nine he's the baby of the group." I pumped the Colonel's hand, which was also very steady and firm, and introduced myself.

"Wisconsin," snorted the Colonel. "That's some cold country up there. I once knew a fella from Wisconsin. Yep, he had hair all over his body, said all folks up there had hair like that, needed it to survive. That right, young fella?"

He looked at me with a serious expression. I searched his eyes for some sign that he was putting me on but there was not a clue. I decided that he had to be and picked up the ball.

"Yeah, it's true all right, Colonel. I had to shave my coat off for this trip or I'd have died in this heat. By the way, I've heard some things about you folks down here. Is it true you all have to pack yourselves into ice during the long hot summer nights so you keep from rotting alive?" I stared at the Colonel with as sincere a look as I could muster.

"Quite the opposite, young fella," says Bowlegs. "You see, we eat a lot of salt down here to ease our minds off the heat. Well, it seems all that salt has fairly well preserved us alive. We couldn't rot if we wanted to!"

Clever nodded vigorously at his feet and agreed, "It's a fact!"

The warm wind blew softly through the trees as the conversation paused and the three of us seemed to drift peacefully through the reality of our choosing. Our wanderings were only occasionally dotted with a random "yep," which I now knew meant nothing could be said that would improve an already perfect evening.

After a good long time of peaceful drifting, Bowlegs up and says, "I know you." Everyone kind of looked up slowly, as if to shake off the trance.

"What's you talking about, man?" says the Colonel. "I know for a fact you ain't come within five hundred miles of Wisconsin."

"No, Colonel, you is right but still I knows this man. He and his momma and daddy was on the TV just today. Yep, they was at the airport in Columbus, sure as I'm talkin' at you today. They was the folks that polished that ol' colored's boots in front of the whole TV world."

The Colonel looked at me hard. "That right boy?"

"Yeah, I guess that was us all right." I chuckled at the memory.

The Colonel and Bowlegs began retelling how my mom polished those boots, laughing the whole time, slapping their legs. Clever just shook his head and grinned. He was so fragile looking you kind of got the idea if he moved too much he would crumble into dust. When the hootin' died down we were a closer group.

Colonel looked at me hard in the eyes and said, "So, you come to fish. Yep, you got the look all right. I seen it a lot after best part of ninety years on this lake. You're a boy who can get the job done. But still this here lake ain't like none you ever fished. It's got a personality all its own. I expect that's why it was picked for the choosin' of the best of Uncle Sam's boys. I know for a fact the Georgia boy who's in the fray ain't never been within a hundred miles of this lake and I'm told the Alabama boy never fished it either. Yep, it's gonna be a true test.

"Now, I jes' happen to know three of the best fishermen in this here part of the state. 'Course, they is 'bout retired, except maybe an occasional run in with a cane pole cat. That don't change things though, they can still make 'em jump through the hoop." He stood there all puffed up like a banty rooster.

I just couldn't resist. "Where can I find these men, Colonel? I think I could really use some help right about now." I looked real serious.

"You northern Yankee fool, boy," he puffed. "You ain't standin' three feet from them! If they was cottonmouth you'd a breathed your last! It's us—me, Bowlegs and ol' Clever there! We know that lake like a baby knows its momma's breast. We could tell you stories that no man alive has a right to believe . . . and all true! You fell into the right bunch a boys here, son." The Colonel rested back in his chair and gazed up into the night sky.

After a respectful moment, Bowlegs leaned way over into the center of the group and said, low-like so no outsider could hear, "You ever hear of a t'aint, boy?"

I admitted I had never heard of such a thing.

"Well, I ain't too surprised." He nodded his head and stroked his bristled chin. "This here lake is full of 'em and they is gonna be the winning story in this here contest." He paused to pull out an old corncob pipe and light up a blend of what smelled a lot like industrial waste.

Just about when I thought he had forgotten what we were talking about, he continued, "Well, these here fish are kind of Frank'nstine type. You know what I'm sayin'? I mean they was kind of thrown together by man. The good Lord had nothin' to do with these monsters. They is half saltwater strippers and half bucketmouth by all accounts, and the Lord never made nothing angrier. So that's why we call 'em t'ain'ts. T'ain't a stripper, t'ain't a widemouth and they t'ain't none too friendly. I expect those fellas, them scientists, kind of figgered these things would pump new life into this old lake but I can tell you this here lake was takin' care of itself long before we was here and I 'spect it won't have no trouble carryin' on when we're gone. Another t'ain't they are is they t'ain't natural. But if a man's gonna fish this here lake he better make them his bread and butter and if he's going to win a contest, he better know how!" Bowlegs sat back, took a long draw on his pipe and blew a perfect smoke ring around the moon.

The Colonel stepped up and began to explain how to snag these rascals. "You trolls 'em deep and slow, boy, and fetch 'em off the bottom."

"No, no, no," said Bowlegs. "You got to keep shallow and shake up the surface!" It went back and forth between the two of them and I could see right off they had a difference of opinion.

Meanwhile, Clever got slowly to his feet and shuffled slowly into the garage. He returned in a moment with something clutched tightly in his fist. Both of the other men quit arguing and stared at Clever.

"What you doing with that, you old fool?" Bowlegs put his hands on his hips and stared at Clever disapprovingly.

"It's for the boy," was all he answered.

The other two started to rant and rave about nonsense and did he know what he was doing and he hardly knew me, but the old man just held out his fist to me and slowly unclutched it. In his palm was the ugliest, most beat-up looking snaggle of wood you could imagine. It must have been a piece of root with the only modifications being someone had roughly whittled a snout on one end and had wired a treble hook on the back. I took the offering and held it carefully, fearing it would break in my hand.

"You have no idea what you got there, boy," said the Colonel. "But if Clever wants you to have it, I know him well enough to know we could never stop him." Clever was back looking at his feet. "I think now we is all tired and you need to rest for your big day tomorrow." Bowlegs nodded and we all got up.

"But what about this?" I stammered and held out the lure.

"That there is Willy," says the Colonel, "and Willy speaks for hisself!"

The meeting was obviously over so I got up and walked slowly toward the motel. When I got to the edge of the gas station lights I was hailed by Clever.

"Hey, white boy," he yelled, "y'all catch some fish now." He smiled and chuckled as he turned and disappeared into the garage. Suddenly I felt very good but very tired and it seemed it was all I could do to get into my room and turn out the lights.

Seems like my head had just hit the pillow when I was awakened by my dad yanking on my foot. "Come on, boy," he said, "you're burning daylight! Come on! Rise and shine!" He was entirely too cheerful for that time in the morning. I groaned but managed to pull myself to my feet. The longer I was up the more energy I was able to muster and by the time I was dressed I was ready to set the world on fire. We hit the restaurant for as fine a meal as the dinner before and a generous portion of the same hospitality. We left with our bellies full and a huge sack lunch to pull us through the day.

The rules said we had to put our boat in on the day of the contest so we pulled out and headed for the public access. The motels were all situated near a landing and ours was just a quarter of a mile or so away. We pulled in and found ourselves around fifth in line. This was fine with me as it gave me a few minutes to check gear and prepare my rod for the first attack. It was when I was putting on my first lure that I realized I had forgotten "Willy" in my room.

The rules stated that you had to clear the landing site as soon as you hit the water and you were not allowed to touch shore again until you quit for the day. There were officials everywhere to lessen the possibility of cheating. I didn't really think that that lure could catch anything, but I had a gnawing feeling it should be in the boat. There was already a line behind me and no way for us to drive back.

"Mom, it's up to you. I know this sounds funny, but there's this old chunk of wood back in my room that I have to have. Could you please hustle back and get it for me? I have to have that stupid thing. It looks like an old root with hooks and it's on my dresser." I handed her the keys and she headed off without a word.

These fishermen were good at what they do, and in no time we were approaching the water. That's when Dad and me went into slow motion. We checked everything over twice, missed our approach and had to pull out and try again, all the time searching for Mom's return.

While this was going on we had our first introduction to Horace Placker, our pal from Iowa. "Come on, you idiots, load it or sink it! Maybe you should get some of your darky friends to help you out. Sho'nuf, masser, yep, yep, yep, bogabogaboga!" He laughed at his well-thought-out humor and looked around for support. Everyone was kind of looking somewhere else and no one was laughing. "Hey, pal, I saw your mother on TV. Yeah, she was really great. Maybe she should get a job on *Amos and Andy*." We were still moving slowly and praying Mom would get there before there was real trouble. "Hey, boy, your momma always go down on her knees for black men?"

My father slowly walked over to Placker. He hit him once in the jaw and it lifted him a full six inches off of his feet. He hit the ground like a sack of cement. Everyone was still looking somewhere else, including the official.

"OK, boys," the closest official said. "Let's get that craft into the water." There was no more time to stall so we dumped the boat into the water and parked the car. We walked as slowly as we could without getting into trouble and climbed into the boat.

I was just preparing to pull the starting cord when I saw my mom. She was running full tilt now and by the look of her matted hair she had been for some time. We were told rather sternly to clear the area, and I was forced to start my motor. I slowly clicked it into gear as Mom ran down the boat ramp. By now we were a good thirty feet offshore. Mom, still running, heaved that lure with all she had in our direction. Even with all of her strength it looked short. It spun over and over as if in slow motion then dropped safely into an outstretched net my dad was holding out at arms' length.

My father held up two fingers and grinned. "Two points, baby, you still got it!" My mom, puffing, could only hold her side and wave. Her grin told us she was all right.

When we were almost out of earshot she had composed herself enough to yell, "Jimmy, go catch some fish with that thing. I don't want that run to have been for nothing!"

I smiled and gave her a "thumbs up" but as I looked at that nasty piece of wood now lying on the bottom of the boat, I wondered. By this time Horace had regained his feet and was screaming at the judge to disqualify us for violence. He couldn't find anyone who had seen the incident though. As we motored away he stood on the shore and threw a stare at us that would have frozen ice. The man had a real problem. I had a sinking feeling he was going to be generous and share it with us.

It was going to be hot enough to fry our catch of fish without a fire, and the wind was so soft it promised to be no help. The lake was so big, however, that there were sizeable rolling waves. I had figured this lake would be more than my twelve-footer could handle so I had convinced Arboblaster to spring for a nifty fourteen-foot Crestliner. It was mostly aluminum with wood around the top edges and on the stern and wood seats. We had a 15 hp Mercury motor, and I had thought we could handle anything.

Now, with the waves splashing over the sides, I wished we had lobbied for a sixteen-footer.

"Well, son," my dad asked, "where to from here?"

I decided to stick to the shoreline. It was impossible to judge a bottom structure in this expanse of open water. We worked the shallows for the best part of the morning and had very little luck. I normally would have changed strategy several times in that length of time but I could not even think of a method. The truth is, I was losing it. I was overwhelmed by the pressure of the event. I had to think.

"Dad," I said, "motor straight out into the wind. I've got to think. I'll just put a crawler down deep and we'll drift back to shore while I try to calm down."

Dad was a little shook, too. From the time I could hold a rod he had never seen me not catch a fish. He did as I asked. As soon as the motor was killed I knew I had done the right thing. I dropped the crawler over the side and lay back in the seat with my legs up and the pole resting between them. I looked at my dad and smiled. He looked worried, but as soon as he saw me smile he relaxed and grinned.

It wasn't two minutes when I had my first strike. I set the hook and quickly boated a four-pound largemouth. Two more quickly followed and I was back in the race. As we drifted toward the shore I noticed that I would catch a fish, then have a quiet spell, then catch another, then more quiet. I figured there were sandbars running the way the river flows all up and down the lake. Now I had something to work with! I limited out on large-mouth then went to pike. Trolling over the edge of bars with large diving plugs produced several. One thing began to bother me. In all of the fish I had caught, not one was a contest winner and I hadn't even smelled a t'ain't. I went to bigger plugs but the action slowed down.

I had just decided to give up on the massive hardware and was reeling in quickly when I was introduced to my first t'ain't. It hit that lure with a vengeance. It fought like a fish possessed. After several jumps and runs I boated the monster. Problem was it wouldn't even go a pound and a half. I gently released the fish and washed my hands.

"You know, Dad," I said, "that little rascal really knew how to scrap. I surely do wish I had a clue on how to tempt a big one." My dad bent down in the bottom of the boat, carefully picked up the Willy and gave me a questioning look. I looked at the sinking sun and realized if I was going to win this thing I needed a miracle. "I guess it's now or never. Come on, Willy, let's see what you can do!"

I snapped on the plug and was preparing to cast when we were almost capsized by a large speedboat. It came so close it lifted our boat nearly out of the water and dropped it with a smash to the lake's surface. As we got back to our seats we could see our attacker grinning back at us—Horace Placker!

I guess we were more mad than anything at him. We shook our fists as he motored away. At that time we figured he was just an off-balance bigot, but we soon realized he was a genuine sicko and meant us real harm. We had motored out pretty far so no one could see us from shore and there were no other boats real close. It soon became clear Horace Placker meant to do us in.

He swung wide after his first pass and barreled down on us like a freight train. I was so shocked he was coming back I didn't have time to even start our engine. Luckily, he intended to toy with us for a while. He passed again within inches while my dad and I sat in shock in the bottom of the boat. The force almost dumped us over. Just luck, or the Lord, dropped us straight back down to the lake. Now I realized we were in danger. I began to pull that 15 hp like a wild man. I must have flooded it in my panic because it didn't start right up. It's a great motor and always starts . . . except then. I pulled and I pulled. All the time Placker was bearing down on us again. He could see I was trying to start our motor and I believe he had decided to finish us off. We could see him grinning with his eyes afire from the wheel of his speedboat. He was totally mad. His boat was big enough to effectively cut us in half and emerge unscathed.

At the last possible second that 15 hp choked and sputtered and finally roared. The little boat fairly jumped out of the way of Placker's speedboat. I don't know how he missed us, but he did, and we rode his wake out of the way. Now there was no anger in us, only fear. I looked around desperately for someplace we would be safe. The only thing I could see was a large rock sticking out of the water. It was only a couple of feet off the surface and probably three or four feet across. Hardly a sanctuary. I decided the best thing was to keep crossways to him and just motor out of his way as he attacked. I was able to do that twice, and then the situation changed.

Two other boats had seen what was going on. I pointed out the big speedboats screaming our way to my dad and we cheered. Then to our dismay the three boats lined up side by side to form a wall of machines with Horace in the middle. As they came closer I could see Confederate flags flying from both of the other boats and I recognized them as the boys from Alabama and Georgia. There was no way we could escape such a charge so again Dad and me huddled in the bottom of the boat preparing to meet our Maker.

As the boats came closer I could see Horace in his glory. He was standing up screaming and laughing and punching the air with his fist. They weren't 100 feet away when they made a sudden shift to the left. Dad and I watched in disbelief as the wall of destruction passed around us. Horace's face changed from glee to question then to horror as he realized what was to take place. Those southern boys ran Horace at full speed up and over the only target they ever intended for him. The rock island. They fanned off in either direction. leaving him to smash into a thousand pieces on that immovable object. They didn't even slow down. Before we could gather our wits they were out of sight in opposite directions. Our motor had died so we sat in silence for quite some time in the rolling water.

"Well, I suppose we ought to see if there's anything left of him," my dad said, breaking the spell.

As we pulled around to the wreckage we were shocked at what was left of the boat. There were splinters of wood everywhere. A seat here, the stern there, but no sign of Horace. We were about to give up when we heard noises coming from the largest chunk of boat.

"Dirty sons of bitches! I'll hang their asses out to dry! Hello! Hello! Get me out of here!"

It was Horace, all right. I was beginning to recognize his mouth. We grabbed on to a side of the hull and flipped it over. There he was, bobbing around in the flotsam like a half-drowned rat.

"You see what they done to me? I'll have 'em run out of the competition!" I guess he had forgotten what he had tried to do to us. "I could a been kilt! The bastards! I'll put 'em in prison for attempted murder! You're witnesses! You saw it all!"

"Are you OK, Horace?" I had to ask.

"Yeah, just a few scrapes is all. Takes more than the likes of them to put me under! Come on now, give me a hand up here."

He was in a good life vest and apparently unhurt. "I don't think so, Horace. I mean, we got a lot of fishing to do, and it's only a mile or two to the shore. I expect you can swim it OK." I was still talking when I noticed him turning red, but he composed himself.

"Come on now, boys, I was just having a little fun with you guys. I wouldn't of hurt you none. Not like those killers that about done me in."

"Well, about that we couldn't really say, Horace," said Dad. "It looks to us like you were running that boat a little fast and didn't see that rock. I expect you ought to be a little more careful next time. Listen Horace, we'd love to stay and chat but we've got a fishing contest to win, and I suppose you want to commence to swimming so we'll part ways. Now you watch out for those flesh-eating bass they got in these waters."

As we motored off we could hear him screaming his most colorful vocabulary at us. We decided without a word to get out of sight and hearing of Mr. Placker. We figured any fish that swam close to him would probably be polluted in some way. It wasn't until we stopped our boat that we realized Horace had hurt us more than we had thought. The stringer was gone. It must've been cut off by one of his attacks. I gazed at the sun and realized there were only a couple of hours left in the competition.

"Well, Daddy," I reasoned, "it looks like this boy is down for the count!" I began to feel real sorry for myself.

"Well, I expect that's true, son, but you know back in the old country sometimes when we fished it meant whether or not we ate, and not just our family but sometimes several families. With all that hanging on it we never gave up. We always tried to steal one more throw with the net. Just one more throw. You know, there were many times when it was the last drag that fed us. I don't see the way clear for you to win this contest, Jimmy, but it's hard for me to picture you quitting just the same."

I knew he was right but all the same I felt pretty bad. "Well, I guess it's up to wild Willy here. Now we've really got nothing to lose!" I took one more look at the twisted root and tossed it out in no particular direction to no particular spot.

The water erupted the moment the lure hit the surface. A t'ain't came straight out of the water, spraying water in all directions, shaking his head. What a fight! These composite creatures are really worth whatever effort went into them. I boated the fish and put him on a stringer. He was definitely the fish of the day.

"Not bad, Willy," I said to the root with a smile to my dad. "Now if you could do that every cast until dark I might be in this contest!"

I had waxed prophetic. The next cast was met with the same result. I quickly had my limit of the mixed breed scrapers.

"Too bad this thing doesn't work this well with other fish," I said wistfully. "We could sure use whatever magic it's got to catch some pike."

I threw Willy again to the same results. The water was smashed into foam the second it hit the water but this was not a t'ain't. Much to our surprise I boated an eighteen-pound northern pike. Now that was spooky!

"Go get 'em again, Willy!" I yelled as I let her fly. Another big pike and more followed. I quickly limited out on the big fish . . . all contest winners.

"Bass, Willy, now bass!" I cried and let it fly. Sure enough a beautiful largemouth in the twelve-pound range!

Our heads were swimming as one large fish followed another. I had but to ask and the twisted root delivered. I pulled in fish one after another for two straight hours. My arms felt like lead and my body was soaked with sweat. The heat was oppressive and my father kept tossing coffee cans filled with water in my face. By the time we hit shore I was so weak I couldn't walk. I had to be helped up the boat ramp and Dad had to load the boat. But the contest was mine. There was no one close. Every fish Willy caught was, in itself, a contest winner.

As I sat on the shore I had a feeling I was being looked at. Now, that wasn't too surprising as I had just won the title of best in the country and the crowds had begun to gather. But this was a different kind of feeling. I looked into the crowd and saw the Colonel, smiling and looking at me like a proud papa. I looked away for a second and he was gone. Bowlegs was standing in his place, nodding his head and holding his clasped hands high like a victorious boxer. I grinned and blinked and he too was gone and in his place was the fragile Clever Tellman.

He was a hundred feet away but I could hear his voice as clearly as if he were whispering right into my ear. "Jim, you done good . . . you wouldn't have needed ol' Willy if things had been straight up all day . . . but we know how they was. Yep, Jim, you got the look."

I was looking right at him and his lips didn't even move. He just stood there with his eyes shining and a little smile. He continued, "I expect yo' won't be needing Willy no mo' so I'll jes' take him on home with me. You're a good boy, River Jim, and I expect we'll see you again some blue-skied day with a soft breeze . . . on the banks of some river where the fish are always biting. Yes, Jesus, someday we'll see you again . . . River Jim." I felt happy and sad all at once, and as I watched him through watery eyes he just sort of melted into the crowd and was gone.

True to his word Willy was gone too. The strangest thing though was I went to the station as we were checking out to say thanks and goodbye. Well, it looked as if no one had been there for twenty years. Everything was falling down and covered with neglect. The chairs were arranged out front just as we had left them but they were covered with dust. I kicked around for a while but never found a clue. I thought about asking about the place at the motel but decided I probably knew as much as anyone and more than most. Some questions are perfect unanswered.

CHAPTER 13
DON'T MESS WITH THE CLAM MAN

Man I can't take it," said Clams. "I just have had all I can stand. If that guy doesn't stop pushing me around I am going to tell him to stick his papers right where the sun don't shine."

"I hear ya, Clam Man," I said. "I couldn't work for that low life if I had to." But we all knew Clams had to. His family wasn't particularly loaded, and if he wanted anything more than a roof over his head and food to eat he would have to work for it.

It was April in northern Wisconsin and me, River Jim, and my pals were gearing up for the end of the school year and the beginning of the greatest time in any twelve-year-old's life, summer vacation. But even with the modest needs of rural kids there would be money requirements. Some new camping gear to replace the old, materials for patching old boats and minor bicycle repair, and of course the latest fishing tackle. There would be the cost of food for the campouts and miscellaneous chip-ins for this and that. Clams would need his paper route.

The issue at hand was a miserable lowlife called Kenny Manderkoin, whose lot in life was to terrorize the lowly young paperboys in his charge. Kenny was an abusive forty-year-old who thought he had the cure to all of the world's problems. He had refused to work for fools and was dismissed from multiple jobs for multiple reasons, none of which were his fault. He currently seemed content with his position as paperboy manager. This was a position where he had control over others and was practically invisible from his superiors who really had no desire to interact with him at all and who were satisfied to collect the revenue generated from the boys and routes under his control. He was the king of his domain.

* * *

Kenny pulled his pickup into the gravel lot, slammed on the brakes and skidded the last few feet to the paper drop-off location. He really liked to skid and also to squeal out. He also liked to push around his young paperboys, especially Clams.

"All right, you pathetic pieces of crap, gather round," he bellowed.

The young paperboys moved cautiously closer careful not to draw specific attention to themselves, fearful of the ever dangerous Kenny.

"I got issues. I got problems that are none of your damn business. I'm gonna have to raise your paper taxes another fifty cents a week each just to make ends meet. If you got a problem with that why don't you open your little pie holes and tell Kenny about it."

Kenny had been collecting his "paper taxes" since he began in his job and it now amounted to about a third of every paperboy's earnings. This was over the top for one of the boys and Jeremy Walsh dropped his sack and began walking away.

"Where the hell are you going, PISS ANT!" yelled Kenny. "Stop in your tracks or I'll kick the livin' shit out of you."

Jeremy took off in a run with Kenny close behind. Manderkoin could run pretty good for a man in his condition and soon had the young boy by the back of the neck.

"Wanna quit, huh? Wanna walk away from old Kenny, huh?" Kenny shook him like a rat. "I am too good for you lousy ingrates. I ought to be getting a fifty-fifty split."

Jeremy was one of the younger paperboys and began to lose his fight with tears. When it looked as if the boy was in for a real beating the Clam Man spoke up.

"Hey Kenny, for pity's sake, leave up on the kid. He's just a kid. Let him go."

Manderkoin stopped and stared at Clams. "Unbelievable," he bellowed. "You fat, slimy piece of crap. You of all people open your lousy mouth. Oh yeah, I got plenty for you."

He let go of Jeremy and made a dash for the Man of Clams. Jeremy made for his bike and peddled off as Manderkoin lifted Clams off his feet and threw him to the dirt. He was on him in a second and lifted the boy's shirt over his head exposing his admittedly blubbery belly. He grabbed the fat with both hands and lifted the kid off the ground. The furious man spun the boy in a circle and sent him flying into the dust. Clams was on his feet and scrambling when Manderkoin hit him again. He grabbed him by the back of his pants, grabbed his underwear and hoisted him off of the ground. He yanked and yanked until the elastic band was over the young boys head.

Clams screamed like a wounded dog, "Kenny, Kenny—stop it, pleeeese! I'm sorry, I'm SORRY!" The slobbering Manderkoin once again spun the young boy in a circle and let him fly into a muddy ditch where the wounded Clam Man skidded to a slimy, muddy, damaged halt.

The panting Kenny Manderkoin strutted to the center of the gravel yard. "OK, assholes! Anyone got any other things to say?"

He dropped the bed of his pickup and demanded, "Get these lousy papers off of my truck and get um delivered. You're already late and you know what I do to the sorry son of a bitch that gets a complaint. All right, fat boy," he spat in Clams' direction, "you're the hero so you deliver Walsh's papers . . . and you better not be late for ANYONE! God you are PATHETIC! I need to wash your grimy slime off my hands. You make me want to PUKE!"

Kenny climbed into his truck and skidded out of the lot, spraying the young paperboys with gravel as he disappeared down the dirt road.

That evening at the river Clams lifted his shirt to show us the bruises Kenny had given him.

"Jesus," spat Billy Wax, "I'm gonna kill that bastard. I know how and no one will ever pin it on me . . . just leave it to me, O clammy one."

"Calm down, Billy," said Scoot. "There is no need for violence. He's just not worth it."

"I agree," I said. "Listen up all. The time is now. We can't let the Clam Man take this abuse anymore, and there is no reason we should have to. This fool is about as smart as a bloated bull-frog and there ain't no reason we can't out-think him and put an end to this. All we need is a plan."

Clams, Mike, Scoot, Billy and me, River Jim, sat around the rock fire that was summer home on the banks of the Apple River. We bounced ideas back and forth.

Clams was pretty quiet but finally spoke up. "I've been think-ing about this and really have come up with some ideas. I know this guy the best and I think, if we do this right, we can get him to eat his own tail. I read a comic book once that told a story that we might bend to our own needs." Clams bent into the fire-light, told his story and gradually over the next few hours the plan evolved.

* * *

Kenny Manderkoin drove his pickup into the parking lot at the newspaper where he was employed as a paperboy manager. It was two p.m. and the papers were waiting for him in neatly stacked bundles. As he loaded his papers in the bed of his pickup he caught pieces of a conversation two kids were having on the far side of a row of bushes that surrounded the parking lot.

"Worth a FORTUNE," a young girl said, "and all for the pickin.'"

Kenny lay down his latest bundle of papers and walked qui-etly closer to the edge of the bushes.

"Keep it down, Mike," said a young black boy. "This is too good to spread around and there is a serious chance of violence."

"Well, how much do you think it's all worth," the young girl asked much more softly.

"I'd say at LEAST fifty thousand dollars . . . at LEAST!"

"Man, what a scam! I can't believe it's soooo easy," said the young girl. "And really no laws will even be broken—your cousin is a genius!"

"Well, I know I can trust you, Mike, and the rest of the gang too. I got to go now, but let's meet by the river at the end of the park at about six. We'll have a fire and I'll fill you in proper."

"OK Scoot, I'll meet you there," said the girl. They said their goodbyes and walked down the street in separate directions.

Kenny stood still by the hedge, shaking his head and mumbling to himself, "Think they're so smart . . . damn! Fifty thousand! Think they're so smart . . . I need to get me that money . . . should be so easy. It would change EVERYTHING! We'll see . . . we'll see . . ."

Hopping into his truck he leaned out the window and looked back toward where the kids had been. As he drove past the spot he spit and snarled, "Damn niggers."

The four kids were huddled around the fire when Kenny Manderkoin quietly sneaked up behind the small shed at the edge of the river. He could clearly see that one of them was one of his paperboys. The one they all called Clams. They were talking quietly but in the still of the woods he could hear them just fine.

"Lateeva Creole is really my cousin I guess but it's three or four times removed," said the young black kid. "She just came up from the Louisiana bayou where she was a princess or a queen or a god or something. Man, I'z don't know, but den agin I hain't too awful smarts as you guys well know." The kids all nodded although they all knew that Scoot was in fact the brightest of the bunch. "So she and my Uncle Jim has got a thing going that's going to change the world and going to be worth the long coin, that's what I'm saying. But weez gots to be careful. My Uncle Jim is one big, mean SOB and he will whip me right into the arms of Jesus if he figures we is messin' with his bidness."

"OK," says Clams. "Scoot, we got the plan, let's run down what we know. Your cousin Lateeva is a master in the ancient arts of Jumbiwe Voodoo. We all know that. We saw what she did to that poor soul who slapped around and jilted your Aunt Pearl. He went from over six feet to four foot two with claws for hands and a body full of hair. The only thing that looked like him was his face and it didn't change at all. You and I and Jim saw that happen, Scoot, and there ain't no denying what we all saw."

I nodded my head and added, "I saw him in Clayton a couple of weeks ago at a penny carnival but I guess he left with them 'cause nobody's seen him since."

"Yep," agreed Clams. "She is what she is and it does no good to deny it, and as everyone knows she is a fortune teller of the highest order. This is where we see our opportunity. The plan your uncle and Lateeva has cooked up is a wicked, devious one.

"Now Widow Johansson was married to the late old Captain Jacob Johansson. Whole town knows he traveled the world on sailing ships and the rumor is he amassed a vast fortune in foreign treasure. Well, it seems that rumor is true. Widow Johansson has been using Lateeva for her fortune-telling skills to contact the late captain and ease her mind about his peace in the afterworld. In these meetings with the dead, Lateeva has found out for sure from the widow that house is filled with treasure. Precious stones, rare carvings and stolen religious artifacts to name a few, and gold . . . yes, my friends . . . gold."

Now, Kenny could barely hold his water. He was hearing

something that had the potential of putting some serious coin in his pockets. His first inclination was to storm the kids and make them work for him on whatever plan they might have. In considering Scoot's uncle, however, he wanted no part of an angry black man who might find no problem with slitting Kenny's throat, and he had no desire to be turned into a monkey by the cousin. He knew no black people personally but had no trouble hating them with a passion and fearing them the same. So he waited behind the shed and listened for an opportunity, some way to get what the world had denied him and was rightfully his, someone else's fortune. It was a pattern that Kenny had followed a large part of his life. He stole from his mother regularly, taking her meager social security checks and giving her only enough to survive. She was terrified of her son and suffered his abuse in silence. Kenny considered this his "fun money" and used it for liquor, gambling and prostitutes. But it wasn't enough. What he was hearing about was big money and Kenny wanted it. He decided right then and there he would do whatever it took to get it.

"As everyone in town knows," continued Clams, "Widow Johansson strings beads and sells them at the flea market in St. Croix Falls. What they don't know is she's been taking the old captain's treasure and stringing precious stones with golden threads and preparing a shipment out east, to New York City where she has a rich buyer. She told Lateeva she plans to move to San Francisco and buy a young husband to finish her days."

Clams stood up from the fire and paced toward the shed where Kenny hid. Kenny crouched lower so the boy wouldn't see him and Clams stopped just a bit short of the shed. He peed on the corner of the shed and the urine flowed under the corner of the building and puddled in a small low spot, the only spot a person might hide and the exact spot when Kenny Manderkoin kneeled. Clams zipped himself up and sauntered dramatically back to the fire.

"Now here," he continued, "is where it gets interesting. Lateeva has been slowly but surely telling the widow that the treasure Captain Jacob acquired is bad mojo. She has made up some conversations with her dead husband that confess of treachery and murder and deeds most foul. She has woven ancient curses into the booty with disaster and death sure to follow. She has convinced the widow that the only way to free herself from the curse is to rid herself of the treasure."

Kenny was beginning to see the potential for someone's huge gain and was becoming more and more determined that that someone would be him. Even the fact that he was kneeling in the urine of Clams couldn't keep him from shaking with excitement.

"Now that sets up the plan so the money is up in the air," said Clams. "All they have to do now is figure how they are going to pluck it for themselves. Well, it seems Lateeva pays for her voodoo lifestyle by playing suckers and she, in this regard, has some skills."

Clams sat on an old log stool by the fire and leaned in. The fire created a ghoulish glow to the chubby kid's chubby face. "This is where the real beauty begins to burst out of this plan," whispered the sultan of slime. "They have told a story to the widow that is as clever as clever can be. It went like this.

"It all began many years ago when Captain Jacob was a young sailor working as captain on a merchant ship off the coast of the dark continent of Africa. He put into port in Kamerun, a

German colony, in search of cargo worth the cost of transport. In those days it wasn't unusual for sailors to seek their fortune from port to port with a sharp eye out for an excellent trade. Now, most traders look to establish honest return and regular routes. Young Jacob was not so proud and often took advantage of an easy quick coin.

"In this harbor, at this time, he ran into an opportunity most cruel. The object was treasure itself of gold and stones. The rightful owner resided in a small village on the banks of Lake Chad. He had made his fortune in honest trade of palm oil, cocoa and elephant ivory. The banks at the time were little more than a strong chest and honest neighbors. The poor fellow was found with his throat slit and his fortune liberated. Captain Jacob spent little time gathering his crew and put to sea. The gold and stones the honest widow wove into her string of beads was the very same ill-gotten gain. What Jacob himself didn't know was that the beautiful Negress wife of the man he slaughtered was herself a local witch of some renown. She cast a mighty curse on the treasure stolen that centered within its very existence and fouled the spirit of all who might seek to gain from its value."

"Holy smoke" said Billy, "That's a beauty of a story! That Lateeva is one fine liar!"

"You ain't just a-kiddin'," replied Scoot. "She cooked that one up jes' fine! Now that old widow is right in the sweet palm of her hand. Yessir!"

Now, Kenny had heard enough to know that this could be his big chance. He thought about showing himself, slapping the kids around some and taking charge but the thought of Scoot's voodoo cousin and a big, pissed-off black dude held him back.

At this point he figured if he listened a bit longer maybe a chance would show itself and he could grab it then.

"OK, so what happens now?" asked Mike. "Does the widow just hand over the goods?"

"Oh no," said Clams, "That would be too obvious and would put the coin in the hands of Lateeva and Uncle Jim should the widow ever gain her senses and figure she was had. No, they want to be clear of any blame should the plan turn south. So they cooked up a delivery boy for themselves to keep things neat and tidy. She told the Widow Johansson that she was stuck with the curse and would surely die a miserable death unless she followed the proper steps to cleanse her of it proper. They took her to a huge swamp at the headwaters of the Clam River and performed a true Jumbiwe Voodoo ritual. There were candles and snakes, incense and moaning. Man, I would've loved to have been there. Scoot followed them up and saw the whole thing, didn't ya, Scoot?"

"Yessir, I surely did. It was something to see. Lateeva was dancing and singing and whirling around like crazy woman. The widow's eyes were the size of pie plates and a time or two she screamed like a banshee!"

"Bottom line," continued Clams, "was that Lateeva told the widow the spirit of the killed man from Kamerun was coming to her very home to get back his treasure. She said he would be black as pitch and smelling of death—a combined smell of rotted fish and skunk cabbage to be exact—and he was coming this very Friday night . . . just the middle of the night they said so as to give them some wiggle room. They have hired one of Jim's friends from Chicago to come up and play the murdered ghost. He's going to smear himself with the required stink and go into the widow's house buck-naked to retrieve the treasure. They knew that widow would be scared to death to be home alone so they told her that she could tell no one and must spend the night alone or the ghost would loose the doors of hell and drag her down, wherever she hid. She had to face this alone but she was also assured the ghost would do her no harm if she only returned the cursed treasure. Lateeva and Jim planned to be in a poker game in town, in case things go bad they would have an alibi. Scoot says they are planning him to be there at two a.m. so nobody would see anything out of the ordinary. So this is what we plan to do."

Just then Kenny's knees slipped in the Clam Man's urine and he banged his head on the shed. We all held our breath fearing a charge from Kenny to foil the plan. We waited but only silence bounced around the campfire.

"What was that," exclaimed Billy, though he knew for sure.

"Just a tree limb, I guess," I said, "bangin' on that old shed."

Kenny held his breath and his position even though it hurt like poison. Slowly we all relaxed and Clams continued with the story.

"OK gang, here's what we are going to do. I know it might make more sense to send Scoot as he is an African by birth but if his uncle and cousin catch scent of him he's a goner. If they catch a glimpse of me or the widow describes me they won't have a clue who it could be. So I am taking the lead on this one. I'm going to beat those guys to the punch and we are all of us going to split that treasure. I'm going to smear myself with campfire ash, rotten fish, and skunk cabbage, be buck-naked as a savage, and walk straight into the widow's house at exactly one a.m. Scoot has been careful as death so they have no idea he is on to them and all the widow will see is the ghost of that poor old soul. I'll get the treasure, be gone way before the thug from Chicago shows up and meet you all at the river to divide the spoils."

Now, it never occurred to Kenny that a group of kids would probably not consider stealing from a widow or that they would not really know what to do with all that treasure. He judged people by his own wicked self and believed only a fool would let an opportunity like this to pass. He considered letting them do the deed and taking the money by force but recognized the word might get to Jim and Lateeva and he wanted no part of that. So he made the decision right then and there to become the ghost himself and be at the widow's at the stroke of midnight. No one knew he overheard the kids and had any idea of the plan. He would be in and gone by the time the fat, slimy punk showed up, and not a person in the world would suspect old Kenny Manderkoin. He had a flash in his mind that there really was a God and he did truly love him by giving him this gift.

Kenny showed up with the papers a bit late on Friday. He had managed to keep his normal state of nastiness, however, and laid right into the clammy one.

"You pudgy, fat worm," he began. "Get your slimy, fat ass over here and unload my truck. I am saving myself for greater things, and I love to watch you sweat!"

As Clams climbed into the truck and began to unload the bundles, Kenny strutted around the lot acting like a just-trapped squirrel in a cage. He was wound tight it was easy to see and mumbled to himself as he paced. Finally Clams finished dumping the papers to the dirt lot floor and Kenny headed for the truck.

"I don't care if I never see you worthless little bastards again as long as I live," he said half to himself. "I may just move myself to Florida, eat coconuts and drink nothing but rum."

He opened up the truck door and jumped in. The window was down, and as he passed by Clams he launched a gob of spit at him and hit him right square in the face. He spun his truck around in the dirt lot and peeled out, spraying the young paperboys with dirt and rocks.

The moon wasn't quite full that Friday night, but the sky was clear and the moon was big enough to light things up pretty good. Clams, Scoot, Mike and me was low in the brush across from the widow's house when Kenny came walking down the road. He had parked his truck a ways away and was naked as a jaybird. Not any self-respecting jaybird, however, 'cause he was black from fire ashes and smeared with a noticeable goo. We could smell him from the good 150 feet away he was. I looked at the hands of my superman wristwatch and confirmed it was exactly twelve midnight. Just about then Billy Wax crawled up from behind and gave us all a thumbs-up. He lived about a mile away, and at exactly eleven forty-five he had called Sheriff Tanner and explained there was a nasty looking prowler in front of the widow's house and he better come check it out. He didn't leave his name.

I guess the timing couldn't have been better. We sure didn't want to frighten the widow and the sight of Kenny would have certainly done that. As the sheriff turned the corner he flipped on his lights and set his siren blasting. Old Kenny was just peering into the widow's front window, up on his tiptoes with his naked ass shining back at the startled sheriff. On hearing the siren he whirled and took off running down the road toward his truck. Sheriff Tanner pulled up alongside Kenny, opened his door and sent the running, naked, would-be treasure hunting ghost sprawling into the ditch.

We could hear the sheriff asking Kenny what the hell he was doing and Kenny crying and saying stuff of which we caught every few words: "voodoo," "Lateeva Creole," "monkey man," "the REAL thieves" and such. He cuffed Kenny but before he put him in the back of his squad car he hosed him off with the widow's garden hose, least as much as he could. Then he planted Kenny in the back seat and spoke for a while with the frightened Widow Johansson who had come out on her porch to see what the commotion was about. The sheriff asked the widow if she knew what Kenny was talking about, but it was obvious she did not. She did not believe in fortune tellers, her husband was a sailor, yes, but in the navy as a cook, and she certainly had no treasure but wished she did. The truth was all three of them looked equally confused.

Finally, the sheriff said his goodbyes to the widow, jumped into the front of his squad car and slowly pulled back down the road from which he had come. As the car rounded the corner there was a young boy standing by his bicycle. As they got close you could see he had a newspaper sack over his shoulder. He was a chubby kind of kid, and as they pulled by Kenny could see his face clearly. The boy softly smiled at Kenny's half-blackened, filthy face in the back window. With a wink and a slow wave the Man of Clams sent Kenny Manderkoin off down the road.

The eventual investigation came up with other foul deeds that Kenny had done and his Mom even stepped up to testify of his abuse. Old Kenny was finally shipped to a place very, very far away where the odds were good that paperboys everywhere would fear him no more.

CHAPTER 14
JFK

After winning the national competition I was an instant minor celebrity. People would come up and say, "Hey, I know you." More often than not they couldn't remember from where but it was still unnerving for a backwoods boy like me. My folks had had enough of the bright lights and scurried back to the river. I was swept away to Washington, D.C., and the president himself. I was as nervous as a perch fry in deep water.

The outer shell of the inner circle is about as hard as a bear's skull. The boys that watch over the president are a serious bunch with no time for jokes. I tried a little small town humor on them but it was like trying to crack rocks with river mud. They just stood tall and strong, always looking around, very serious. I got the feeling that when their shift was over they probably were led to a small room where they lay on a stone slab until their next go-around. Don't get me wrong, they were well-dressed and well-mannered and, believe me, if some joker was after my skin they're the boys I'd like to look after me.

Anyway, I was directed through the bear's skull to the brains and people let me tell you that's a good comparison because as hard as the outside was the inside was just that soft! There was a party going on that was literally fit for a king—King John! There were people of all ages and descriptions. They all had two things in common, they were all beautiful, by the world's standards, and they all looked genuinely happy. There were jugglers and clowns dancing around and roving minstrels playing their fare for small groups of merrymakers. I'm not much for judging crowds but I would have to say there were at least four hundred people there, and there may have been twice that. But for all the people there was no mistaking the center of this world. Your eyes were automatically pulled to the young American king and his court. He was tall and quite handsome as were the folks around him, most of them his relatives. They all acted as if they were no strangers to good times.

"Ah, Jim! Yes, that's it . . . ova he'a." (I don't know if I can keep up this accent!) "This he'a is Jim a Bordell and a is thee a reason a for this a little get-together." The room applauded loudly but without losing its good looks.

"Jim is thee a best fisherman this a great country of a ours a has to offer. I believe a with all my heart a that he is also thee a best the world has to offer. I have, as you all know, made my feelings a plain . . . to Mr. Khrushchev."

The room, once again, erupted in applause with a few cheers and whistles thrown in for good taste.

"Perhaps a Jim would honor us with a few words . . ."

He stepped aside directing me to the center of attention. How does one speak to a bunch of professional speakers? After the polite (yet strong) applause I stood before our country's best feeling like a crayfish addressing an elite gathering of trout. I decided to take a radical chance and try to be myself.

"This is really something! Do you folks really live like this? We are considerably more than miles away from the river!" They laughed at the right places and I got the feeling that they really were proud of me. I waxed bold: "I feel like Marco Polo must have felt when he stepped into the palaces of Kublai Khan. Makes a person want to polish his boots!" Again laughter. "I guess I should tell you that I'll do my best to win for America, 'cause I will, but there's some other stuff I'd like to tell you all too, since you seem obligated to listen." In an instant the room quieted to a hush and the mood changed from merrymaking to semiserious respectful attention.

I continued, "Now I'm not a politician and Lord knows all the things I don't, but perhaps you folks don't get a lot of chance to hear from a regular joe like me, and I expect I won't have a lot of chances to talk at you when you're forced, out of politeness, to listen." Light laughter, then quiet.

"I expect you know all about the problems with the colored folks down South. I've just been there and I can tell you they're real. I suppose you know how the country feels about the bomb. Even I have bad dreams. Hunger and poverty are problems in this world and I guess they always will be, but there is something very good in this country also. It's a feeling that the government, you folks, really do care. I just want you to know that the guy on the street is saying good things about what's happening here. You all praise what I did and wish me good luck, and I thank you for that, but I just wanted to praise you a little and wish you the same because the contest you have to win is a lot more important that the one I'm in.

"Now to lighten up a little bit I'd like to invite you all to my river in Wisconsin for the finest fishing and a thick slice of living the way God intended!" I said my thanks and stepped back and by the sound of the applause I guess they liked getting a few strokes. The rest of the evening was a blur. I'm sure the wine went to my head although I guess I didn't embarrass myself too badly (didn't get down and gator or anything!) I remember plainly the president wandering around telling people that he never had a rubber swan but did bathe with a pink duck and would happily give all the beautiful girls at the gathering a party goose! They really knew how to kick off their shoes (in their own way). I woke up the next morning with a sore head and a terrific memory.

Yeah, I remember 1963. The Mona Lisa was in Washington. Communist China was making nuclear devices. "Nonviolent" India got some fighter planes from the Russians. France exploded an underground nuclear device in the Sahara. In Yugoslavia Tito was made president for life. Martin Luther King was arrested in Birmingham. Khrushchev was talking about hanging it up because of his age. American death count went to eighty in Vietnam. France was considering Tahiti for nuclear testing. Telstar 2 was launched. U.S. astronaut Cooper made twenty-two orbits and landed right on target in the Pacific. The Supreme Court said that schools had to desegregate without delay. Kennedy signed a bill saying equal pay for equal work in regards to sex. A woman was launched into space by the USSR. The Dodgers beat the Yankees four straight to win the World Series, and on

November 22 in Dallas, our thirty-fifth president, John F. Kennedy, was shot to death.

Things were real quiet on the river for a while.

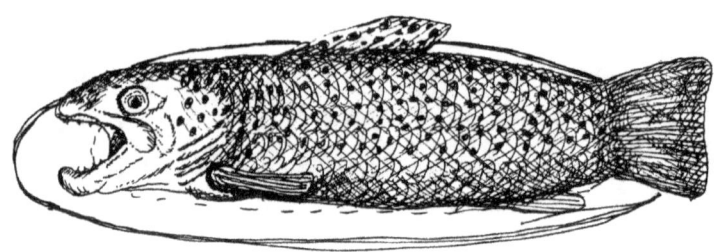

There were eight or ten of us, I reckon. All of our eyes were on that one plate of steaming trout and all of our hands were on our revolvers. It's sweet smell pulled like a woman to a sailor. Sweat poured out of us and hit the floor making the sounds of a summer rain hitting the buckboard but no man dared make a move.

—BASTON MOLSEN*

*From his historic novelle, "Lives lost over steaming trout in the old west."

CHAPTER 15
LYNDON JOHNSON

Things were real quiet on the river all right. We just hung around trying to guess what would happen next. I thought that the chances were very good that the fishing part of the Olympics would be called off. It was just a bet between leaders, and ours was gone. We didn't hear anything for the rest of the year and as time dragged on I was sure, like so many of our country's young and budding blossoms of hope, the idea of an international fishing competition was destined to wither and die.

I was surprised indeed to receive a letter in early January 1964 asking me to please come to the White House for some pre-Olympic briefings. I was also invited for some fishing input from the big Texan himself.

If there was ever a back room politician, Vice President Lyndon Johnson was one. It must have been difficult to be so outshined by the Kennedy Boys. I, along with the rest of the country, was watching to see how he would stand up to the impossible challenge of filling JFK's shoes. At this point, all I could think of was that the thrill was gone. He did go on to do some great things for the common American with the Great Society, Medicare, Medicaid, and race relations and such, but at this moment I was just pleased that the competition was still on and surprised and honored to have him ask to talk to me personally. The meeting was for the first week in February and as the time drew near I became more and more excited about my second trip to the nation's capital.

I was surprised when I was met at the airport by the presidential limousine. It was early evening, there was a party in progress at the White House, and I was invited. As I entered the ballroom I was struck by the transformation that had taken place. Where there had been cultured, East coast money, grace and charm in the Kennedy regime there was now a look that could be best described as "old West," with the new money Texas oil tycoon at the front. Wing-tipped shoes were replaced with cowboy boots, and pearl buttons replaced French cuffs. The women looked somehow more "down home" but the change in the men was striking. There were many new faces, but I was surprised by how many old ones I recognized even in their new images. In talking to some of them I found out that many of their families had partied with the various presidents for generations, and although they'd truly enjoyed the previous administration, they would do what it took to survive through this one. They prided themselves on their adaptability so in Stetson hats and snake-skinned boots they strutted around the room with their thumbs tucked in their belts.

Again it was not hard to find the center of this crowd. Even though they were as different as two men could be, Jack

Kennedy and Lyndon Johnson had one thing very much in common. They were both the president and in that capacity were both very powerful men. I wandered over to my host and prepared to introduce myself.

"Well, if it isn't James Bordell," he said as I approached. "I don't expect you even noticed me at the last gathering here, did you son?"

He took my hand and held it firmly and gazed deeply into my eyes with an unfaltering, piercing look. I tried to think of where he was at the last reception but I couldn't honestly say I had seen him at all.

"Don't let it bother you, boy. I was so buried in that administration I couldn't even find myself to go to the restroom." The group around him chuckled with practiced perfection. "In a few minutes I would like to talk to you in private if you don't mind, Jim."

I assured him I was at his disposal and wandered off to one side of the room where I could watch the show. I had barely begun my people watching when I felt a hand on my shoulder. I turned around and LBJ was there, lumbering over me like some kindly old giant. His back was bent and his head leaned down to my level. His large nose with the tiny specs he wore made him look like a prehistoric bird. He tilted his head with a kind of questioning look and pressed his face very close to mine.

"Jim, would you-all care to talk to me now?"

I, of course, assented and was led to a small study off of the party area. The room was, I believe, a hideaway of his because it was too small for any serious presidential work yet filled with many personal things, including a hand-tooled leather chair that I am certain came with him from Texas and fit him like a friendly old pair of shoes. I sat on an overstuffed chair across from him and with the door shut somehow I felt as if we were in Texas.

"This room suits you, Mr. President," I offered as we dropped into our resting places.

"It's about the only thing in this damn town that does then," he replied with a sardonic grin. "You see all of those brand new cowboy boots out there? I guess you can't blame them for trying, and although I hate hypocrisy I guess it's better than to have folks hate you to your face. That's too hard on a person's insides and if you look close it's pretty easy to tell who your friends are."

He offered me a large cigar and lit one for himself.

"You know I struggled with that young pup and hated his punk brother. I know everyone loved him and the country was happy. I know all of that. He had a gift all right. He could shoot himself in the foot and come out of it looking like a sharpshooter. A real thoroughbred. Then I come in looking like a tired, old, plow-footed mitre-messa mustang. You know they ignored me when I was here. Just flat ignored me. I may not be pretty but I have more experience and downhome savvy in my big toe than that whole group of womanizers!"

He took a long puff on his cigar then visibly sagged.

"It was so sad, Jim. That young man killed that way—and in Dallas! So sad. I may not have liked the way he was doing things but you couldn't help but admire his love of life and pure honest optimism. In so many ways he was like a child. He must have stirred up some bees somewhere. You can forget that single nut theory about his shooting. No, it was bigger than that. Then that Ruby guy taking out Oswald—much too clean. I doubt anyone will find out the real story, at least not until I'm in the ground.

It was the saddest thing I've been through, and I watched my momma and daddy die. But you know they had their lives, full and sweet."

He paused and stared out a small window at the garden below, but I think his mind was a million miles away. He slowly turned my way and looked at me with sad and compassionate eyes.

Slowly he smiled. "So you are the best Fisherman in America."

I smiled and I must have blushed.

"Now don't be embarrassed, boy. You're the best here and maybe the world. We're proud of you. Country needs something to be proud of."

I mumbled something about trying my best.

"I know you will, boy. I talked to Mr. Khrushchev last week and he has a boy over there he says will bury us . . . in fish. I personally picked up Mr. Kennedy's wager. You know, as a boy I did a bit of fishing myself down near Stonewall. I hope to do some more after I'm done here and go back to my ranch. I never was that great at it and maybe you could give me a pointer or two."

We talked for hours, and I wondered about the room next door filled with very powerful folks that had planned on having the president's ear.

CHAPTER 16
ROCK AND ROLLIN'
ON THE RIVER

I wonder if a person ever grows up. I mean, I'm forty-six years old and I can honestly tell you I still think of myself as eighteen. I really haven't changed that much, inside I mean, behind my eyes. Someone wrote a line, "Every old crone in her wrinkles and bones is still a young girl in her heart." That really says it plain. I like that. I wonder if we all aren't kids in our hearts. I'll bet it's true.

I've had a lot of folks come to the river to fish. I'm often asked to guide for someone with connections. Sometimes it's a lot of fun and other times it's a lot of work but I have a hard time turning down anyone. I've guided for everyone from underprivileged kids to multimillionaires, and there's a story in every box!

One time that comes to mind was in the middle sixties. There were these four mop-tops from over the big water that had started a mania with their brand of rock and roll. Well, it seems that someone up there figured that what they needed was a taste of "real America" so they stayed on a dude ranch for a few days then came to the river for a couple of days of fishing and solitude from their screaming fans. Now, I don't know much about that "rock and roll," and back then I knew even less and hardly ever listened to the radio. I had, however, heard of the boys and knew they were probably the most popular thing in the world at that time so I was curious to meet them and see what all the fuss was about.

My folks had just recently moved to the road. While they built their place there, Arboblaster built my new cabin on the river. I was so proud of that place I would have entertained royalty (and later did!). The band (I'm told by my editor not to mention their band name or their full names as I don't have permission and getting it would take years if it could be done at all), arrived in a black limo that reached from Milltown to Fox Creek.

"Up your income, Brian, we don't need no friggin' body-guards in the friggin' woods!" A tall, thin young man with very sharp features and apparently a tongue to match spoke to a shadowy figure within. "Just be back in two days and bring along a couple of birdies 'cause we'll be ready for 'em."

The doors closed, and the big black car sped off down the road leaving the five of us and about a ton of "stuff" in its wake.

"The things we do for our bloody public! I'd rather be in a bloody pub!"

"Me too, Josh (changed name), I'd ruther be swillin' in a pub meself!" said another young rocker with a friendly, simple look and a rather large nose.

"Come on, lads, break out of it! We're on holiday! Check it out now . . . quiet for a change," piped up another young star who had lots of energy and good looks. "This could be bloody wonderful! I know if I had to meet another friggin' birdy I'd turn meself inside out!"

He turned to me with a grin. "I'm Pal, this crabby one here is Josh, young wallflower over here is Geo and finally our man Dingo! You, of course, are fisherman Jim."

He held out his hand, and I shook it and all the others in turn. After the amenities I stood looking at all the baggage. There were a couple of small clothes bags, but the lion's share of the pile were instruments.

"You boys fixin' on holding a concert on the river?" I asked.

"We always stick with our gear," replied Josh, the tall, moody one. "You can't tell when a song might come along . . . even in this bloody wilderness!"

I thought about their yeah, yeah, yeah song playing at that time on the radio and wondered if there was any inspiration for that kind of thing on my river.

"Well, boys," I said with a shrug, "it's a long and winding road to the cabin and we have to walk it. The only way we'll get in any fishing is if I get a little help from my friends with this stuff."

The one with the sharp features seemed to be very serious about his craft and must have been a genius in writing songs 'cause he was always jotting down ideas. We all grabbed a share and started down the path.

"Make sure you are comfortable with what you have," I shouted, "'cause you're gonna carry that weight a long time, but I've got a feeling that we can work it out!" and off we trudged toward the river.

I tried to take it slow 'cause it was obvious that the boys were slightly out of shape. This was their time off and the last thing I wanted to do was make our time together seem like boot camp. About halfway I called a halt and we took a short rest.

"Well, boys," I queried, "what do you think of my world so far?" I could tell by their moans and groans they were not overly enthused. "This here land belonged to my folks before me and an old Scandinavian before them. I only met him once but I remember him clearly. I can almost hear him saying, 'Little-a fel-la, vat do yoo tink-a my yoost-a be land? Isn't it a gud, my Norvee-gin-a voods? Yah shoor!'"

Three of the boys laughed, but the serious one was off in his own world writing down ideas. I doubt if he even heard me half the time. I guess I admire his ability to pick hit songs out of the air, just like leaves off a tree. I guess that's why they were such a bit hit . . . pure genius!

"Well boys," I said after a spell, "let's get rollin'. When we get to the cabin I'll treat you to some wild honey pie; that'll pick you up! While we're walking don't pass me by 'cause there are some cliffs along the river where you might step out into the air! I'd hate to see you crashing helter-skelter into the drink!"

After what I'm sure seemed to them like a lifetime we arrived at the cabin. Even as tired as they were I could tell they were impressed. We dragged the last of their stuff into the cabin and they collapsed into the easy chairs. I could see it would be hard to get them fishing for a while so I decided on a meal and some small talk. Before they could catch their breath I whipped up some of my "bass a la Jim" deep-fried in secret egg batter. They devoured two four-pounders and the promised honey pie without much conversation.

I also had my share and pushing back my chair on completion patted my belly and commented, "I don't care what they say, boys, I won't stay in a world without fish!" They all smiled (even Josh), and I could tell this was going to be all right.

It was still the heat of the day so we decided to digest for a while and hit the river an hour or so before dusk. The boys tuned up their instruments, I brought out my old banjo and we commenced to pickin'! I dug up an old Indian tom-tom for Dingo and I'll tell you right now those fellas were famous for a reason. Not only could they ride a tune with the best of them, but they truly had fun doing it. They even let me sing a couple of my ditties.

"Hey bass, don't make it bad. Take a hot day and make it better. Remember when you take it into your mouth and try to swim south, you make it better!"

With all their "la, la, la, ladadadas and hey bassy bassy bassy bassy bassy bassys they turned that little jingle into a real rocker.

Then there was "There's nothing you can catch that can't be caught. No lure you can throw that can't be bought. No fish around that you can't learn how to catch in time. It's easy! All you need is bait . . . All you need is bait . . . All you need is bait . . . bait . . . bait is all you need!"

We had a grand time! I picked along with some of their tunes and we played some old standards. God bless the three chord progression! Folks can play a lot of good tunes if they just keep it simple enough. Before we could catch our breath a couple of hours had scooted by, and it was time to show the boys why they had come so we put aside our music boxes and headed to the river.

It was a beautiful afternoon. The sky was so blue it looked

unreal with white fluffy clouds so perfect it almost looked like a cartoon. The air was so clean you could bathe a baby in it with the temperature hovering around the mid-seventies. We couldn't have asked for more. The river sang to us with a gentle swish and hiss and we stood and looked at it for the longest while.

Finally, the gentle Dingo said, "It sure is loverly, Jim!" They all nodded and smiled softly.

"Yes," I said, "it's really kind of magical, isn't it? I mean, it's always coming and always going and always right here. Kind of like us all, wouldn't you say?"

I knew it was and I knew this river. I realized that if we didn't get moving she would seduce us into spending the rest of the day sitting on her banks listening to her tell her stories of long ago and far away. Not a bad way to spend a few hours, but the boys had come to fish and that's what I intended to do. We all piled into two canoes and pushed off the bank. It was my plan to float to a small lake downstream, then near dark we'd paddle back upstream, and I felt the boys could handle it. Pal seemed to be at his most adventurous so I put him and Josh in one canoe with Dingo, Geo and I in the other.

As we paddled down river I could see that Geo was a little nervous. "Relax, Geo," I said. "Turn off your mind, relax and float downstream. It won't kill you!" I smiled and soon he began to loosen up.

In no time at all the river widened and we poured into the picturesque little lake. We held our canoes together while I tied lures onto the boys' rods and explained the methods we would use. It was my opinion that they would not be overwhelmed by blue gill fishing so we were going after bass with surface lures that might also bring a rise out of a northern or musky. I explained how they must think like a wounded bait fish and make their lures act the same.

"If I'm gonna think like a bloomin' fish I'm gonna need some 'elp!" said Pal, taking a bag of something out of his jacket.

He rolled a skinny cigarette out of the stuff while Josh, Dingo and Geo looked on with hungry eyes. I guess I was green but there were no real marijuana problems in my world at that time, and I honestly didn't know what they were up to. They held their breath, choked, and giggled as they smoked the sweet-smelling weed. They told me right away what it was and encouraged me to try some, but in my realm of experiences I had been assured one puff would be my undoing.

Also, I was in charge of perhaps the four most popular young men in the world, on a river that can sometimes be unforgiving, and with those responsibilities I had no intention of drifting off into Never-never land! Besides, it was up to me to see to it they caught some fish. That was not going to be as easy as it sounds. Within minutes I was transformed into a babysitter. They lost all sensibilities. First, they began laughing and splashing each other with the paddles. Then they stood up in the canoe (never, never, never) and tried to rock each other off and into the lake like a log rolling contest. I was beginning to think I was in over my head. These were just overly indulged children in men's bodies, and they seemed to have no regard for me or my equipment.

"Easy does it, boys," I yelled, waxing angry. "If you're going to act like piggies with no regard for anyone but yourselves I'll be happy to get off here and bill you later for the canoes. I reckon I'd rather not sit here and watch you crashing obladi oblada all over the lake like you was ten years old and it was your birthday! If you think it's your birthday well it's my birthday too, yeah, and I came to fish. If you want to swim we can go back up to Molly's Hole and that's all right with me. Now, you've been doin' all this rowdy stuff all your life I'm guessin'. I like that stuff too. But this ain't the time or place. This here lake is mostly river with some strong current. You can plainly see the weeds, and let me clue you if you get in that you're a goner! Even the beaver stay out of that stuff! And on top of it all, my guess is that none of you are what I would call strong swimmers so please put her in low gear and let's get what we came for."

I really thought they were beyond me. We stared at each other for a moment or three, then Josh spoke. "There's smoke comin' out of your ears, Jim."

The other three giggled softly. I felt like a school teacher in a rough part of town. For a second I could see the devil in Josh's eyes and I figured I had lost, then in an instant it was as if the clouds lifted and he saw me clearly.

"Oh Jim," Josh said, "right you are, rascal—so sorry, just a bit of madness. We'll behave, won't we boys?"

The rest smiled and agreed and within seconds we were all seated and talking fishing techniques, but it was several minutes before my heart regained its natural rhythm!

It is hard for me to accept the possibility that not everyone is cut out to be a fisherman. It just doesn't sound right. If there are four on this earth I was convinced I was looking at them. I don't know if it was the drug they had waterlogged their minds with or maybe the level of energy they were used to but fishing proved to be only a forum for their ongoing nonsense. I started out admonishing them and I would try to slam their gears back into fishing mode. It would stick for about two or three minutes then something would distract them and away we would go on a comical carnival ride on the wheels of their playful reality. I ended up just making sure they knew enough of the severity of each situation to keep them reasonably safe.

Pal caught one hapless bass. It was less than a pound and became the center of their living theater. That poor fish was passed between them; first it was Pal's lover, then a singer in Josh's hands with Josh working its large mouth to the songs of Bo Diddley and Fats Domino. Then Geo made it their manager, nag-nag-nag! The soft-hearted Dingo finally felt sorry for the little fish and turned it loose so it could, as Dingo put it, become famous for having sung with the group. None of them hurt the fish and they really did know how to have fun.

It became harder and harder for me to maintain my adult role so I suggested we get off the lake and paddle up to Molly's Hole for a swim. After many off color jokes about the name of the swimming hole they agreed and we headed off in that direction. When we got to the hole we were greeted by a half tame raccoon that I had named Rocky. He was on a large, flat rock on the edge of the water, washing his face and fur. He wasn't too concerned with our arrival. He just gave us a quizzical look then returned to his grooming. The boys were delighted. They jumped out of the canoe and hustled over to the little critter. I told them to be careful because Rocky was only half tamed. Someone suggested "bopping him with a rock" but claimed he was only kidding when I threatened to bop *him* with a rock.

Like everything else Rocky only managed to hold their

attention for a short while, and we were all soon skinny dipping in the river. Rocky climbed up on the old wooden footbridge that crosses there and watched us as if we were crazy. When we would do something extra loud he would cover up his eyes with his paws and kind of peek. The boys loved it. There was a rope swing out over the water so we could swing up fifteen or twenty feet in the air then drop into the deepest part of the hole. Dingo was the only one that couldn't swim at all but it didn't slow him down one bit. He would jump and sink then one of the others or I would drag him back to shore to do it all over again. After what seemed like hours they began to slow down and we made our way back to the cabin.

This wasn't turning out at all like I expected. I figured I was hired as a fishing guide but fishing was far from the minds of these young Englishmen. I just resigned myself to staying loose and not trying to force anything on them. When we got back to the cabin we found it locked up tighter than a walleye's alibi. I just told them to stand by and went to the back of the cabin. When I arrived at the door to let them in they looked surprised. They knew there was only a front door.

"Did you have to break a window or such, Jimmy?" asked Dingo.

"No, it's a darn pain in the neck, though. You see that there lock on the front door is out of kilter. When it gets slammed it locks itself. This ain't the first time I can tell you! So I have to break into my own cabin. See I came in through the bathroom window. I jacked it open with a silver spoon that I keep in a hollow willow by the banks of the old lagoon. It's a pain, though. I mean, I don't even know why there's a lock on that door at all. I haven't got a lot of valuables here and who would hike all the way back to do the job anyway? I mean, this is in the middle of nowhere. I'm the nowhere man in my nowhere land."

I kept on yackin' as we piled into the cabin. "I'm just a kind of fishin' fool. Sometimes I climb up on that hill out there and sit and watch my river for a whole day . . . sun up to sundown. I know it sounds crazy but when the sun's going down I can feel the whole world spinning round from up there."

I kept jawin' while I fried up some fish. Pal, Geo and Dingo were polite and tried to nod their heads at all the right times. Josh was back in his creative world, writing like a maniac. I don't really think that any of them heard a word but I didn't mind a whole lot. I'm alone so much of the time (wouldn't have it any other way), when I do get around people I tend to exercise my jaws a tad.

"You know, as I sit back in the woods here I think about all the hate and wars in the world . . . back here it makes so little sense. I guess I take a simple view of the whole thing but, well, with all this rambling on, all I'm saying is, why don't those rascals just give peace a chance?"

The fish was eaten, a song or two was sung and the sun set on the river . . . like it's done ever since God breathed life into it.

The next day was spent just hanging out near the cabin. I expect what they needed most was just that kind of quiet therapy. Evening found us at the road with their mountain of packed music. The limo arrived on time. When the door opened I could see the same shadowy figure within along with several young women who were trying to suppress giggles. Pal jumped right in with an eager look. Dingo bid me farewell and dove in next. Geo thanked me with sincerity and climbed in next.

Josh was the last. Throughout the two days I guess I felt the most distant from yet at the same time the closest to Josh. We stood looking at each other for a long moment.

"There's a great power in you, Josh," I said. "It's not an easy road you've got ahead of you. I feel that you're like a salmon swimming upstream, trying to fulfill some primordial purpose that even you don't know. I won't tell you not to give up 'cause I don't think you have a choice but I somehow feel deep down inside that a lot of things and people are going to come together. They're going to come together . . . over you."

He dug deep into my eyes with a sad and serious look then all at once the clouds lifted and he smiled. "Must be off, Jim," he said with his hand on my shoulder, "me public awaits!"

Then he climbed into the back seat of the limo and was swallowed by a sea of giggling flesh. The car pulled away and in an instant I was alone. I couldn't help but feel the weight of the quiet.

I had another group coming that afternoon so I just sat by the road. It was a beautiful day and in little time the woods had wooed me solidly back to her side. My next group were also rockers. I was told they were also big time, but I couldn't place them. All I could think of when I tried to remember their names was "gathers no moss." For whatever that was worth.

I was almost asleep when their limo came screeching down the road. The first guy out had long hair and big lips and I tried not to think of him as ugly. By the time the other three were out I was convinced that the first one was handsome indeed. They all looked like they had come from a street fight where they had lost badly! One of them walked to the side of the road and relieved himself. It isn't often that I think of guiding as a job. This was one of those times.

"Well boys," I began cheerfully, "let's grab a load and head for the river!"

"I ain't carrying no friggin' baggage, you sot," said one who was so stoned on something he could barely walk.

"Now, now, Bryland," said Mac (the first one out of the limo) let's be gents and help the river man."

As we hiked to the cabin I made a note to myself to screen my customers myself from now on because at that moment I felt very strongly that I was going to lose my lunch! I tried to be cheery.

"Well, Mac," I said, "back here in the woods is where you go when you can't get no satisfaction anywhere else. I like it fine, though. You may not get everything you want back here but if you try I think you'll find what you need."

I rambled on thinking I was just talking to four stones. I'm sure they never heard a word I said, and I was thinking it was going to be a long couple of days!

CHAPTER 17
THE FISHING OLYMPICS BEGIN

Washington is a true adventure but truly not for me. I enjoy my visits there but don't really feel relaxed until I sit squarely in my favorite chair at the river. So after my LBJ encounter I was more than ready to put my feet up. The competition was set for July so I had five months to gather my strength. I remember sitting back, closing my eyes, and thinking I was going to need all of it.

Meanwhile the wheels were turning at Olympic central. They still had to choose a way to fairly find the world's best. There were hundreds of countries represented and millions of lakes to choose from. The first stipulation was that the lakes offered had to contain lakes in which no competitor had fished. The next was that the lake could not be in the country of any of the participants. The contestants themselves were divided into groups of four by some mysterious means known only to the Olympic committee. The lakes chosen were deemed to hold similar stocks of fish in similar stages of development to allow any participant to catch winning sizes and numbers in any one of the areas.

The Russian and myself were together, of course, along with the Chinese and the English. We would be allowed a person to motor the boat who would also double as an interpreter. This person was also a member of the Olympic committee and so would assure fairness. We would be allowed on the lake one week in advance to familiarize ourselves with our quarry. I expected to be fishing some lost river in darkest Africa so was very happy indeed when Lake Mangor in Ontario, Canada, was pulled from their hat for us.

What a fabulous lake indeed! If all the other competitors had lakes with the same good fishing in them there are hundreds of lakes in this world that I must someday visit. The only access was by float plane, which departed from Rainy Lake (an excellent fishing lake of its own!). Since the competition was set for the first week in July, our plans for the last week in June were to be motoring north to the shores of Rainy Lake to connect with a flyer by the name of Somp Paulson. I always get as excited as a gray squirrel when I'm heading out on a fishing trip, and that feeling along with the excitement of the competition had me almost totally useless. My mom packed my things and my dad agreed to drive me to the plane.

It had been a long wait that spring but this day had finally come. The morning was a perfect one and I thanked God again for my little piece of paradise. The car had been loaded the night before so all we had left was the lofty job of grabbing the Thermos of coffee and bidding adieu to my biggest fan, my mom.

She mushed all over me and we drove off in the soft light of a coming dawn.

It was about four hundred miles to the plane and we chattered all the way. My dad is a fine fisherman himself, and he had lots of tips for his seed. The time and miles flew by and by the late afternoon we were pulling into "Somp's Hotel, Marina, Fly'n'Guide" service. There was a large cabin with three or four smaller cabins in back and a giant garage to one side that had a huge sign on its roof that yelled "BAIT." It was right on the shore and we could see a battered old float plane half bobbing, half sinking in the water. It looked as if it was only held up by the dock to which it was tied. I felt a little sick. A crusty old dude met us as we drove into the parking lot.

He began to cover us with patter. "Got to be! Got to be! Jim Bordell! Yessir! Yessir!" He began to pump my father's hand.

"And you must be Somp," guessed Dad while accepting a steady gush of praise.

"That's me all right, Somp Paulson, and who's the sprout?" He pointed at me.

Well, I'm not very tall, and in my mid-twenties I probably didn't have a lot of hair on my face (if you looked close, a small mustache), but I hardly considered myself a "sprout"!

"Oh, that little pup?" I watched Dad decide on how far to ride this situation. "That's just the greatest fisherman that ever lived! You've heard of him. Now you've met him! You just can't help but love him! The one, the only, JIM BORDELL!"

The old duffer looked at my dad, wondering if he was having some kind of fit and maybe ought to grab his tongue. After a moment he gathered his wits and figured out that I was his passenger and that my dad was putting him on. "Then, who the hell are you?" he queried.

"I, my good man, am the roots of this greatness! I am the boy's father."

He was visibly unimpressed. "Well, whoever you are, your cabin is over there, and if I can pump out that pontoon we'll fly to Mangor tomorrow morning." He was obviously miffed and shuffled back to his cabin shaking his head.

We backed the car up to our lodging and unpacked. We agreed that it was not in our best interests to have the person who was going to have my life in his hands mad at us so after unpacking we made the short walk to his lodge to mend fence. My father apologized with sincerity and in minutes we were enjoying conversation and a cup of the old guide's Red Rose tea.

"Don't matter how old you are, boy," our host reasoned, "when it comes to fishing, I've heard lots about you—all good. I've already flown up the other three. Strange group, I can tell you that! To be honest the Russky is the most normal of the three. Can you figure that? 'Course, what is a 'normal fisherman,' huh? That would be like a 'prudish lady of the night.'" He laughed at his slightly off-color simile.

I thought about my competitors and realized what he was saying was true. The state department had put together a detailed history of each of them for me. I guess they figured it would help me catch fish. I don't know. At any rate, they were a "pack of cards."

Nang Tang Hue was the Chinese representative. He was a Buddhist monk from the Chinese province of Chianghsi. He was born in the city of Nanchang and spent most of his life at a monastery on the shores of a lake called Poyang Hu. It was rumored that he could catch fish whenever he desired. That seemed to be his gift and weakness. It seems that, being a Buddhist monk, he had nearly rid himself of desire. He understood why the fish was there and why he was where he was and that things were really "perfect" the way they were. Most times he caught only enough to eat. (He was well over three hundred pounds and had a special taste for raw fish.) He also understood that we are all one in the greater sense and competition was, in fact, fighting yourself.

You might well ask how he won the Chinese competition. Well, another function of the Buddhist is to "take on the karma," or sins of others to allow the whole world to achieve enlightenment. Only when we as a whole reach this plateau will heaven be attained. Soooo . . . he was surrounded by people in China who were not as attuned as he was and who had an overpowering desire to catch fish. He burned up their sins by catching fish after fish, thus winning the competition while burning out their desires. Just as it is said Christ died for our sins, Nung fished for his people's sins. I know how strange all that is and if I'm wrong in all that, blame the state department because before I read their sheets the only thing I knew about Buddha was that he had the extreme bad taste to sit around showing the world his overly stuffed belly button.

The English contestant was a rather unusual fellow as well. His name was Sir Edmund Stitsel. He was reported to be as prim and proper an English gentleman as was ever born. It was said he packed around an inflatable pontoon boat complete with surrey to fish off of. He was attended by a very correct manservant,

"Chives," who looked out for his every need. When he left the dock, however, he was always alone because he felt that any advantage over the fish that Chives might give him would be "unsporting." He was known in his part of the world for fishing for creatures "broad of beam" and was a favorite to catch the largest fish in our competition.

He'd received some publicity for hooking something "of great size" in Scotland's Loch Ness. I guess he was dragged around for weeks but would not give in. He became so tired that he was forced to tie the pole to his wrist. Both hands had become ineffective because of cramps, but he would not tie to the boat as that would not be sporting. In the rain and fog he was dragged. Chives stood on the dock for ten days, waiting for his return. He finally collapsed and was rushed to the hospital. A mild pneumonia was diagnosed and treated. Meanwhile, time and Stitsel dragged on. After three weeks he was intercepted and the line was cut. He was totally unconscious. He was found with his arm stretched out over the side. He'd been kept from being dragged into the deep only because the toes on his right foot had a "grim lock" on the pole at the center of his craft. He was in bad shape indeed!

I guess he always wore wool and the ever present rain and mist of the Loch Ness had shrunk that material so tight that he had to be taken to the nearby shepherd where he was put in line with the other sheep (the shepherd was a very busy man) and duly tied and shorn. The tying was unnecessary as he was unconscious but the shepherd knew no other way. It's said he was trimmed between a ram called Gentle Tom and a ewe named Hildy. He was then rushed to the hospital where it was found that he suffered only from exhaustion and a lack of tea. He was placed next to his manservant for recovery. It said that Chives, despite his own weakened condition, worried over him day and night until he finally came around.

My Russian counterpart was a man by the name of Ivan Petrovsnick. He was reported to be a gentle man who carved all of his own lures and talked continuously to the fish while he was fishing. He was from the small town of Gdov which lies on the "Chudskoye Oz," formerly Lake Peipus, about 150 miles southwest of Leningrad. He was a man who spent much of his time in the wilderness. Like many Russians, he had a strong taste for vodka, but his ability to catch fish "even in a bowl of borsch" made him the only logical choice.

The morning brought with it a dreary, misty day. A thick fog blanketed the lake and I had trouble picking out the dock a scant fifty yards from our cabin. I could, however, pick out Somp's voice, ringing clear in the misty gloom.

"Sonsabitches! Can't nothing be easy! Not one blessed thing! I wouldn't know what to do if something came easy. I'd up and say I must be dreamin' or dead. I'd say, 'Lord, if I'm dead tell me now so's I know not to wake myself up 'cause if I ain't dead and something went easy I must be asleep!' Why me? I ain't such a bad fella. COME ON, PUMP!"

WHAM! The sharp sound of steel on steel rang loud through a morning air so thick with moisture the sound felt like a blow.

"Suck, you worthless piece of scrap iron!" Then he changed his approach. "Come on, baby . . . Just one more time for ol' Somp. I'll fix that leaky pontoon tomorrow and change your oil to boot! That's it, baby. Sweet baby. Come on now, come on … .…Suck, you son of a bitch!" WHAM!

We hustled down, as much to protect ourselves from the sound of his blows, as to help. From all the bellowing it was pretty obvious what the problem was. The antique pump was being more antique than pump and Somp was trying to bring it back from the dead. By the looks of all the dings and dents in that old pump, I would guess that he'd dragged it back a hundred times before.

"What seems to be the problem, Somp?" My father tried the obvious approach.

"Well, both your eyes sewed shut or something? Any belly-up bullhead could see the problem!" He gave the pump another smash with a huge pipe wrench he was holding. "WHAMM-MMM!" The force of the blow and our position right next to it nearly knocked us to the ground.

"You old fool!" My father grabbed the wrench and waved it at the old man so as I thought he was going to ring his bell with it.

"Now calm down, Mr. Brodell….calm down. No point getting mad at old Somp. It's the pump that won't cooperate! I'm sorry as a pup if I was a bit testy with ya but this here machine has me so worked up I ain't thinkin' right."

There was silence for a moment, and all I could hear was the sound of the lake lapping up against the badly leaning plane, and the heavy sound of my father's breathing while he held the tool aloft as if deciding whether or not to crack the old man's coconut. Soon his face relaxed into its familiar smile and he offered to take a look at it for him. Somp was so glad to be out from under that sword of Damocles that he accepted the assistance cheerfully.

My dad was used to working on machines that should have

been left for the earth to reclaim. His garage was so full of the same that there was never, from the day it was erected, any room for a working vehicle. He had the knack of milking out one more job from such creatures so I left in search of a coffeepot with the solid knowledge that, if it was at all possible, that pump, in short time, would sing like the fat lady.

I was right in my thinking because I had barely lifted my cup when, with a cough and a sputter, the pump pumped, the water flew and the plane righted. The next half hour flew by as we loaded my gear. I wished that Dad could come all the way with me, but I guess the accommodations were limited at the lake. He claimed he had things he had to do at home but I really couldn't imagine what they could be. I guess he just didn't want me to know how disappointed he really was. Somp started the plane and we stood on the shore shuffling our feet trying to think of something to say that would be of value.

"I wish you could come, Pop," I mumbled.

"You know they won't let me, boy. Besides, I got too much to do at home. I can't just run off for a week any time I get the feeling. Nope, it's better this way."

"Sure, Dad, but it would have been nice to have you there."

We hugged and he said, "It sure would, boy. It sure would!"

I climbed into the plane and slammed the door. The little plane screamed as we skimmed faster and faster over the surface of Rainey Lake. The fog was quickly burning off and was only thick in small valleys that led down to the water so we could see fairly well in all directions. I'm glad it's a big lake because it seemed like forever until the pontoons lifted clear of the water. We climbed slowly into the air, making a big circle over Somp's lodge. I could see my dad waving from the dock and I could see him continue to do so until the hills and the trees made him and the lodge disappear from sight.

The trip up was uneventful, I'm glad to say. I had never been in a small plane and enjoyed it very much. Somp gabbed and gabbed but never expected an answer. Mostly he talked of the country we were over and the life he lived there. I'm sure, from all I heard, his life would look real fine in print. Yep, he had some tales to tell! In a short hour or so we were coasting up to the lodge's dock.

It was midmorning by the time I arrived. The fog had melted away and the sun shone bright and warm, its strength intensified by its mirrored image in the lake. Somp helped me unload my gear then taxied off with a smile and a "good luck." The airplane's drone slowly melted away and I was left in the quiet warmth unique to the north woods. I allowed myself a moment of rapture then grabbed an armload of stuff and headed for the cabins. There were exactly five cabins arranged in a semicircle facing the lake. In the center was a large fire pit, in front of what I gathered was the main lodge. The whole area was surrounded by giant white pines. It was as beautiful a spot as exists on God's green earth, but then I'm partial to the country. It was a quiet spot, though, and I began to wonder where all the people were when a tall Indian, dressed in buckskin, stepped out of the main cabin.

"You must be River Jim," he said and held out his hand.

"Some people call me that," I replied, "but just Jim will do fine." I smiled and took his hand.

"Well, Just Jim, we've been expecting you. Go on in. You can eat while I bring in your gear." I wasn't about to be waited on so we both went back for a load, found my bed and unloaded, then made our way back to the kitchen.

Come to find out this wild-looking Indian was named Taracoot, spoke nine languages and was my motor man and interpreter. I was pleased indeed as he was, by all appearances, someone I could work well with. Although he had been educated all over the world, it was his choice to live his life in the north woods of Canada. I could relate to that! He was a "no nonsense" kind of guy and made it plain that everything was to be played by the rules. I liked his attitude, and we began to be friends. It seems the rest of the competitors were out trying the water and I was so excited to begin, I actually ran around getting things in order so we could head out. While I unpacked, Taracoot loaded the boat. We finished at about the same time so all I had to do was walk down to the dock and step on board. I could feel my heart pounding as we pushed off into the waiting lake.

"So, Taracoot," I began, "how'd you get so smart?" I was confident he would not think I was being disrespectful and he returned my question with a ready smile.

"I don't know, Jim," he said, "must a been a white man in the wood pile back in my family tree!"

I smiled and continued, "Seriously, it must have been hard for an Indian to learn nine languages in the fifties. I mean to say, your people are not exactly a pampered class!"

His face softened when I mentioned his people, and a very deep pain glowed from him like an aura.

"It's as you say, River Jim, life is not easy for my people. There were two hundred children in high school with me on our reservation. I am the only one I know of to make a success in the white man's world. I am thirty-five years old and there are already fifty of the two hundred dead that I know of. Many, too many, of the rest are "whisky warriors" living in the vapor world of imagined valor.

"I don't judge them harshly. They are warriors in a world without a fight worthy of a warrior. They are hunters whose hunting is done for them by a society that calls their quarry welfare, their meat, food stamps. Only a fool would pack up a mountain and carry an elk down on his back when he returns to women and children who would rather walk to the government store and trade their stamps for cola and candy than eat the meat of the elk. The white man was careful not to give his red brother any land near population centers so there is no real work for an Indian. So in order for him to have success he must leave the people he loves and live with people he does not. And, just to keep it from being too easy, he must also fight their unreasoned fear and hate and compete with them for their jobs. So he ends up, if he tries as hard as man may try, with a job so menial that no white man wants it, with pay so low he must add food stamps to it to feed his family and accept welfare for his family's health.

"Native Americans are very proud people . . . very proud. So what is he to do? He lives in poverty on the reservation. He watches his children, so full of life in their youth and innocence, slowly die in their hope as they recognize the challenges they can never hope to conquer. Self-respect is life to the red man and woman. Without it they will take their lives. Many do. But then there is the whisky, to them a magic herb. It is the only thing the white man has brought that has given them self-respect. And they take it with a relish! It takes sickly women with cola-rotted teeth and makes them beautiful. It takes weak, unhealthy men, dressed in white man's rags and fills them with power. While they are in its control they are, once again, children of the sun. They dance and sing the old songs. The women dance and laugh and flirt while the men tell each other how they would have hunted the elk, fought the mighty bear, drove off the white man. They wrestle and lie and pat each other on the back. For awhile they are Geronimo, Cochise, Black Elk and Sitting Bull. No difference. For you see, River Jim, in their hearts and souls they are warriors and princesses, it is only in their flesh that they remain in squalor. So the whisky performs two valuable services for the Indian. It eases the pain in their souls enough so they can know their hearts, and at the same time it destroys their flesh, which has become their torment."

The boat's engine died and we quietly drifted into a small bay on the northwest corner of the lake. There were large white pines and birch on land with beaver-chewed giants, head under water and feet high on ground all along the shore. Between the fallen trees existed small quiet pools, and it was to these pools we had come. Taracoot watched as I tied on a small surface popper and flung it to the heart of one hopeful spot. We waited as the ripples ran their course. After a minute that felt like ten, I gave the tips of my rod a gentle twitch. The lure made its pop then lay still as if wondering what it should do next. The water was fairly deep but crystal clear, and I saw the rising smallmouth an instant before he hit. I had set the drag on my Mitchell spinning reel light so the line peeled off and I had to sacrifice my thumb directly on the line against the rod to slow the fish enough to keep him out of the tree tangle. He did turn, however, and was soon flopping in the boat.

"Well done," said Taracoot with a smile. "We will be a good team, River Jim." I smiled back and agreed because I liked this man.

We fished for an hour with very good results then headed for the resort. As the boat sliced through the water and the motor droned I was left to my thoughts. It wasn't about big fish that I pondered, however, but about strong men like Taracoot, and whiskey dreams.

We were the last off the lake and by the time we had put away all of our gear the sun was giving up the ghost. We climbed the steps to the main cabin, opened the great door and stepped in. It was like entering another world. In contrast to the calm serenity of the outdoors, the lodge was filled with people, all talking different languages and straining to be understood. They were all similar in one way, however. They sported the ruddy cheeks and laughing eyes of fishermen. I hadn't realized how much fun this was going to be!

CHAPTER 18
A STRANGE GATHERING
AND FISHY TALES

I guess the closest thing I had ever seen to the spectacle I was now witnessing was when I was a kid and my folks took me to the circus. This gathering at the lodge was a three-ring feast for the senses.

In one corner of the large common room the British entry, Sir Edmund Stitsel, was bathing in a large wooden tub while a large, disgusted looking man dressed in buckskins scrubbed his back with a huge brush. At the same time Sir Edmund was blowing bubbles out of a pipe the size of a medium to large saxophone. Across the room my Russian counterpart, Ivan Petrovasnick, was trading belts on a bottle of vodka with what looked like a member of the Royal Canadian Mounted Police, who looked anything but royal. His coat was undone, his pants were down around his ankles, and his hat just barely clung to his head. He appeared so intoxicated that I felt his conscious departure to be imminent. Even though he swung to and fro, however, he refused to fall. I watched him swill another glass of the stuff that had so effectively robbed him of his royal bearing.

Ivan was as steady as a rock but addressed the Mountie loudly, "You ride horse, Mountie? Ivan can ride horse, Mountie? Boy, oh boy! Hush, you muskies!" He laughed from his belly and slapped the dazed lawman on the back. I thought the blow would put him down for sure but he only bent like a palm in a hurricane then sprang back up and continued swaying.

In the center of the room, up against the far wall, sat the Buddhist, Nang Tang Hue, looking a lot like Buddha. The man was as bald as a river-washed rock with a head as huge as his body and ears that stuck out dramatically and moved like radar antennas. He was stripped down to the bottom of his long johns and wore slippers that looked like bunny rabbits. He had no shirt on and his three-hundred-plus pounds bestowed on him a belly the size of a Buick and breasts that would have turned Jane Mansfield green with envy. He sat cross-legged on a sturdy-looking table (thank goodness), chanting at one moment, "oommmmm," then giggling like a schoolgirl the next. At his feet sat a small man with a thin mustache. He stared at the huge man with a look that can only be described as awe. As I was introduced around the room I learned that this proper looking little man was Pierre Le Monde from France. Much to his dismay he had been selected as Nang Tang's interpreter. He was French and very civilized and considered his man an abomination. He tsked and rolled his eyes while Nang giggled, chanted and played with his belly button. (At least in that area as the button itself was so far from daylight I'm quite sure Nang's probing fingers never came close to striking bottom.)

The Mountie was a man called Sgt. Bill Yukon and was Ivan's interpreter. The buckskin clad backwoodsman was an American trapper introduced only as Beaver Dan who was to be Sir Edmund's interpreter. Those two also seemed like a strange match. I guess all the interpreters were, in their own rights, good fishermen and very professional in their jobs. They were chosen with all of these things in mind so as to make a fair competition. Even though they might have been awkward in their situations, they would do all that was possible, within the rules, to aid their competitor.

Taracoot and I had arrived just in time to freshen up a tad then head for the dinner table. Dinner was just a continuation of the circus and I found myself staring at the interaction between guests. Nang ate with both hands and gusto; Pierre was proper and properly grossed out. Beaver also ate with his hands and without manners while Sir Edmund tried to explain, "A fork, Mr. Beaver. I say, do try a fork!" Ivan and Yukon Bill ate with both hands and utensils and seemed to get along. Taracoot ate fairly normally and seemed not to be impressed at all with the gathering. I think I stared more than ate and I ate quite a lot.

After our meal we all sort of settled into corners to digest. It was quiet for several minutes then Yukon Bill took the floor.

"You know," he began, "I never been around a stranger group of fishermen. Fishermen in general are known for their ability to tell a tale. I wonder if you all might oblige me and each recollect one. I expect it might make for worthy time spent." We all agreed it was a good idea and began the evening with a tale from Sir Edmund.

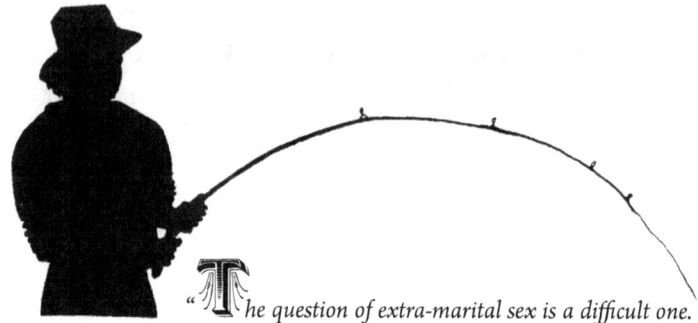

"The question of extra-marital sex is a difficult one. It is the Church's position that when life's passions would have you commit an adulterous act, you should, immediately, in protection of your immortal soul, escape in pursuit of the fishes, not with net or seign, but rather with a sportsman-like approach. It has been found that the successful search and capture of these creatures, in this manner, releases in the human body, a feeling of intense rapture and afterwards a feeling of gratification, that is, for all intents and purposes, the same as bawdy, lustful, extra-marital release, but in no way endangers man's eternal rewards in the after-life."

—POPE PIUS IV IN HIS 400 AD BLESSING AND CLARIFICATION INVOCATION ON THE EVE OF THE FEAST OF THE FAITHFUL*

*With permission, reprinted from the Vatican transcripts, subhead three, titled, "Faithful fishers."

CHAPTER 19
A PROPER ENGLISH TALE

Sir Edmund was a smallish man with great handlebar mustaches. This night he was scrubbed so clean he glowed, with his moderately long hair parted in the middle. He was dressed in his WWI English issue gray wool riding pants with straps under the feet and suspenders. For a shirt he sported the tops of his wool union suit. On his feet were what looked like some sort of East Indian slippers. He walked slowly to the hearth, which was aglow with a blazing fire. He put one foot up on the wood box and began to fill his pipe.

"If it suits our company," he began, "I'll tell a tale passed down from the days when Mother England was but a child and the ancient ones still wandered the earth. Before our Lord and Savior pushed them into the sea. It is said that act was necessary but it seems so harsh that along with the evil ones that roamed the forests and glens, the kind and gentle spirits and the powerful and wise wizards were also destroyed. That mighty race, who since the earth was set to spin held back the tide of evil domination were replaced in a breath's time with no allowance for a place of honor in the minds of men. Our God is a powerful and jealous God.

"It is said that in the deepest wood in the most farthest dale in the clear, warm summer skies of England when the moon rises round and bright as a peasant girl's smile, the old ones come out from where they hide and for a short spell they sing the old songs and dance and give thanks for what little they have left. But they are weak and only if you listen very hard can you hear their ancient song. But I drift like a ship without a tiller yet I won't ask your pardon as it is said that the best tale tells itself and the wisest teller listens with the rest.

"My tale begins many and yon year ago when strong men were knights and women were the fair and gentle sex and happy to be so. It was a time when England was giving birth to the notion that all men were equal but had still not recognized what it was that she wrought. Kings were kings, both good and bad, and divided countryside suffered or prospered accordingly. In this country near a place now called Cheltenham in a valley in the Cotswold Hills lived a knight with whom I am distantly related. Sir Darniel Stitsel was his name and word of his courage and honor spread throughout the land. The peasants within his lands ate what they could grow and sold what they could not eat. They prospered greatly and only owed their lord their services should a war arise. Sir Stitsel was content with what could be grown within the castle walls by the folks that lived there and it is said he even, on occasion, wielded a hoe himself saying that such labor kept an unused sword arm strong. The wealth of the family was secure because of noble adventures the knight, from time to time, embarked upon. My tale is one such.

"It began on a morn, fair and warm, in the old English countryside. My ancestor, being much like myself, was a confirmed fisher. When the king had no need of his sword and the crops no need of his hoe, it was his want to take his hand-carved willow pole to a creek nearby and try his luck at some crafty English trout.

"On this day he had barely begun his quest when he was spied by a water nymph, who upon seeing his comely countenance, fell madly in love. This is not surprising as the Stitsel men have always been handsome, and water sprites are notorious for being impetuous, without thought for tomorrow or consequences. Even though sprites are lesser immortals they are more than a match for a man. And before poor Darniel could gather his wits he was swept beneath the water, carried handily to the creature's lair. I don't mean to imply that the creature was a monster or anything of the kind. Far from it. Nymphs are as comely a creature as any on this fair earth and this one was no exception. Though she was old in our time, years beyond count, she had the flesh of a young woman with breasts full and legs long, and golden hair that reached to the ground. She also possessed a power over love and an appetite for the same.

"But Darniel was a knight and as such faithful to his wife, Lady Stitsel (a somber and plain woman). Try as she might, the nymph was unable to turn the brave knight's head. She was not willing to use her magic upon the man as that would be the same as admitting her lack as a woman. So she worked with skill and patience, singing suggestive songs and dancing with a rhythm that turned the damp, underground cave into a room that breathed with a life of its own. The knight's heart was strong, but his flesh could not hold off the assault. When his manhood became proud she attacked and had her way with him. He turned his head as she pleasured herself and tried to be far away, but her power was great and soon she was drawing from his cup. They lay upon the earthen floor for a time he could not judge, for there was no sun nor moon to tell the time's passing. When they awoke she pleasured herself again against his will but with the full and lurid consent of his flesh. When she was full she arose and stretched and he watched with wonder for few men had ever seen beauty so great.

"She was well pleased with his manhood and kept him for a great span of time, feeding him fish and young green plants. Water nymphs are second only to the god of the sea, Neptune, when it comes to gathering fish. It is said that when the Christ came they hid in the bodies of otters, also known for their fishing abilities and their appetite for pleasure. But for now this one was very much in the body of a woman.

"Sir Darniel never weakened and showed his want but stood erect and as she ravaged him turned the other way. It became obvious to her that he would never surrender. She, being a creature that loved laughter and mirth, began to grow tired with her sober captive. Finally, she deposited him back on the shore, calling him a noble knight, kissing his feet. He reached down and touched her head, repaying kindness with kindness, and smiled then turned and walked to the wood with the nymph swearing her undying love loudly until he was deep within the wood and out of range of her mournful cries.

"He stumbled his way back to the castle, for he was weak from day upon day of unending exercise with little time for sleep. He made his way straight to the Lady Stitsel and confessed his situation. He swore undying love and lay his sword upon her lap that she might smite him should she bear him ill. She had no stomach for a mess so she simply spat upon him and went straight forth and joined a nunnery. They were without child so Sir Darniel lived alone with a shame he bore with dignity, and the seasons passed.

"Finally, a cold and lonely winter gave way to spring but the heart of the poor knight refused to thaw. He did not really miss his wife as their marriage was arranged by their parents and she was a woman with a bosom as cold as creek water born of spring-thawed snow. But he felt himself a failure as a knight sworn to purity. It was about at this time that a rider came to the castle bearing a bundle wrapped tight against the cold. It was a good knight, who had been on a quest of truth and light. He had ridden many a day and on his journey he had been athirst so had stopped at a creek in a fair glade to drink. As he lowered his head to the brook his lips were met at the water—not by a refreshing fill but rather with lips, full and demanding.

"A beautiful water nymph emerged from the deep and stood naked before the shocked knight. He offered her, not his manhood, but rather his cloak to cover her shame. She stopped her advances and asked if he be a knight, true and pure. When he replied that he was she begged his pause and dived back into from where she had come. She returned quickly with a bundle and a tale of a brave knight whom she had used most unfairly. She swore true love to this knight and promised she would never abuse one of his kind again. The traveler finished his story, 'If you be Sir Darniel Stitsel, she begged me deliver this to you.'

"The proud knight unwrapped the bundle to expose a

newborn man child. It was of Stitsel flesh she had confessed, and a baby was not the kind of fun she craved so she begged Sir Darniel to rescue a nymph from the dragon of responsibility. He was a knight and now a father so the burden of this babe was light indeed.

He summoned a peasant woman to suckle the child in its mother's stead and the child prospered. He grew into a fine knight. Being half immortal he was long lived, lasting a lifetime times two and had many a noble quest, but his most outstanding asset was his unequalled ability to catch fish. It was the water nymph in him that gave him the gift. He could summon fish at will! It was from this seed that I have come and from these roots that I credit my ability."

Sir Edmund drew a long breath on his pipe and blew three perfect rings to the center of the room. The gathering was silent as the Englishman sat down and the rings vanished into our memories.

Rather than be overwhelmed by the tales we elected to have one a night. Sir Edmund's left us with food for thought and I know at least I needed a day to digest it! The next morning brought with it a soft rain with a cool breeze from the north. It didn't slow us down much, though, and we spent the day on the lake. I can't be sure how it went for the rest of the group, but Taracoot and I did fairly well as I began to get a feeling for the rhythm of the lake. We were fairly chilled as the day drew to an end and the entire group figured it must be about time to fire up the camp's sauna. We had a delicious hot bowl of chili for dinner then met in the small log house built for that fine Finnish pastime.

This sauna was a small log house, as I said before, and was heated by a barrel wood stove. It was very small for the size of the stove and lined with cedar. It was large, however, for a sauna and there was plenty of room for the eight of us. The idea of this type of bathing is to get her stoked to between 190 and 210 degrees. Then when she's good and hot, water is thrown on rocks that are piled on top of the woodstove. Some saunas are dry but the true Finnish bath is more of a steam room. There are seats in levels and the heartier the soul the higher he or she sits. Sir Edmund and Nang Tang sat on the top row with Pierre and myself in about the middle and Yukon Bill, Ivan, Beaver Dan and Taracoot down fairly low. We sat for quite awhile in silence then Nang began to speak.

CHAPTER 20
AN ENLIGHTENING TALE

My friend and honorable fisherman, Sir Edmund, has told a memorable tale of his illustrious past. I would like to make a humble attempt to relate a time in my past that you might have some small interest in, as it does deal with our common brother fish." Pierre rolled his eyes at me and it was obvious that he would rather rest in the intense heat than interpret.

But Nang looked as cool as stone and continued what he had begun. "It was a time, many years ago when I was only nine seasons into this incarnation. It had been decided by ones much wiser than I that I was reborn from a wise master and would continue in an enlightened role. I admit I knew not, at that time, much wisdom and wanted only to play like others my age. It was decided, however, and not my time for decisions.

"I was to travel to Lhasa in the newly "liberated" Tibet to spend time at the feet of the universal master, the Dali Lama. I am from the City of Nanchang in Western China so the distance to the Lama was great. China was a new communistic state with no religion as the official mode of worship. The good chairman was none too happy about workers who could not see the extreme importance of our newly socialized state because of some idiotic interest in the purpose of our existence in the universe."

Nang giggled and giggled and rocked on the top seat of the sauna like Humpty Dumpty. Then he seemed to drift off with a soft "oommmmm." His eyes were glassy and I thought he was going to fade away when he began again.

"Travel for the purpose I wished to travel was forbidden. The people, however, still recognized a small need that I could fill and aided us in our quest. The group most angry and most committed to the new ways were the students and to them we gave much space. Our country is very large and the people are many. One teacher and myself made the trip and two peasants among so many could pass unnoticed. We carried nothing except our wooden bowls and the clothes on our backs.

"I learned much about poverty and suffering on this trip and saw much starvation. It would be many years until I could recognize God in such places. I would not have you believe that communists caused the suffering. Oh, no, not so. In fact, they were feeding people who, before the revolution, would have certainly starved. I fault them most, I reflect, on their lack of humor. Most truly, they had no time for jokes and I suppose many fault them for their lack of compassion for the ways of their ancestors. But, indeed, they were perfect, of course, it is the way of the Buddha to recognize the perfection in all things at all times. We are only limited by our interpretation of events. Only angered by what we believe to be, rarely by, in fact, what is. The time was not for prayer or understanding, for who can hear the Buddha over the growling of one's own stomach? The time had come to eat! I believe that when the people have their fill they will again refocus on the things of the soul. One who has starved never forgets hunger but even this horror too will be blurred by the passing of time. China has already softened for who is their fishing champion? A fat Buddhist!" Giggle, giggle, 'oommmmm.'

"We traveled from Changhsi, through Hunan, Szechuan and Chamdo into the Himalayan Mountains in western Tibet. The Lama was in the center of the country, deep in the mountains at a retreat along the Brahmaputra River, a most holy place. I would love to tell of the wonders of my travels for it is a story filled with pearls of wisdom that hint at some of the truths that are China. We would sit for days, however, before we even approached the Lama and I fear we would come out of my tale on the other side of our most important contest. So let me only say that the answer to what is true is often in the search and many teachings for young Nang were taught before I reached the teacher.

"The Himalayan Mountains are most marvelous and my travels through them were magic indeed. I met and talked with creatures that our scientists have proved do not exist. It was equally magical leaving the harsh beauty of the mountains to descend into the retreat of the Lama. The weather was warm and the trees laden with fruit. The river sang its soft song without pause and a feeling of peace was in command. Even as a nine-year-old I remember so well feeling I was standing at the threshold of something very profound. The retreat was a group of thatch huts in a circle around a wonderful garden. There were stone walkways everywhere, and although all was in good repair, it was evident that this place was old beyond memory. We were met at the edge of the area by an old man. We had no idea how he knew we were coming as he could not observe our approach. He simply said we were expected and the Lama would see me the next day. We were led to a hut filled with fruit that had been prepared, it would seem, for us. Our journey was long and the vibrations so peaceful we drifted quickly to sleep.

"I was woken in the pale morn by someone pulling on my ear. Just a gentle yank, yank. 'Wake up, little fish,' he said. 'The time has come to swim upstream, little one.' I awoke to gaze into the soft eyes of a man with whom I was instantly in love. He was a man who had no age. He might have been forty and he might have been eighty. I could not tell. He was, however, overflowing with life. He giggled and said softly, 'Welcome home, little fish.' I walked with him out into the courtyard, and it wasn't until I was seated with him at its center that I realized I was crying. It was not the tears of pain that I cried but rather tears of joy and peace. I felt, for the first time, that I was where I belonged.

We sat and ate fruit all morning. I am sure that we spoke no more than a few sentences. 'So you like to fish, little one.' 'No, master, I have never.' Giggle, giggle, 'You are so funny, little fish!' Time would pass. 'So what kinds of fish do you fish, little one?' 'But master, I have never.' Giggle, giggle, 'You are so funny, little fish!'

"Most of the time I gazed into his eyes and without words I grew greatly in knowledge. The teacher I had traveled with knew the Lama and took on a role of servant with the rest of the students. I was so taken by the holy one I didn't even realize that I was being honored greatly by commanding his side. I only knew that this was where I wanted to spend eternity.

"In the early evening the Lama arose and began to walk away.

I started to follow him but was stopped and told to return to my hut. I was slow to leave the master but did as I was told. I did not again see him for three days. During this time, I too did chores around the retreat. There was cleaning and fetching wood and harvesting fruit. Fruit and raw fish were the main diet of the retreat. Almost everyone seemed to be on some kind of fast. I simply did as I was told and, with my eyes, searched in vain for my master.

"It wasn't until the morning of the fourth day that I was again woken by a gentle tug on my ear. 'Little fish, little fish, arise and greet a wonderful morning. Today you will be born! Arise little one and celebrate the birth of one little fish!' I embraced him and climbed out of my little straw bed.

"'Master,' I began, 'Where have you been?' 'Why ask a question whose answer has no value? I am your teacher now, am I not? Is not WHAT I teach to you why you are here? The teacher is to talk, the student is to listen. Now come.'

"We left the tent and I realized for the first time it was still very early for it was almost dark. We walked directly to the river. His pace was so quick I had to run to keep up. He stopped when we reached the banks and he turned to me. 'Happy birthday, little fish,' he said to me, then he picked me up and threw me into the deep, fast moving current.

"I did not know how to swim. It was never taught to me. I was thrown into the water so quickly I had not time to fear. Now that it was done, I felt nothing except the flow around me and saw nothing except the dark. I did not swim or thrash. I simply was there. I did not breathe but did not lack breath. I simply was there. Suddenly, in front of me, was a large fish. Its face was pressed up against mine and I remember thinking . . . there is something familiar . . . then it spoke, not through its mouth but through its eyes.

"'Happy birthday, little fish!' I realized with a start that this fish was my master. I wondered if I was dead. 'Can you feel your feet, little fish?' I could not. 'Can you feel your arms, little fish?' I could not. But I was moving. I could feel that. Then I realized the truth—I too was a fish. I remember being afraid for an instant. I swam in a large circle, and then once again faced my master.

"'Do not fear, little one. There are worse things than being a fish!' I saw his eyes and they twinkled, full of mischief.

"I remember trusting him and loving him, and if a fish can laugh, I laughed. We both laughed, and then we began a chase that must have gone for miles. He swam and I chased. Under logs, around stones, deep down and over the shallow rapids. Then we turned and I swam with him right on my tail. Up and down and around. I jumped straight out of the water and splashed right on top of him. We laughed and laughed and I never knew such a time. After this mighty chase I was tired and when we were done laughing we found a deep, slow moving pool, and together we sank slowly to its murky depths.

"'Swimming is great fun, is it not, little one?' I believe if it is possible as a fish, I smiled. 'But there is so much more.'

"As the Lama said this, I began to sense a change. I was losing my identity. I was, at first, terrified, then I felt a blanket of warm, secure feelings from my master. All would be well and I drifted off into oblivion. It is hard to explain clearly the sensations with the words that we have created to clarify our world. There are no sensations like these for us. But please allow me to try. First off I shed my Nang. That is to say I was no longer a person and I had no idea what one might be. I also was no longer a fish because this too was a word and not a tool of a fish. I developed into one overall being that I can best describe as . . . purpose. All my senses were sharpened. I saw with great clarity. I felt the motion around me with an understanding that allowed me its command. I felt warm and cold more intensely but with no discomfort.

"Every sense was geared to purpose and that purpose was . . . to feed? I began to move at once. I glided smoothly, picking up great speed. My senses knew where to go. Too warm, deeper, too cool, go up, too swift, deeper water, and so on. I knew where they would be—minnows. I hit them with a total ferocity. First one in my teeth, chewed and swallowed, then another. In a matter of seconds I had attacked and mauled many little fish. I cannot say a number because I had no aptitude for recording such a thing. I had only purpose. I dimly ceased my frenzy and settled to the bottom as bits and pieces of torn apart fish floated around my head. I must have felt as the sun feels with the chunks of matter that we call the planets floating perfectly around it. Or as a molecule feels with its parts spinning and wheeling. I felt perfect, complete, void of purpose, left only in a state of blissful being.

"Suddenly I felt a tinge of purpose again. This one was different and struck me like a blow. Flee! Danger! I was in motion at the instant I felt purpose. I swam as I never swam before, darting here and there. I saw nothing at first but my heart pounded and I was living terror. Then I saw the shadow behind me, swimming with me, behind me so close. I tried every escape but it followed me like tomorrow follows today and there was no escape. You see, I understand now, he had purpose. I wheeled around a large rock and as he cut me off for an instant I recognized this fish, dimly, as one, at one time, I had no fear of, when I had begun my own purpose. Now my terror was ended as I felt my bones crush inside his mighty jaws.

"The next thing I remember was waking in my tiny straw bed in my hut. I searched for my master, for explanations, but he was not to be found. I spent my next few days in contemplation of this thing.

"'Wake up, my tasty little fish!' The morning of the fourth day, I awoke to my master's pulling, again, on my ear. He led me to the center of the retreat where we sat and ate fruit and raw fish. 'You see little one,' he told me, 'We are all related in this universe, we are all tied together like pearls on a string of prayer beads. We are truly all part of the whole. So we are related to all things. There are brothers and there are distant cousins. The brothers are more the same and cousins less but related none the less. You are fish in nature. Very close. In this connection you may find liberation and your own purpose. As you look around can you not see the animal world in your human brothers? The timid field mouse, the relentless wolf, the powerful yet senseless snow bear? Can you see the graceful deer and the playful otter? Can you recognize the brutal and self-serving shark? Once you know your fishness you will know all animals and so your fellow men. They all have their own purpose and are all part of the purpose that is God's. So at the end of your learning you will cease to be the fish, recognize the purpose of God and become Buddha. There are many paths to enlightenment. This is yours, my little brother.' He stood then and walked across the retreat. I left with my old teacher the next morning and never saw the Lama again. That is my story, my friends. It is my fish tale."

His head stood out like an incandescent balloon in the steamy room. He pursed his lips, sucked the air out of his cheeks and made his lips and giant ears wiggle. This made him appear to be some sort of fat, tropical fish, found only in exotic waters in places with names like Borneo. Giggle, giggle, "oommmmm."

CHAPTER 21
PLEASE CONTINUE...

Well, after listening to Nang's story, I come out of that sauna about as clean as a bass in a reservoir. I had sweat out so much moisture I had to hang onto things on my walk back to the main lodge for fear of just liftin' up and blowin' away! I could see about everyone was about ten pounds lighter after they got out of there, everyone but Nang, that is. If he lost a pound or fifty, I couldn't see where. But I did enjoy every part of the evening. I was so pooped, all I could think about was where my bed was and what was the quickest route there!

The next morning was a beauty with the bluest of blue skies. Small, fluffy, white clouds just hung like cotton in the air. The wind was straight out of the south and was sweet and warm as a mother's breath. Taracoot had put all the gear in the boat by the time I roused and ate my breakfast, and he was waiting on the dock.

"Well, River Jim," he said, shaking his head like a disappointed school teacher, "all the fish will have eaten and gone home by the time we arrive."

"Sorry, Taracoot," I laughed. "That sauna and story really sapped my bones. I was both tired and hungry and it took me a might longer than normal to refill my supplies!"

Our fishing wasn't as good as it had been, which I blamed on the change in the wind but my partner couldn't help but continue to give me good-natured jabs about my late departure. We learned a few things about the lake, though, and that was what this week was all about. Toward the end of the day I was content to just hang my feet over the side and enjoy the day's heat. My mind wandered to days past and stories told, searching for the perfect one to share with my new friends. I can't say that I made a decision that day but I surely did watch some fine memories on my mind's stage, and somewhere in my drifting I drifted off to sleep. I awoke with a "thud" and realized that Taracoot had also nodded off and we had drifted ashore. We gathered our wits and washed our faces in the cool lake. Then, as the day was nearly spent, we motored slowly back to camp.

"I say, Jim old boy," greeted Sir Edmund, "I thought I saw a boat adrift as we motored in this evening. There were two bodies in it that looked dreadfully like Taracoot and yourself. I was about to call the constable around to make certain there hadn't been any foul play afoot!"

The cabin came alive in hoots and laughter at our expense.

Taracoot explained that we had merely closed our eyes to listen intently to the voices of the fishes so we could better understand our quarry. Everyone but Nang laughed at that, and he just looked around like he couldn't understand why that would be funny. The group soon settled into normal chatter about the day and the lake and time dissolved like a fizzy.

The next event was dinner and I do mean event. It was a complete Russian feast. Everything was served, from caviar to dishes I can't begin to pronounce. It was all fabulous! We ate with relish with Ivan proudly explaining the ingredients and backgrounds of the dishes. We topped it off with vodka toasts, and with full bellies and a gentle glow we all headed for the main room and a period of mandatory digestion. The fireplace was roaring and the comfort and warmth of the cabin gave us feelings of security that must have been akin to the warmth of a mother's womb.

I was about to stand up and commence talking when Ivan arose and addressed me: "If you do not mind, River Jim, I would like to speak tonight. My belly is full of good Russian food and my heart is aglow with good Russian vodka. It is a condition in which I must speak . . . if you don't mind."

I smiled and nodded, and Ivan commenced like this . . .

CHAPTER 22
THE TALE OF
IVAN PETROUSNICK

My name is Ivan Petrousnick and I am Mother Russia's son. I was born to a man and a woman who I knew for only a short time. My father was a soldier, as were most young men in the 1940s in our young republic, and he was assigned to a lonely post in a northern town called Igarka on the Yenisey River. My mother was a soldier's wife and dutifully bundled up her seven-year-old son, and we all boarded a plane. It was unusual for a soldier to bring along his family but since there were to be only three military personnel in the town it was deemed necessary that the families go as well. It was arranged for my mother to work in a local job that was found to be suitable to her.

All plans are subject to the whims of fate and ours were never to be fulfilled. Igarka is very close to the Arctic Circle and in that country the weather is cold and harsh. Although it was mid-May and the rest of our country was basking in a gentle warmth,

Igarka was to have her last taste of snow. We were a mere fifty miles from our destination when it hit. The skies turned gray and the winds began to rock the plane. As time passed the rocking became move vigorous and the windows became filled with the sight of waves of wet, swirling snow. The plane held only soldiers and soldier's wives so the only expressed fear was in the eyes of a seven-year-old boy.

I must have whimpered because my father suddenly looked at me sternly. "Do not be afraid, Ivan," he said. "You are a son of Mother Russia and Mother Russia will always take care of her sons!"

I tried to look brave, and I remember my father's eyes softening as a look of pride came to his face. He held me tight to his chest, and at that moment the whole world lost control with the sounds of screams and cries and twisting steel! There was a final impact and my mind surrendered to the beckoning void.

When I awoke I was still enveloped in my father's arms. I could hear the wind and felt the cold and from the lack of motion I knew we had crashed. I remember asking my father, "What are we to do father?" There was no answer. I became afraid and pulled from his still tightly enclosed arms. His head fell to his knees and I knew he was no more. My mother was on the floor and I ran to her and shook her, but her life too was over. The plane was broken in half with bodies everywhere. The snow and wind enriched my nightmare. I could not breathe. There was a man's coat on the floor, which I grabbed in some sort of unconscious fight for survival, and I burst my way out of the plane.

I ran blindly through the storm, crashing over logs and bushes, fighting aside the thick underbrush. I fell and arose, fell and arose. I fought on as if I could only break through . . . if I only could break through. I must have reached a ridge in my terror and stepped off into the void. It seemed as if I had indeed broken through for an instant. As I fell through the air I remember only relief. Then I hit the ground and was rescued from my situation again with unconsciousness.

A dark, damp warmth surrounded me as I slowly awoke. I felt somehow secure in my half awareness. The only discomfort I felt was from the bruises and scratches I'd received in my flight and from a gnawing hunger that suggested I had been out for some time. I was nestled against a warm, slowly breathing body in some hole in the ground. When I became awake enough to wonder where I was I slowly rolled over and stared into the face of a giant mother bear. I cried out and tried to run but she pinned me to the ground with one of her huge paws and held me firmly until my fighting cased and I only whimpered softly.

Then the she-bear licked my face and hair, carefully picked me up by the collar of the oversized coat I had grabbed and pressed me to her belly. I struggled to get away and was promptly returned. I tried again and was cuffed hard enough to cry out and was pressed again to her belly. Then I saw the object and realized her intent. She was pressing me to her to eat as she was heavy with milk. I was horrified and tried again and again to escape my nightmare. Again and again she returned me with a cuff. In time I lay without moving, my face pressed to her bounty. I could smell the sweet fruit she bore. Finally, in hopeless despair and gnawing hunger, I took one giant teat in my mouth and I drank.

The days that followed are a blur in my memory. As it was dark in the cave I cannot tell you how long I was there. It seemed like an eternity. The she-bear left on occasion, but when I tried to escape she seemed to hear my attempts and quickly return to destroy my plans. It was quickly apparent, however, that she meant me no harm. In fact, to my discomfort, she appeared to be very fond of me. A seven year old is a very adaptable creature and soon I accepted my role as the only answer to my survival. After what must have been weeks, she relented and allowed me to, at last, exit my tomb. The sun was so bright that it physically hurt my eyes. I held my hands over them until I could stand the change.

As my eyes focused in the cool morning air, I was within moments aware of what had transpired. The hole I had been in was part of a much larger cave. The great bear had, undoubtedly, wintered in these quarters and the spring had brought her twins. Our crash had not only taken my parents but had also taken her twins as one whole side of the cave had been plowed under by a giant wing. I could see amid the wreckage two small bodies carefully covered in sticks and grass. It was now obvious, even to a seven year old, that I had been adopted.

The sight of the wrecked plane, once again, filled me with despair. I sat on the ground at the mouth of the cave and wept. The mother bear came to me and sniffed my sobbing form, then, sensing my distress, became overcome with her own grief. Swinging her huge head back and forth she howled and barked. I stared at her in amazement and although I have since been told it was not possible, I swear our eyes met and hers were overflowing with huge tears. At that moment of deepest pain, we understood each other and a bonding took place. I held her around her giant neck and we mourned together. There was no longer any fear in me, but my overwhelming thought was to leave that place. It was as if she understood. After we could cry no more we both stood. I placed my hand on her head, and, without looking back, we walked together into the wilderness.

The fierce winter of those northern regions had, with that fatal snow, finally given up her grasp. In the weeks that I had been confined most of the snow had melted and by now was working its way north to Ust port and the Kara Sea. We, on the other hand, were working our way west into the mounts we call the Gory Putorana. There was no urgency in our flight, and for that I was glad. It was difficult enough for me to keep up with her relaxed, effortless gait. It is amazing how they cover ground. Up hills, down hills, it makes no difference. When I seemed to take too long for her, she would circle me and bark as if to encourage me. Since our time of mourning, it was as if she left that all behind. Now her spirits were always good, even cheerful, often playful as we followed her instincts into the mountains. When I would become sad from my loss she would comfort me with purrs and licks and would often put on a show—rolling, jumping, making faces—until I would have no choice but to leave my sorrow. She allowed me to crawl all over her. I was now her pup and she would do me no harm.

It was quickly apparent that I would not, however, be capable of keeping up with her. I took it upon myself to remedy the situation and once when she circled me I grabbed her by the hair on her neck and I swung onto her shoulders. There was a moment when she was not quite sure what I was getting at; she took a few steps, and I hung on. She took a few more and then it seemed to dawn on her. She was elated! She ran in circles and cavorted in silly jumps and side steps that made me laugh so hard, I lost my grip and tumbled to the ground. She was seemingly concerned for my safety and sniffed me from head to toe. I was fine, however, and when I dusted myself off, I remounted her and we were off. You just haven't lived until you have ridden a nine foot tall, 800-pound brown bear. There is no vehicle on land that can cover ground like that. We crossed mountains, plains and swamp in equal time. She never seemed to notice my weight and never, that I noticed, tired at all.

We seemed to be headed in no particular direction with the one exception of altitude. As the lower elevations warmed, we headed up and lived in a constant temperature zone around, I would guess, 60 degrees. We stopped regularly to play or eat. Our diet was mostly berries, nuts and roots with an occasionally honey tree. She would dine on dead and rotten creatures but even though she offered I would repeatedly decline. I did still drink from her bag regularly, and I believe the nutrition there helped me in the early part of the spring to survive. Later the fruit and such were plentiful and I gradually tapered off and she dried up.

Sometime, not too far into our adventure, we climbed a ridge and looked down into a secluded river valley. The big bear stopped and sniffed the air, and I could tell by her excitement something new for me was in store. She galloped to within fifty feet of the riverbank then stopped abruptly. She once again sniffed the air then began to slowly approach the rapidly moving water. I climbed down off of her and watched. She stood at the bank, stretched her massive head out as far as it would reach and slowly turned it from side to side. She eyed the water with first her left eye, then her right. Then she stood perfectly still. It seemed like ages, then with a deft flick of her wrist she struck the water and neatly lifted a ten pound salmon from the surface and placed it, flopping, well back on the shore.

I jumped into action by grabbing a rock and killing the big fish. She watched my efforts then lumbered over and, with one bite, swallowed half the fish. It wasn't until the third or fourth catch that I was able to join her. I was not used to eating anything raw, and it took some mustering of courage before I could accomplish this. I found the flesh to be chewy but sweet and in no time at all I was tearing off chunks with my teeth. It is amazing to me how quickly a man can revert to being an animal if the need arises. Within two weeks I was running around half naked and half wild and I remember the feeling was exhilarating. Soon we had eaten our fill and both lay, stomachs distended, sleepily in the sun.

The next few days I spent in intense training. My big mother bear was a rigid task mistress and would accept nothing less than perfection. When I became tired and tried to leave she would block my retreat and woof at me until I returned to task. Fishing is survival to the great bears, and I believe she would have trained any of her cubs the same way. To watch her casually one might believe that her methods are simple and crude. Believe me, that is far from the truth. Her skill is carefully planned with intricacies that approach art. She had several approaches within her skill.

One attack was exactly that, an attack. If she was fortunate enough to find a hole filled with fish, she simply jumped in with her giant paws striking deep into the water. I have seen it literally raining fish as she harvested with this method. Most of the time, however, it was not so easy and stealth was applied. She would slowly approach the water and her head peering over the bank must have seemed like a slow moving cloud to her prey. If the hapless quarry was near the surface the story ended with a slap. If the water was deeper, a more delicate system was employed. She would *very* slowly lower her massive arm into the water. This was done so carefully I can't remember ever seeing a fish frightened away. Then as the fish lay unsuspecting, she would again, with a flip of her wrist, launch the game to the bank.

Finally, there is the lure method. If the fish are deep in the middle of the river it is impossible to use any of the above approaches. Also, salmon are swimming up the rivers to spawn and eventually die so they seem less concerned with self-preservation and they are easy targets. But they are only available during their spawning runs and at other times we were forced to stalk the wary trout. These we had to lure. She would carefully approach the water then slowly lower her paw and arm into the river. She would let her paw wave slowly underwater much like a huge fish's tail or giant plant being gently moved by the current. Eventually, some luckless trout would come to lie in the protection from the current that her paw afforded and to nibble at her fur. In an instant he would be on shore. I have seen her stand, stone still, for the better part of an hour before catching a fish. I never saw her give up without a catch.

In my primal state it only took me a short time to perfect my own form of the art. I was not strong enough to slap a ten-pound salmon out of the water, but I did learn to use my stealth to put both my arms slowly under a salmon's belly and flip him to the shore. I also became an expert at luring fish with my hands. Again, I had to use two hands, and I was eventually able to have the fish actually lie between my immersed forearms for protection from the current. When they were in there, they were mine. I believe you must actually coax fish with your mind and at this I became an expert. I learned many things about my prey that can never be guessed by the normal angler. I use this knowledge today in my efforts and am well served.

We enjoyed many long weeks of fishing, gorging on berries and just romping around in the summer sun. My foster mother was as fit and beautiful a creature as exists on earth. Then about midsummer we experienced a severe drought. The lush grasses turned brown and the bubbling creeks turned to dust. It seemed that within days our paradise was lost. There was no hiding from the searing heat and little water for the parched tongue. My she-bear seemed to have an idea, however, as we continued to move, steadily, in one direction. The days turned into a colorless drone in my mind, and I believe I was slipping in and out of consciousness.

I awoke again to the world with my guardian standing in a cool, slowly moving river. Our heads were the only parts above water. The sensation was fabulous. My dehydrated body drank deeply from its pores. I gulped with my mouth and dunked my head in the sweet relief. She too was relieved and within minutes we were romping around laughing and splashing in the clear, cool water. We were exhausted from the travel and relieved at finally being safe. So within minutes we were both sound asleep on the shore.

I awoke to the sound of a deep, guttural growling. The she-bear was standing over me. Her hair was standing on end, her ears were laid back and her teeth bared. I looked beyond her and saw the reason for her wrath. We were surrounded by giant brown bears. This was refuge for many from the dehydrated earth. All the other bears, too, were growling and staring at my she-bear. Then it was obvious to me. It wasn't the mother bear they were alarmed by. It was me. Several of the others had cubs and there was no way they were going to share their space with a human.

One huge bear made a lunge at my she-bear and she whirled to meet him. Another immediately charged from her rear. Again she whirled. The fight became a frenzy. Fur and flesh began to fly in all directions. I remained between her legs hugged into a ball. Even in all of her fury, she never even touched me. It was obvious to me that it was only a matter of moments and she would be dead. I think at that moment I didn't really realize that if she died I would quickly follow. I only feared I would lose another one I loved. This thought was too hard for me to face so I jumped out from my protector and yelled with all my strength. The attackers jumped back in confusion and some even ran stumbling over others. In an instant I was on her back. We broke through the startled ring and ran for our lives. Several followed in hot pursuit but dropped away as we left their territory. As we climbed out of the river valley I looked back and saw the remaining bears splashing and lying in the coolness of the water.

Now, I did not know what we were to do. We could not return to the valley for fear of another attack, and the alternative was to face the bareness of the earth in her drought. The she-bear must have had some kind of idea, however, as she headed steadily in one direction. It wasn't until an hour or so had passed that we finally stopped for rest. I climbed down from the big bear and stared in horror at her condition. There wasn't a part of her that wasn't torn and bleeding. I hadn't realized it but she was laboring in her breath and was losing a lot of blood. She lay panting on the ground.

We rested for only a minute then she was on her feet again. She crouched down for me to mount her. I hesitated with tears in my eyes but she looked at me, deeply panting, with her huge tongue hanging from her mouth. Even in her condition it would be much faster if I rode. There was little choice. I climbed on her gently and we continued. This time we did not stop for hours. The huge animal's condition got steadily worse and worse. The heat and lack of water also began to take their toll. There was little protection in these altitudes from the sun. The trees that did grow were small and thick and only served as a nuisance to passage. Even I, unhurt and without exertion, began to swoon in the oppressive heat. Finally, upon climbing a very steep ridge, my dear she-bear crashed to the ground and could go no further. She breathed heavily with her tongue in the dirt and her eyes half closed. I stroked her massive head and cried to her.

After my moments of despair I came to the realization that if we were to live it would have to be me that saved us. I would not just let her die. I picked up a large, flat rock from the hillside and began to chop down a fair pile of scrub trees. I covered her with these to afford her some relief from the unrelenting sun, and then I headed out in the direction we had been traveling. I ran at first in some sort of unconscious frenzy but several crashes to the ground shook me to my senses and I began a steady walk. I was never in better condition in my life, thanks to the life I had been leading and to my youth. But my immediate condition was very poor indeed. I was not only weak from heat and lack of water but perhaps more serious I was losing my sensibilities. I began to wander. It became harder and harder to keep a straight line or to even remember why I should. Finally, I topped a large ridge and stumbled sliding down the other side on my stomach, ending with my face immersed in a pool of cool water.

I'm not sure how long I lay there. I know it was only long enough to regain my senses. I knew without immediate action I would lose my dear she-bear. There was nothing I could see close by that would serve as a container so I stripped completely, soaking the tattered remains of my clothes, and I headed out. I vaguely knew the direction I had come from, and I sensed that it was not too far. Now I did run with renewed strength and purpose. The sooner I reached my bear the more water that would reach her tongue. I believe it was new animal senses that led me to her. Even though she was hidden by branches I walked right to her. I kneeled at her head and dripped the warm liquid into her gaping maw. It was just enough to wash out her mouth and afford her a little relief. I wiped her face with the last dampness in my rags then headed back for more. After many trips she was able to lift her head. I had stumbled back in the dark on my last hike and feared if I left again I would not be capable of finding her. So I lay at her side and the cool evening breeze bathed us to sleep.

The next morning I awoke and I was alone. I made my way to the pond and found her lying by its side. She was now refreshed but still horribly wounded. I tended her where she lay. I cleaned her body and slowly she began to heal.

A bear can live a long time between feedings but a human is not so blessed. At first I ate the few withered berries on the surrounding hills but they soon dried to worthlessness. There was plenty of cool spring water in the pool but unfortunately no fish. I began to roam wider to find sustenance but soon became too weak for this. My bear was healing but still too wounded for travel and to where I did not know. She seemed content to linger by the security of the water until the drought had passed. I doubted I could last that long.

It was about noon on a typical sun-scorched day that I heard the helicopter. It circled above us as I waved for my life and my bear struck at it as if it were some giant bear-killing bird. It landed above us on a plateau. I ran to greet them but was stopped by my protector. She couldn't understand why I didn't flee. She circled me and mentally begged me to climb on her back to escape as we had done before. I could only think of rescue and ran past her toward the still humming bird. She dared come no closer and ran to the opposite ridge. She would not abandon me entirely, though, and lay watching.

Two men climbed out of the now silent craft and barraged me with all the questions one might ask a child in the company of a great bear. When they could think of nothing else to ask they gave me one of their lunches and explained their purpose. It seems they were from the great Moscow Circus and had come in search of a great bear to add to their count. It was my she-bear they were searching for, not me. My family's plane had been found. Several bodies had been missing and were presumed eaten by a large bear evidenced in the area. No one was thought to have survived so there was no search. As they spoke they kept looking toward my she-bear.

Finally one spoke. "Can you help us catch her?" I was shocked.

Catch my bear? Put her in a circus? Then I thought of the hardship we had known, the starvation, the mauling. I could not stand the idea of my bear out here alone with the constant danger.

Yes, I said, I would. I had them fly their draft a distance away then return with their nets. They hid in the brush. I called her to me, she came and was captured. That is all. There is no more. She was slung in the net under the craft and flown that way to Igarka. There we boarded a large plane and landed next in Moscow. It was thought that I would stay with her and be the "Great bear boy" but soon it became clear, to my dismay, that she would no longer tolerate me. She was trained in the normal way and for years danced as a clown in the Great Moscow Circus.

I never returned to see her until the day she died. I could barely recognize her. She was old, thin and toothless. She still wore part of some foolish costume and showed plainly on her legs the marks where the shackles had been. They had probably taken them off for my sake, and in her condition she needed them no more. I held her giant head in my lap and talked of our adventures and cried. It was there she let out a giant sigh and breathed no more. I argued strongly in my mind over what I had done. I still argue. But I was correct! I was correct! Is it not better to be fed than to starve? Is it not better to dance than to fight? Is it not better to suffer some loss of freedom than to chance losing one's very life? Yes! Yes! To be able to live is the answer! Life is PRIMARY!

CHAPTER 23
THE RAINS CAME

Ivan took a long drink from his ever present vodka then marched, head up, to his chair and sat down. The group disbanded almost immediately after his tale. No one really commented on its content and I guess we all went to sleep with our own thoughts. I was truly moved by his story and lay awake, it seemed, for hours.

The morning arrived with the first real nasty day of our stay. The rain was steady with a wind from the north that made it feel more like sleet. Everyone went out, though, because we all knew the day of the contest would bring whatever weather it wished and we would have to make do. The only exception would be lightning, hurricanes, tornadoes, high winds or other such life threatening conditions. So a flotilla of "rubber-men" pushed off from the shore of the camp and scattered across the lake.

I have often fished in the rain and wind so it wasn't an impossible situation but as chilly as it was that day I can't say it was fun. Pierre le Monde, Nang's interpreter, got hypothermia about halfway through the day. Sgt. Bill and Ivan had to tow them into camp. They found Pierre motoring his boat in a tight circle, singing ribald French songs. Nang thought it was very good fun and was laughing and clapping his hands. Hypothermia affects your judgment early on in its symptoms and you could say Pierre was definitely altered. A little soup and a warm fire had him back to earth in no time, but they stayed in the rest of the day and the seriousness of the weather was impressed on all of us. Taracoot and I did fairly well as far as fish caught but came in in the evening totally exhausted. Fighting the wind and just moving in our heavy rubber gear made for a tough, physical day. Everyone was in the same condition so it was decided I would put off my story until the next day. I was so tired I was thankful.

The next morning brought with it the same weather. Everyone stood on the porch of the cabin and sort of groaned. It was decided (to everyone's relief), that we would fish half the day, and I would begin my story after everyone had had a hot shower and a noon meal. The morning seemed to drag but eventually we tied up to the dock and made our way to the refuge of the camp. As I stripped out of my boots and my rain suit I thought of the story I would tell. I had decided which of my adventures I would relate in the middle of Ivan's story so now I just lightly reminisced as I showered and dressed.

Everyone looked clean and refreshed. Even Beaver Dan's cheeks were pink, and his hands had a scrubbed look. We gorged ourselves on a fine bean soup with large chunks of ham and Wisconsin cheese then all stretched out in front of the fire. We all digested for awhile to the sound of the rain on the cabin's roof. In a short time I ambled to the hearth, and I guess I commenced my story thus...

In Greek, the word for fish is **IXOTE**.

These are the first letters in the words of the phrase

"INOOVS XPIOROS OEOV TIOS EMENP"

which is Greek for,

"JESUS CHRIST, SON OF GOD, SAVIOR."

I think that speaks for itself!

—R. J.

CHAPTER 24
JIM'S TALE

I guess it was August about three years ago now. The fishing had been slow but that never slowed my enthusiasm any. I keep my canoe in my pickup in the summers so I hiked out to the road and headed off to a small lake I knew that was part of the Apple River. It was at the end of a rough road and was very lightly fished. As usual there was no one on the lake, and I felt like a king with all of this paradise to myself.

It was early morning with a slight overcast but the birds were wide awake and they greeted me merrily. I couldn't imagine what could be finer than to be in a place that I loved doing a thing that I loved. I felt like a character in a children's story. A small piece of someone's perfect imagination. I slid the canoe off of the truck and into the water. In an instant I had loaded my gear and was pushing off. There was no wind to speak of and the water was as smooth as a mirror.

Paddling through the reflections of the trees and shore I felt like Alice and I half believed I was going to fall through the reflection into some kind of topsy-turvy world of distorted images. I guess looking back that was a shot pretty close to the mark! It was so peaceful and calm I just kept paddling, watching the reflections on the water and paying little attention to the direction I was heading. It was almost as if I was being lulled into a peaceful, very pleasant trance.

I was gradually aroused from my mental drifting by the sound of crashing water. I looked up to see a high waterfall cascading off a shear wall and falling a strong one hundred feet to the pure crystal water below. This was interesting to me as the small lake on which I was fishing was surrounded by gentle rolling hills. Also the sky had lost its gray and was boasting the most beautiful aqua blue. There was no fear in my mind, only wonder. There were animals on the shore, birds flying in the air and fish jumping right out of the water. The slight wind carried music in its arms, and its breath was as sweet as a spring flower. As I neared shore, a lion, a deer and an eagle intoned in voices that sounded like musical instruments, "River Jim, River Jim."

As I pulled to the shore I verbalized the obvious: "I guess I must be dead, huh? What'd I do, swamp my canoe? Will I be able to stay? Did I live my life okay? Where are the humans?"

The lion spoke, more with his mind than his lips. The words blessed my mind and although his lips did move they seemed to be just slightly ahead of his words.

"Easy, fisherman Jim. It is not as you think. Your time on earth is not yet through. When you do pass over it will not be here that you will come.

"This is a place the master has set aside for his animal kingdom. It is true that your holy men have no knowledge of our afterlife, but it is a truth that does not concern them. Although man is master of the beasts of the earth the great one loves us no less. We of the animal kingdom, in that time before time, kept our covenant with the Lord and throughout eternity have remained without sin.

"Man, alone, coveted more than he was given the capacity for, and in doing so listened to the evil one and smote the will of God. So it is man alone that suffers a pain of soul. Lo those many upon many years ago he took a piece of his God from his heart and since tried without hope of success to erase the pain by filling the void with the shadows of knowledge and the opiate of possession.

"The lives of the simple animals know only pain of the flesh, which is, by comparison, small and essential within the fullness of life itself. Their souls are ever at peace, being ever one with the purpose of the creator. We are still challenged by the master, however, for bliss cannot be whole without the motion of growth. You have been chosen by us as a solution to a simple challenge of the perfect one. You must do this with your own free will and with the joy of service. Will you assist us?"

The air was so thick with joy and purity I'm sure I was crying. As he stood waiting for my reply, tiny birds circled his head singing softly, "River Jim, we know he can; he will help us, the river man."

I stammered that I would do anything I was capable of, and he replied casually that he knew I would.

They turned and proceeded down a gentle woodland path. I followed. The forest was alive with animals of every description living side by side—creatures that on earth would be mortal enemies. They sang in voices that were animal but that my mind could understand, in tones that were as sweet as honey and as soft as down fur. They made up words that included me helping them. I felt small and unworthy but very good indeed! I seemed to move in a slow motion, but at the same time I seemed to cover a lot of ground. Time was nonexistent and in a minute or a lifetime I was standing on a ridge overlooking a small pond.

"Look yon, River Jim," breathed the eagle. "There is our challenge."

The pond was about one hundred feet across and perfectly round. Into one side flowed a shallow brook that came from the main body of water on this lane. I was about to question my purpose when a large musky broke surface and made a ferocious attempt to swim up the shallow creek and escape to the water beyond. It seemed all the animals were watching and gasped as the large fish struggled mightily to reach its destination. Gradually it weakened, however, and was eased gently by the current back to the pond. The creatures sighed as one, and I looked at the three next to me with questions in my eyes.

"You see a great fish, River Jim," began the deer. "It is a mighty female pike, filled with young. Can this be bad in this place? There are no young here. There are no old. This is a place that has no reason for the lessons of age. This fish does not speak, it is with simple purpose, to eat and to have young. This creature is not from our world. We have judged it to be a challenge from our Lord. We happily accept it as such.

"We have judged the conditions like this: If this fish should reach the main water, which with much effort it is capable of doing, it will survive much the same way as it does on earth. It will kill and eat our numbers, have its babies, which will do the same, and our lives will be affected by a drop in our closeness to the master. This may seem harsh to you, but it is now as it was from the beginning. The Lord would not give any of his creatures a chore they are not capable of achieving, and if there was no consequence for failure there would be no reward for success. There would no challenge to begin with.

"We have approached this already from our own number. The great bear tried, with great skill, but the water is too deep and the fish too wary to be lulled to the shallows. The stream is, as you can see, bordered by high cliffs so we are unable to attack her there. The cliffs are also too narrow for the eagle to swoop upon her. We have creatures stationed at the Lake of Life but she is blessed with slimy hide and we believe that if she makes it that far we have lost. So we had a great meeting to meld our minds to arrive at a solution. How do you catch a fish? The solution became obvious to us. With a fisherman! We would have, if he were available, used Peter but he has many duties tending his world so we searched elsewhere. There are many fishermen on your world but it is to you we have come."

The birds began singing again, "River Jim, we have come; save our world, oh Jim of the river."

I stroked my chin, gazing at the pond and pondered that pike.

Jim, oh Jim, with the dreary and the dire road
Pike and nasty pike with her teethies all shiny-o
'Tis an rhodum dire an fear
Legen rile and pithrel near
Canna mis no rel mid hurt me as we an them an they
Cast an reel and set line squeal an take yon pike away!

I stood looking over the pond and tried to focus on what was certainly my greatest responsibility. I could see fish in the lake that looked up at me with hopeful eyes. I turned and looked at the lion, but before I could mouth my question he answered it.

"Yes, River Jim, the fish know who and what you are. Some of them, no doubt, ended in your frying pan. That is, was and always will be fine with them. The lion is created to kill and to eat. The doe's life is to run and to hide and to one day be eaten. The worm is eaten by the bird is eaten by the fox is eaten by the worm. The fish is fished by the fisherman. It is purpose, and without it there would be no motion in the dance of life. It is how the master created creation and it is perfect in all ways."

The burdens of life that I seem to pack around seemed suddenly insignificant and left me. I began to feel very good about my life and my Lord and the perfection of his creation. I'm sure I just stood grinning. "Jim"—I was aroused by the eagle and the memory of their situation. I realized it would take all my skills because the challenge was also to me. I picked up my rod and tackle box and made my way to a position closest to the creek that connected the small pond to the Lake of Life.

I guess I've caught a number of musky in my time, and I know a few things about them. They are the most undependable creatures on earth. They don't seem to have regular feeding habits. They don't even seem to have regular fears. One day I saw a huge musky in about three feet of water in Bone Lake. I threw every lure I owned at it and couldn't get a bump. Finally, I motored my boat in a tight circle around him, just to vent my frustration. That fish never moved! He just lay on the bottom glaring at me! Later that day a young kid came into the dock with that same fish. He had caught that fish with a worm on a hook and bobber! All my skill and no luck, and he caught it with a worm. There is just no explaining this breed of fish.

Now I was faced with the chore of not only catching one but catching it in time! I started at the beginning. There was no feed in that pond, but she had only been there for a day or so earth time and was probably not too hungry yet. Still, I crept up to the water's edge and tried every artificial bait I had. She ignored them all. She seemed to have one purpose . . . escape. It seemed as if every attempt she made brought her closer to success. I felt a slight panic. This would take all my skills, all my skills and more. My mind raced. A plan—I needed a plan. Lord help me!

Then I had an idea. It was farfetched, really way out, but somehow I thought it might work. I took all the hooks off of a large diamond spoon I had. The next time that pike made a shot at the creek I nailed her with it. It took my best casting but that's what I'm good at! She seemed to be hindered by the attack and didn't make it nearly as far as she had been. Again she tried. Again I smacked her. I retrieved the spoon as quickly as I could so she had no chance to strike at it. But she saw it. In her simple, basic mind she was beginning to recognize an enemy. Again and again I slapped at her when she tried to escape. Again and again I pulled the spoon from her reach. Now she was beginning to reach a frenzy. She swam round and around the pond, and I feared that if I didn't make my move soon she would use her hatred of my weapon to boost her escape effort. I replaced the hooks.

Now she made her move. Up and up the creek she swam while I watched helplessly. Higher and higher until she teetered on the edge of the lake. I could hear the moans behind me. Then she slid back a few feet, but with renewed energy she burst again toward her goal. I thought of making a desperate cast in hopes of snagging her but knew that the only place I could catch that fish would be in the hard bone of her mouth. The hooks would easily tear her soft flesh. Up and up she swam like a huge salmon following some primal drive. Again she tottered on the edge and again she slowly slid back.

Now I made my move. I dropped that hated spoon inches from her snout. I pulled it to me at a speed that equaled her slide. She struck at it, I pulled it from her reach, again she struck, again it eluded her. By the time she hit the pond she was wild with fury. Now I began my retrieve. Not too slow, not too slow. Wham! She hit it like an express train. I set the hook with a yank that bent my pole in half. Never have I fought a fish that was as mad as that creature. Even with the hooks imbedded in her jaws she bit at it and bit at it again. She thrashed her mighty tail and made runs across the pond that peeled off my line. Around and around she swam making giant leaps, twisting and turning and shaking her head like a cat shakes a rat. She fought a great fight but once I had set the hook, I knew she was mine. The stakes were too great. I would not play with this fish. I guess it must have taken about thirty minutes or so to land her. I grabbed her carefully by the gills and dragged her to the shore. We both lay on the banks with our sides heaving.

I asked only two things of those kind creatures as I departed. That was to be allowed to take the musky with me, and to be able to leave soon so I would be able to release her, in my world, unharmed. This was granted to me, and as I paddled my canoe through crystal clear water that looked like air, I could hear their song…

Jim elst while amby nin rench o pike did
Wonder Jim catch her swim jump o thrash and fight id
Fair padded Jim wish well fisherman do
Never fear we be near . . . thankin you thankin you!

The song and the drum of the falls faded as I found myself back in Polk County. It had started to rain softly as I slid the tired musky into the cool waters of the lake. She has spawned many feisty babies in that place and I have already caught several of them. They are some of the toughest to lure, roughest to fight, fish that this fisherman has ever known. But they came from a good seed.

With that I ended my story and sat down. We spent the rest of the day loafing and I think we all needed it.

CHAPTER 25
A BATTLE ROYAL

The remaining couple of days leading up to our contest sped by in a blur. The weather gradually cleared and the night before promised that the big day would be a beauty. Our little nonofficial Olympics didn't draw the attention of the main competitions but we did draw in a fair group of reporters and spent the last night telling our personal stories. It was all very exciting and I can't really say with honesty if I slept that night at all. The morning didn't hesitate a bit in its coming. The sun didn't even seem to notice a handful of fishermen waiting nervously on the shores of Lake Mangor in north central Canada. The boats were lined up on the shore. Our interpreter-guides were all set at the rear, waiting to motor their competitors in the direction of their choice. There was a short speech by some local politician and a handgun shot into the air. All three of us climbed into our boats and it began.

Taracoot and I motored directly to the north end of the lake where I had been having my best luck catching walleyes. I was going to take no chances. I've been skunked more by those fish than all other species put together so I wanted to be sure I had them covered. I began using a silver spinner and a minnow and quickly netted two three-pounders. The action ended abruptly so I quickly changed to a jig and a crawler. Bouncing it across the rocky bottom produced lots of fish but the great percentage were too small. I was having great fishing but it was taking too much time.

Again a change. Next I went to a deep diving plug of my own design. The lure, together with deeper water, produced some bigger fish but, as usual, the walleyes had been tough. I had a limit minus one with all three- and four-pounders. Not contest winners, and I had worked most of the morning for them. I decided to save my last fish for the evening when a large one would be easier to catch.

Midday was the time for big pike so we attacked accordingly. The summer sun bore down on us like a winter's roaring fire but there was no corner of the cabin we could retreat to. The reflection off the lake made us feel like two trout sizzling on the skillet. Dragon flies fluttered their paper wings around us like some kind of miniature, primitive air force in perpetual reconnaissance for some tiny army escaped from the mind of a science fiction writer. We fished on. The heat became so intense we had to, repeatedly, soak our hats in the water and drench our near-boiling brains. The northerns, too, were tough with me, and it wasn't until afternoon that I finally hooked a worthwhile fish.

Taracoot had been motoring near the shore, and I would cast a large daredevil and retrieve it quickly. Classic pike attack. We were off a small bay that was filled with tall reeds. Classic pike territory. I tossed the spoon just to the edge of the reeds then began my retrieve. I saw a flash and braced for a strike that didn't come. Again I cast to the same area and again the flash. This time his aim was better and the rod tip made a dive for the water. My line squealed off the reel as he made a run into the reeds. I knew at once that this was a large fish and I cursed the weeds into which he had made his run. Slowly I stopped his retreat and inch by inch began to haul him toward the boat. Reeds fell over like trees before a tornado as my line became a sickle.

The big fish made a sudden change of plans and made a bee-line straight for me. Down, down he swam into the deep water. Straight under the boat. Taracoot had the motor off by this time and now lifted the prop out of the water to protect my line. He yanked and yanked at my resistance and the tip of my rod dipped into the water. Then up he came like a launched missile. Straight out of the water on the opposite side of the boat. I stuck the tip of my road still deeper under the boat, praying that my line would keep away from the rough underside. He was a beauty. I knew I had to land him. The battle raged. He tried attack after attack and I would counter. He was a noble fish but I was not to be denied. After twenty very long minutes, Taracoot slowly slid the net into the water and hoisted him, still thrashing, into the boat. We figured him at around thirty-five pounds and I was tired but pleased. Finally I had hooked a decent fish. Now I hoped my luck would continue.

Sgt. Bill and Ivan motored by and informed us of the rest of the company's progress. They had one very nice bass but nothing else of any size. Nang had caught many fish but had eaten a quite a few and seemed to be having problems being serious. The big story was Sir Edmund, in keeping with his reputation, had hooked something huge and had been battling it for hours. As they passed, Ivan hooked and landed another nice bass that must have been in the five- or six-pound class. I suddenly realized that these were some of the best in the world, and I was truly running in tough company. I continued after northerns and in the next hour boated three between fifteen and twenty pounds. At this point I was satisfied and turned my attention to bass.

Now I've caught a mess of bass in my time but I'm not really a bass fisherman. There are guys that just foam at the mouth when they think of the old "bucketmouths" and I can't say that I blame them. Pound for pound there's not a tougher scrapper and God made them easy keepers so almost every lake has a healthy population. I guess maybe that's why I haven't fished a lot of them. They're a little too easy. But when it comes to catching big ones there is nothing easy about it, and I believe that north woods giants are the toughest of all. But doggone it the time had come to dig in. Somehow I was fishing distracted. I was doing a fair job but I had the feeling that fair wouldn't be good enough. I watched Ivan land a very nice northern and I began to get a feeling somewhere between panic and nausea.

"Pull the boat to the shore," I direction Taracoot. He did as I asked and watched as I hoofed it into the woods. I suppose he figured I was going to relieve myself and I guess I was but not in the way he thought.

I found a little break in the woods and sat down cross-legged on the ground. I laid my face in my hands and felt the sweat that had built up on my brow. I stared at my wet hands and noticed that they were shaking. It's not supposed to be like this, I kept saying to myself. Not like this. What's the matter with me? I began to shake all over. I wasn't cold and I remember detaching mentally and watching myself shake. Then the shaking sort of took me over mentally and I remember hearing a buzzing sound that was like a dentist drilling in a tunnel.

The next thing I knew I was sitting, still cross-legged, in front of a fire. Across from me was an Indian. He was dressed in clothes that didn't somehow look like a costume but rather looked ancient and as much a part of him as his hands or face. I knew him but it seemed like from a place far more ancient than my short span of years. He looked deeply into my eyes and I loved him and I cried.

"River Jim," he breathed, "my brother." He reached his hands into the flames. "Take my hands, Jim." I stared at his hands in the fire and was afraid. "Take my hands, Jim."

He smiled and my fears disappeared like a smoke ring in the wind.

I reached into the fire and took his hands in mine. I felt flames lick my arms. I knew they were real. I could feel them but they were more like an experience than pain and, somehow, I refused to allow my flesh to be devoured. It was my decision. We sat in silence for a moment then he spoke.

"The flames do not touch you, River Jim." I nodded. "It is your decision." I nodded again. "Then why, my brother, do you bend before the flames of life? Are not the happenings of earth only a passing parade? Fame, gain, pleasure and pain merely the colors on the portrait of your life? Be true to what you are and let the portrait paint itself. Are you Jim the winner? I think not. You are and always have been Jim the fisherman. When you force yourself to be 'The Winner' you cease to become 'The

Fisherman.' A man may never become that which he is not. He may force himself to become a reasonable copy but it will be a flat and lifeless representation that will only fool other copies. Rest in yourself and your feet will find the path, keep your steps on the path and the mountain will come to you."

I began to mentally shake again, but it was more like a peaceful vibration. Then I heard the buzzing and the next thing I knew I was sitting cross-legged in the break of the woods, alone.

I returned to the boat and Taracoot. He looked at me and smiled. "Are you relieved, my brother?" he asked.

"Yeah, let's go." I grinned as we pushed off into the lake.

My mind was filled with the realization that I truly loved to fish. This was my life and calling and one way or another it would see me through. The contest became secondary to the love that I had for my sport. I could not wait to drop a line over the side. It was obvious to me instantly that fishing bass in the middle of a hot, sunny day was not my style. Sure, Ivan was doing well at it but that was HIS way. I decided to fill up with pan fish.

We motored to the shore and I directed Taracoot to several trees that had blown down into the lake. The bases of the trees were on land and the branches disappeared into the water below. A perfect, sunny hole. On the way over we passed Sir Edmund and Beaver Dan. I guess that Sir Edmund was also fishing pan fish on very light gear when he hooked into a giant northern. Dan was strongly recommending that he cut his line and get back into the contest because to land a fish of that size on that light gear would take hours. Sir Edmund would have none of it.

"Never, Mr. Beaver," I heard him yell. "For a fish this grand, the queen will understand!"

I knew exactly how he felt. His life and nature was catching BIG fish, the greater the odds the greater his joy. He was being, pure Sir Edmund, and was joyfully complete! I must have been grinning from ear to ear as I bounced a small fly off the surface of the water. A large fish was instantly mine. Another followed then another and another. The action became frantic as I filled the boat with fat one-pounders. I was hookin' 'em and dancing and feeling so good I thought I might turn inside out.

We were soon joined by Nang and Ivan. It wasn't that they were after my spot, it was just that our purpose had become the same in a larger sense, and I had a sure knowledge that something pure and wonderful was preparing to commence. Nang began laughing when he saw me dancing and grinning. He had a little cane pole in his hands but I never saw it catch a fish. His boat was almost standing on end with the tiny Pierre at the motor, his end up in the air and the huge Nang at the front. The prop of the motor was also out in the air but the boat still moved, it seemed, wherever the giant man wished. He never caught a fish on his tiny pole, as I said, but he gathered fish nonetheless. They jumped into his boat, making an arch like a "fish rainbow." He just laughed and clapped his hands with an occasional "oommmmm." Ivan had begun to harvest one right after the last. He was, in contrast, serious and mechanical but effective none the less. Sir Edmund was playing his monster like it was a violin. The big fish made run after run and was carefully turned by the English master. He moved so quickly and with such fluid motion that even Beaver Dan had quit his protestations and watched in awe. The ever present pipe sent a continuous flow of rings into the flawless blue sky.

I was just proud to be there. Proud of my competitors, proud of their skill, proud of our art. For this level of fishing was art in its purest form. I joined my fellows in their rhythm and was soon catching fish at a pace even I had not thought possible. Taracoot began a drumbeat on the side of the boat and was soon lost in a chant that lifted us even higher.

Sgt. Bill began a military cadence that went, "Here it comes and here we go, now up and up into the flow now, sound off, one two, say it again, three four, king's count, one two three four, one two… THREE FOUR!"

Each repetition brought a new verse that described what was happening to us all, and Taracoot's wordless tale rang of ancient truths. "Hey ya, hey ya, hun nun nun na, Hey ya! Now we're catching fish like crazy, pullin' petals off a daisy, sound off, one two . . . Hoy! Ha na na na Howy! Ya ya yah un na na . . ."

Nang ceased to put fish in his boat and began to float the fish around his boat like a giant halo. They spun in a huge circle, then circles within circles. Nang rolled his eyes and held his hands aloft and we all began to rise. We continued to catch our fish. Fish of all kinds. The lake rose with us. A ring of water about an acre in size began a slow spin in the air. It wasn't just Nang, it was all of us. We were united in a way that spoke of greater mysteries than we could have imagined. No one stopped what he was doing, no one was really surprised because once we reached that place where we were exactly true to our natures, the truths of the universe lay before us.

I can't say I could explain them to anyone. I can't say there ever were words for it. Something so outrageous, like touching the face of God, and I must admit that time has paled the colors of my memory. I tried to cling to them for awhile, to hang on, but that wasn't right or natural either. Everything fades in time and new things that glow bright in their time also fade. It's a small part of the truth that the mind is capable of grasping. Suffice it to say that four fishermen, boats and lake and all, spun in the universe and caught more than just fish. There was no Nang, no more Ivan, no more Sir Edmund. There were no more Sgt. Bills, Dans, Taracoots or Pierres. There were no more River Jims and none of us had the slightest idea of what one would be if there were one! There were fishermen and fish and it was basic and we all danced to the rhythm of Gabriel's horn.

I don't remember coming down. I vaguely remember the day ending. I barely remember being told that my boat held the most fish. That I had won. It all seemed so trivial at the time. We had fished together as no one else had, I would wager, since Peter threw his net with the Lord. Somehow, my boat had held the most fish. Such a small thing in reality. Now they said I was the greatest in the world. They still say that. Well, now you know the truth. I won't say I am or I'm not. All I can say is that I believe I've stood shoulder to shoulder with the best—and, man, did we catch some fish!

CHAPTER 26
THE FISH

I guess I couldn't really allow a book about my life to pass without tellin' ya about the fish. People talk about this tale and I hear it on its way around and it strays about as far from the truth as a story is able. I have heard that I, personally, whipped the devil—the devil, can you imagine? Daniel Webster or someone out east claims something like that. But I can tell you, whatever it was I met with, ol' Jim wasn't even in its weight class! No sir, not even a contest. Whipped it? Even the good Lord had to roll up his sleeves to do that! No, that's just how it was. But let me explain . . .

I got up with the sun that morning, as I always do. I figure that the early morning is about as fine a time a day as there is with the world all clean and rested and all. The sky was about as blue as it can get and still—it was so still it kind of set me back a tad as I recall. It was almost more like a postcard than a day if you know what I'm sayin'. I remember that path down from the cabin. The roots from the pines seemed to swell out from the ground like veins on a farmer's arm. You could almost see a pulse. The ground seemed alive, with the pine needles soft and gentle, almost like flesh. I sort of slid down the winding way and before I could spit I was standing in front of the fish house.

Now, I've lived on the river all my life. The woods are no stranger to me and don't I know it's alive! It lives and breathes like you and me. It can be soft and kind and it can be trouble! But I didn't realize how strong it was that morning—not until after . . . the fish. I guess I was thinking about fishing. The good lord made mornings and evening for fishing. Especially in the summer. The fish just rest in the middle of the day. They hide in the deep water under them big rocks, out of the hot sun. They just, sort of slow and easy, rub their bellies in the cool sand and work terribly hard at being lazy. Hard to catch 'em then I can tell you. But they're just like children, they get mighty feisty first thing in the morning and just before bed. That's when old Jim likes to flutter a blue fly about an inch or two above the river. The trout 'bout come to blows over who's gonna land in Jim's frying pan first.

That was my plan for this morning. I was just going to catch my breakfast . . . no trophies or anything. If I had a dollar for every time things worked out the way I figured, I'd have about a dollar or so! It's only about twenty or thirty yards from the fish house to the river, but somewhere in that small span I got swept away. I can remember walking. I knew I was going somewhere. I didn't fight it really. In my mind it was, almost, my idea. But every time I tried to remember why I was headin' upriver I kind of got confused until my mind was blank again, and I was just hoofin' it up the path. I recall the trees moving like they do in a heavy wind, back and forth, in and out, but the air was as still as death and I should have had a clue. I walked a long time…a long way… upriver. I didn't think about time and the longer I walked the less I was aware of what I was doing. The next thing I remember, I was standing by a large pond in the river. In this spot there was no sign of life or movement. The trees had stopped their motion and it was as if the entire world was holding its breath.

The pond talked to my mind, "Jim . . . mighty fisherman . . . fish me . . . fish me." It called in a way that can only be described as seductive. "Try your skill on me, mighty fisherman," it mocked.

I felt my hands move to my fishing pole . . . I pulled a fly from my kit. I watched myself go through the motions. I softly danced the fly lightly on the pond's surface. I watched it dance. I played it like a marionette and, as I do sometimes, I marveled at the way I could make it act like a real fly. For a short while the pond was silent, and I became absorbed in my fishing.

Then came the strike. The big fish came straight out of the water with my lure in its mouth. Then came my last moment of control. I believe that my adversary thought I was a little farther gone than I was for it reacted with outrage as I leaned into my pole and with a might yank set the hook. It pulled with fury with repeated leaps into the air and all I could do was hang on. It was as if I had hooked a power line and energy coursed through my body.

Then it quickly regained its composure and began to taunt me. "Oh, mighty fisherman . . . could you catch me? Oh, mighty fool . . . can't catch a little fish?"

It laughed with a howl that frightened me and all I could do was watch and shake. The sky had turned an awful gray then black as thick and powerful clouds covered the area. I began to sink into my mind. It was like I was walking back into a tunnel, and I recessed farther and farther from my eyes, into my head.

I could still hear its laughter, and it continued to taunt me—"Mighty Jim, pure and simple fisherman . . . taste the fruits of life . . . roll in the richness of the flesh."

I began to have visions of vulgar scenes, of naked women and men with intermingling, pulsating flesh. Of unnatural acts and violence. At first I was repulsed, but soon my own flesh began to respond and I knew my mind and soul would soon also be lost. I fought inside, but my interest was again and again drawn to the ongoing visions. I began to fight less. I began to enjoy more. I began to care less. Yes, I remember beginning to crave to be in the soft, wet flesh and all the while the fish's laughter rang loud and hideous. It must have been my last attempt to withdraw—my last desperate fight for my soul. I could only cry, "God help me," as I sank into the pit.

I have no idea how long I was submersed. It was probably only an instant but the separation from God and all that is good I can only describe as if I had thrown up my heart. I was lost and I wailed and gnashed my teeth.

Then I felt a warmth on my forehead. It quickly eased some of my suffering and gave me sight to see through the slime. I was led out of the mire and I gathered strength as I withdrew from that dark region of my soul. As I slowly regained my outward sight I could see that there was a small hole in the black clouds and a ray of perfect white light was beaming to a spot in the middle of my forehead. The fish was lost in its own revelry and laughed and jumped in the center of the pond. My pole was dangling from my hand but the fly was still hanging loosely from the creature's mouth. I still was helpless, physically. The power of the evil one was complete on earth and I didn't have a clue as to what to do.

Then I heard, in a deep and melodious voice, these words: "JIM . . . KEEP YOUR TIP UP!" I hesitated and the voice came again. "TAKE UP SOME LINE, BOY!"

I slowly started to wind in some line. The unholy one must have felt the tension and in an instant understood the situation for he stopped his wicked dance and stared. Then he screamed a mournful scream and made a mighty run, peeling off line.

"CAREFUL, BOY, CAREFUL. TURN HIM SLOWLY—KEEP HIM OUT OF THE ROCKS!" As the battle raged I became less and less in its spell and more and more was I able to be a fisherman. "THAT'S IT, JIMMY . . . THAT'S THE IDEA . . . HE'S COMING AT YOU . . . TAKE UP SLACK . . . TAKE UP SLACK!"

I did as I was told and could feel myself begin to smile. The fish screamed and yelled, "No fair! No fair . . . he was mine! HEEEESSSS MINE!" He made one more terrible leap directly at me. He hit me full in the chest, and I was knocked out cold on the ground.

When I awoke, I awoke to a beautiful day. There was the biggest, most beautiful brown trout I had ever seen lying, quite dead, next to me. I pushed myself up on my elbows and took a deep breath. The clouds had all but disappeared and the few that were left were outlined in brilliant silver. I thanked God for helping me out and got shakily to my feet. I buried the trout 'cause I figured it wasn't a natural trophy and I didn't want it in my cabin and I sure wasn't going to eat the thing. It seemed a deep grave was the best solution. By the time I had finished it was getting onto late afternoon. I was quite a bit farther upstream from where I normally traveled but I recognized the area. I was still shaky and I had a long walk to my cabin. I suppose I should hoof it back, I remember telling myself. But there is a pool just a tad downstream. I know there's a fat rainbow trout that hangs out there. I've seen him a couple of times but always in the heat of the day. I'm sure if I just hung one of my best yellow ties about an inch or two over his nose he'd come bustin' up. Yep, he'd be mine this time of day. I could still feel the weakness in my knees as I crept down the path that ran alongside my river. I recall laughing to myself, "Jim, you're just a fishin' fool!" And somehow I just knew that God agreed and was up there smiling.

❧ ABOUT THE AUTHOR ☙

Gary Belschner spent much of his childhood in the land of many lakes featured in his stories. His education included Shattuck Military School in Faribault, Minnesota, where he attained such distinguished designations as "Captain of the Work Squad" and "President of the Privates Club." He was also captain of his varsity soccer team and was the recipient of an excellent education.

After attending college in several locations Gary headed north to Alaska in 1972 for adventure and riches working on the Alaskan pipeline. In Valdez while working as a surveyor on construction sites he met his wife and soul mate, Rosemarie. They were married in Anchorage in 1977 on the day they first sent oil down the pipeline.

After enough adventures to write several books they moved in 1981 to a small farm in Polk County, Wisconsin. They were blessed with two perfect daughters, Jennifer Rose and Rachel Marie, who continue to warm their hearts to this day.

Gary continued to do surveying but a very poor local

economy limited their income and other strategies were set in motion. Being very conservative and blessed with a strong business sense Gary decided raising thoroughbred racehorses would be a sure source of steady income. Again after enough stories to write several books the horses were all sold at auction and Gary began selling real estate.

Through all of this the patient Rosemarie was working as a facilities maintenance engineer for a plastics company in Stillwater, Minnesota, about forty miles from the farm. The family funding fell to Rose as the real estate market produced riches about as quickly as a the horse venture. In 1992 Gary went to work as a salesman for a company manufacturing the finest surveying instruments in the world, WILD. In the mid-1990s WILD went corporate and changed its name to Leica Geosystems.

Gary had found his legs and was very successful working in this excellent company. He went back to school and earned a better-late-than-never degree in marketing management. He was made part of the senior management team and was promoted to vice president. The company was promptly gobbled up in a hostile takeover, which involved replacement of management. Gary persevered in spite of having his neck under the boot of the new regime until October 2010 when he decided to follow a different brick road.

www.ingramcontent.com/pod-product-compliance
Lightning Source LLC
Chambersburg PA
CBHW061559170626
46811CB00001B/257